C000174689

About the author

Susan Parry began writing when her twin daughters were small, and she was working full time as a university professor at Imperial College. She now devotes her time to consultancy work, including forensic studies and archaeological investigations that form the basis for her writing. Her husband, Mark, is retired so they are now able to spend more time together in the family home in Swaledale, where the views from her house provide inspiration. Together they have walked many of the areas described in the books, accompanied by their Airedale terrier. Her grown up daughters, Elspeth and Alice both have careers in crime – on the right side of the law. Visit her website at www.SusanParry.co.uk.

By Susan Parry

Corpse Way
Death Cart
Grave Hand
Craven Scar
Purple Shroud
Frozen Ground
Grand Depart
Potent Poison

POTENT POISON

SUSAN PARRY

Viridian Publishing

First published in the United Kingdom in 2016 by
Viridian Publishing

Viridian Publishing
PO Box 594
Dorking
Surrey
RH4 9HU

www.viridian-publishing.co.uk
e-mail: enquiries@viridian-tc.co.uk

ISBN 978-0-9567891-5-0

For Andy

Chapter 1

'There's fennel for you, and columbines. There's rue for you and here's some for me. We may call it herb of grace o' Sundays.'

Sofia shut her eyes and leant back on the bed. 'Damn, what comes next?'

Mae had been standing at the window watching a run-through of the fifth act. Her friend, Leanne, who had the part of Hamlet, was rehearsing the fight scene out on the open stage in front of the school. The girl playing Laertes had fencing lessons so she knew what she was doing and she'd worked out all the moves. It looked pretty awesome from where Mae stood. She sat back down on the bed and picked up the open copy of the play, running her finger down the lines.

'Sorry, where are we?'

'I know it, don't tell me!' Sofia was holding up her hand in protest. 'O, you must wear your rue with a difference! There's a daisy. I would give you some violets, but they wither'd all when my father died.'

Madison, who'd been lounging on her bed on the other side of the room, jumped up as she twisted her long blonde hair into a tight ponytail.

'Gee, no more please guys! I can't take another afternoon of Hamlet. I'm outa here!'

Her southern drawl grated on Mae's ears.

'Don't take any notice of her, Sofia,' she said softly. 'Americans just don't get Shakespeare. They don't understand the significance of the words.'

'Really?' Sofia asked, looking anxiously across at the American.

Mae nodded. 'Take what Ophelia is saying about the herbs – every flower has a meaning and a purpose you know.'

'Do any of them repel mosquitoes – that is the question!' Madison was rubbing her calves. 'My legs are covered in bites! You guys will be bitten to death at the evening performances, you do know that!'

'Do they itch?' Mae enquired. She had a bedside locker full of herbs and Chinese medicine – her mother didn't trust western doctors.

'Like crazy!' She pulled up the leg of her shorts and scratched her thigh.

'Then you should rub them with the inside of a banana skin,' Mae told her.

The girl looked up and put a finger to the side of her head. 'Crazy!'

When Madison had gone, Sofia burst out laughing. 'Are you serious, Mae?' she asked. 'Is that true or were you teasing her?'

'Of course it's true. My mother always rubbed our bites with banana skin when we were small. It stops them itching right away. And she used to make her own insect repellent. I have some with me.'

'Shall we continue?' asked Sofia, indicating the copy of Hamlet that was now closed in Mae's lap. 'I'm supposed to be word perfect for the rehearsal in… oh my God… one hour!'

'I think you're doing really well,' said her friend. 'Considering English isn't your first language.'

'Excuse me!' Sofia pretended to take offence. 'I happen to have been cared for by an English nanny in Moscow, so I am virtually bilingual. But some of these speeches are very difficult to understand.'

'Don't worry, they are for me too and I was born here. After all, they were written five hundred years ago.' She flicked through the pages until she found where they'd left off. 'Thought and affliction, passion…' she began

'No, no,' said Sofia, 'I'm not doing the singing bit – Mr Young agreed in the end.'

'In that case… that's it. We don't see you again until you drown.'

'Yes, well that's the other thing; I told Mr Young I wouldn't do it. I'm not jumping into the swimming pool with my clothes on.'

'But that's the best bit,' said Mae. 'And Fran has spent ages getting the lighting right so the audience can see you from far away.'

'I said he could get someone else to do it. I even told him who to ask.'

'Who? There's no-one who looks like you,' said Mae.

She was jealous of Sofia's height and slim build. She was small in stature but, as her mother would say, the western diet didn't suit their metabolism and she simply piled on the pounds.

'It won't matter,' said Sofia. 'The pool is such a long way away from the stage and they've covered the diving board in foliage so it looks like a tree. A figure in Ophelia's costume would pass at that distance. All Cecile would have to do is pretend to fall out of the tree. They've even recorded the splash to play as she goes in.'

'Cecile?' asked Mae.

'Of course. She's an ace swimmer. It's a no-brainer.'

Madison sat with her back against the warm stone of the barn, waiting for Jeremy to arrive. She liked to watch him unobserved before he caught sight of her.

It was exciting to see his expression change when he finally spotted her in their secret meeting place. She was being bitten by insects again but it was worth it to spend time with him, away from school and her juvenile room-mates. The gate slammed down by the road. She counted to a hundred and then again until he appeared on the track. Head down, he was walking up the field fast and didn't look up until he was almost in front of her.

'Madison.' He looked serious.

'Hi sweetie!'

She jumped up and grabbed his arm.

'Steady!'

She kissed him on the cheek and pulled him to sit down beside her. She handed him a cigarette and he inhaled absently and sighed.

'It's no good, Madison. It can't go on like this.'

'Why not?'

He was looking at the ground. 'I'm concerned about my family. I think we should stop meeting.'

'It doesn't matter if no-one knows.' She pushed her shoulder against his. 'It's just a bit of fun, for goodness sake.'

He groaned and scratched his head. 'If someone found out, if someone saw us here, I'd get thrown out of school, you know that.'

Madison shrugged. 'I thought you liked me.' She was undoing her ponytail and shaking her hair loose. She turned towards him, put her arms round his neck and kissed him. 'Let's not discuss it any further.'

When he finally pulled away from her, he looked at his watch and stood up. 'I've got rehearsals in half an hour. I only came to tell you that we've got to stop seeing each other.'

Madison was lighting a cigarette. 'I don't believe you, Jeremy. I don't think you really want to break up. You just think you *should*.' She shaded her eyes as she looked up at him trying to read his expression.

'Have a good rehearsal and say hello to my brother, won't you?' she called to his back.

She inhaled slowly as she watched him make his way down the track, wondering what she needed to do to hang onto him.

High Fell Hall was hidden from the Richmond road by a long drive that swung sharply to the right as soon as Mills turned the car through the gates. A series of humps in the road slowed her down sharply, ensuring she observed the 20 mph limit indicated by frequent signs. She seemed to crawl up the gravel drive to beyond the line of trees and out into a large area of lawn in front of the stone house. She recognised the façade from the website; it had been an old rectory but now served as the main school building. Accommodation for the boarders was scattered in the grounds apparently. She'd assumed their quarters were quite comfortable when she saw the termly fees.

Mills had gone straight to the website as soon as she'd finished speaking to Fiona. It was so unusual to hear from her father's wife – she couldn't bring herself to call her stepmother – that she initially thought there must be something wrong. But no, Dad was fine, Flora was fine, it was about a girl, some distant relative, who was in a sixth-form boarding school near Richmond. Apparently, once Fiona had discovered it was the Richmond in Yorkshire, she'd immediately thought of Mills because this French woman was looking for someone to teach her daughter archaeology.

Mills wasn't averse to a bit of tutoring. Although she'd started her new lecturer post it was still not full-time so money was tight. She'd been used to the income from acting as temporary manager of the forensic science laboratory but Brenda, who owned the company, was now well enough to return to work – which was good news, of course, but left her own position there uncertain.

It appeared from the website that this private sixth form college had around one hundred girls, all studying for their "A" levels, which presumably meant they were between about fifteen and eighteen years old, possibly nineteen. It was a boarding school with separate student houses, each holding up to ten shared bedrooms. The long list of staff covered the arts mainly, but Mills wondered if they were all permanent. She suspected her own name would be added to the list if she accepted a few hours tutoring each week. The school aimed to bring the girls to a standard for university entrance but the results in the league tables did not impress Mills and she wondered whether the foreign diplomats and parents in military service overseas were sufficiently ambitious for their daughters' academic achievements.

She passed groups of girls sitting or lying on the lawn and, in the distance, she spotted a tennis court where a game of doubles was in progress. She noticed a large raised construction, where two girls appeared to be having a fencing match. Mills pulled into a space in front of the school and climbed out, turning to watch the action. They were certainly using swords but weren't dressed in the outfits she associated with the sport.

'That's Leanne. She's playing Hamlet.'

Mills recognised the plummy voice of Mrs James from their phone conversation and turned to meet her.

'You must be Dr Sanderson. I'm so glad you could come.'

'Mills. And thank you for inviting me.'

'Yes, we decided we'd have a female Hamlet and some of the other male parts are being played by the girls. But not all; some of the boys from our partner school are helping out. In fact the drama teacher from the boys' school is producing the play this year.'

She led Mills through the front door and into a panelled entrance hall. It was cool inside and smelt of furniture polish.

'This way, we'll have tea in the music room.'

Mills was glad she hadn't been late because a tray was already waiting on the small table beside the window. Much of the room was taken up with a grand piano and several music stands but there was a worn leather sofa, just large enough for two. They sat side by side while the headmistress poured tea and offered biscuits, which Mills refused. She was actually rather nervous about the impending interview.

The Head turned to her awkwardly with her cup in one hand and a biscuit in the other.

'I was so pleased when Mrs Fleurot told me that you worked at the university. Sometimes we find we have to seek expertise outside our little community and when Miss Porteous said she wouldn't be able to cover the practical assignment part of the course work I was rather worried.'

'Miss Porteous is an archaeologist?' Mills asked.

The headmistress pulled a face. 'More of a historian and classicist, to be honest. She's very much "old school". Retiring soon.' She snapped at her biscuit. 'Anyway, let's hear about you. Very highly qualified with your doctorate, of course, but what about practical things? Do you do digs and that sort of thing?'

Mills suppressed a smile and described some of the fieldwork she'd been involved in.

Mrs James nodded frequently, waiting until she had finished establishing her credentials.

'That all sounds most satisfactory, dear. More tea?'

Mills declined and the headmistress replaced her cup on the tray.

'I've asked the girls to come down to meet you. They can show you round and tell you their ideas for the assignments next year. Now they've taken their AS level exams they should, apparently, be deciding what to do.'

Mills assumed she had passed the interview and had been accepted for the task.

'I've been looking at the syllabus,' she began, 'and it seemed to me that if the girls want to be involved in any fieldwork it would have to take place over the summer or early in the autumn before the weather gets bad. Do you know what they are going to work on?'

'I'm sure they can tell you all about it,' said Mrs James, standing, 'I'll go and find them.'

Mills waited until she'd gone then reached across to the plate on the tray.

'Hey! Is your car the red Mini?' The American accent surprised Mills.

A girl was standing in the doorway. She was tall and slim, with long tanned legs.

'Er, yes,' she replied.

'I so want a car like that when I get back home.'

The girl wandered slowly into the room and took a biscuit from the tray.

'Are you here to do tutoring?' she asked, looking out the window.

'Yes.'

'What d'you take classes in?'

'Archaeology.'

The girl seemed unimpressed. 'Ugh, history! I'm taking politics.'

'Madison!' Mrs James had returned. 'Have you seen Frances and Cecile? I told them to wait in the common room.'

Madison shrugged.

'Well go and find them, please,' the Head demanded crossly.

She watched the girl help herself to another biscuit before moving slowly to the door. Mrs James waited until she'd left before turning to Mills.

'It's rather chaotic at present. Well you saw the stage being erected outside. The first year sixth always produce a drama for the end of term. It keeps them occupied after exams have finished. Of course the upper sixth are still in the middle of their exams.'

She peered out of the window.

'Frances is doing the lighting. Of course Cecile isn't involved because she goes swimming on a Wednesday afternoon when we hold rehearsals. She's a very accomplished sportswoman – but I expect you know that?'

She must have detected that Mills was puzzled by the question.

'I thought you knew the Fleurots? Cecile's mother said you were related.'

Mills smiled. Mrs Fleurot was Fiona's brother-in-law's sister. 'Only very distantly, and only through my… stepmother.'

'Mr Fleurot works in the French Embassy in London,' she explained. 'They have a flat in Kensington I understand.'

The Head clearly enjoyed bragging about the parents of her charges.

'Cecile was boarding in France,' she went on, 'but there were some issues, they didn't go into them. Anyway she's a quiet girl, with good English and it turns out that she is an excellent swimmer. She goes to the university pool every week to practice.'

There was shouting outside and Mrs James jumped up to look through the window.

'Oh, it's just the rehearsal. We have to keep the noise down because there are girls revising. Where was I? Frances, poor girl. Her parents have been out in Afghanistan, Kabul I believe. He's something to do with the reorganisation out there. She doesn't go, of course.'

There was a knock at the door.

'Come!' she called.

Two girls dressed almost identically in shorts and T-shirts entered the music room.

'Come in, girls. I want you to meet your tutor, Dr Sanderson.'

Mills struggled to her feet and they stood facing each other awkwardly beside the grand piano. Through the window Mills spotted the American girl sauntering down the drive, cigarette in hand, her hair falling loosely round her face. Mills wondered whether the Head had seen her smoking and if she would reprimand her if she did.

When she was left alone with the girls, Mills suggested they showed her where they might have their tutorials. They took her to a small room off the main entrance hall with a table and four chairs. The only window was high up the wall with no apparent means of opening it.

'It's going to be hot and stuffy if we sit in here for any length of time,' said Mills. 'Is there anywhere else we can go?'

They both shook their heads so Mills suggested they had their chat outside.

'It's such a nice day. You can show me round the garden.'

To her surprise, the girls took her to a back door that led into a rose garden, where there were benches arranged at intervals along a central gravel walkway. One or two of the benches were occupied by girls who were reading or writing. Instead of sitting on one of the empty benches, they took a right turn that led them to the far end of the house. They came out onto a sunny patio where there were wicker chairs and tables scattered round a small pool.

'Is this for swimming?' Mills asked, wondering whether it was big enough to be called a pool.

'Yes, but it's not used much,' said Cecile.

Her French accent was barely discernible.

'It's not kept very clean,' added Frances.

They found three chairs and formed a small circle round a low table.

'So tell me about what you've been doing for your "AS" level archaeology this year,' Mills began.

From what she could gather, Miss Porteous had struggled through the syllabus with them as best she could. Neither of the girls expected to do well in their exam and they were disappointed. Mills got the impression they were bright students only lacking the right direction from their teacher. She could help them but had only been asked to assist with the fieldwork.

'So, what plans do you have for your practical assignment?' Mills asked.

Frances looked at Cecile and they both looked back at Mills, sheepishly.

'We thought it might be interesting to do something about Richard the Third, since his remains were found quite recently.' Frances was waiting for her reaction.

'Right,' Mills said slowly. 'So what had you in mind?'

She couldn't see what she could offer with respect to that project since the discovery had been made three years earlier, the excavation was complete and as far as she knew, the spot where the body had been found was now reinstated as a car park. But if she rejected that idea they would have to come up with another. She explained the dilemma and advised them to think of a topic that was geographically closer to home, wherever that was, if they were to work on it over the summer holidays.

Frances looked surprised. 'My parents are abroad so I'll be staying here over the summer.'

'Me too,' said Cecile.

'Oh, I thought your parents lived in London,' said Mills.

'They do. But I want to stay here with Fran.'

'We thought it would help our project,' her friend added in a rush.

Mills could hardly argue. She advised them to look around Richmond to see if there was a historical building or feature they could investigate and reminded them that their projects had to be carried out and written up separately.

She left them to discuss their plans and made her way behind the school to the back door. As she entered the corridor she could hear raised voices and recognised the American accent immediately.

'You don't have any rights over me! I'll do exactly what I want, thank you!'

A door slammed and it went quiet. As Mills made her way to the hallway she could see a young man in jeans and a hoodie marching down the drive and jumping into a white van. In the dimness of the hall, Mills caught Madison pushing a small plastic bag into the back pocket of her shorts. If that was what Mills thought it was, she was certain Mrs James would not approve.

Chapter 2

'Have you heard Jake's news?' Nige asked, when Mills returned to the office.

'What?'

It had been a long morning: a lecture with the second year forensics group followed by year one archaeology. Mills wasn't sure if she could cope with this constant hopping between subject areas.

'He's only been offered a professorship at Columbia University, New York!'

'Is that where his girlfriend comes from?' Mills tried to sound disinterested but knew that Nige wouldn't be fooled.

'I don't know. Anyway, he wants to be there for the fall semester.'

'The what?'

'The autumn term to me and you.'

'Will they let him go at such short notice?'

Nige grinned. 'Depends if they've found a replacement, doesn't it?'

Mills sat down. 'What d'you mean, Nige?'

She knew he'd know what the department had in mind; Nige was on all the academic committees and would have a hand in choosing a replacement. Was this the opportunity she'd been waiting for?

'Nothing really. I expect there will be a decision made about it in due course.'

She wasn't going to let him get away with that.

'Have you heard something, Nige?'

He shook his head and smiled.

'Nigel Featherstone – all the babysitting I've done for you and Nina over the years! Taking over your classes when you were on leave! You must've heard something?'

'Honestly, Mills. I'll let you know when there's something definite.'

'Just tell me if they'll replace him with a full-time lecturer.'

'You wouldn't be interested in that, would you?'

'I would if it was a permanent position.'

'What about teaching on the forensics course?'

It would be a shame to lose that but Mills needed to find a suitable niche for the future that guaranteed a monthly salary.

'I would miss it,' she said. 'But I can live without it.'

'Well, they may decide to change Jake's post around, you never know.'

He began working on his computer so Mills didn't quiz him further.

That evening, as they cooked together, she told Alex about Jake's position becoming vacant and asked whether he thought she should go for a full-time lecturer post in the department. He seemed convinced it was the right thing for her to do.

'It can't do any harm and if you get a permanent post at the university it will solve Brenda's problem.'

'What d'you mean "Brenda's problem"? Was she at the laboratory today? What's she been saying?'

This was exactly what she had been concerned about. Alex was still hanging on in Yardley Forensics despite the understanding that he would have to go when Brenda returned to work.

'Oh, nothing much. Just the usual. I told her I was looking for something else but it's not easy.'

But you're not looking are you? Mills thought, then immediately felt guilty. 'I'm sorry, love. It doesn't seem fair that you have to leave Yardley.'

Alex was standing at the stove with his back to her.

He said, 'But if you get this university job it'll solve everything. I get to stay at the lab on a permanent basis and you have a full-time permanent job. Everything's sweet.'

Mills knew that hadn't ever been the plan. Taking Alex on was a hare-brained scheme of Brenda's to expand into digital forensics. Mills had been pleased with the arrangement at the time because it meant they were together and she was happy for him to move into Laurel Cottage with her over a year ago. Digital forensics work just hadn't materialised and Brenda was still dependent on Mills for her expertise in soil forensics and other analytical techniques.

'You know, there are no guarantees that I'll be considered for Jake's replacement,' she warned Alex as they sat watching television later that evening.

'Don't be so negative. It'll all work out – you see.'

Before Mills could respond, the landline rang with a tone that told her it was family, which could only mean her father or his wife. Since Dad rarely rang, she guessed it would be Fiona wanting to know how she'd got on at High Fell School.

'Did you meet the Headmistress? What is Cecile like? I haven't seen her since she was a baby. Are they taking you on?'

'Yes, it's fine. The two girls seem pleasant enough. I'm going to see them for a session tomorrow afternoon.'

'Marianne has told me that Cecile is in the school play.'

'They're doing Hamlet. I saw the stage, it's being performed outside.'

'She said she's travelling up for the performance. It's in two weeks.'

She paused and Mills waited.

'She asked if I'd like to go with her.'

Mills was thinking fast. How long would she stay? Would she bring her daughter? The child was quite sweet but Fiona fussed over her so much.

Mills asked, 'Will Flora be with you?'

'Heavens, no! She has school and her nanny, Agnes, will cope for a few days.'

Suddenly Mills was paying attention. 'You're very welcome to stay with us,' she offered now she knew it was safe to do so.

'That would be lovely, Mills, but Marianne has asked me to accompany her to a rather lovely spa hotel in Harrogate. It's just the break I need at the moment.'

Mills asked after her father and Fiona talked for a while about their difference of opinion over leaving Flora with Agnes so much of the time. Apparently the woman's English was poor and Hugh was concerned that it would impair their child's speech development.

'Where does Agnes come from?' Mills enquired out of politeness.

'Poland. Her name is actually Agnieszka but no-one can remember it.'

Mills assumed by "no-one" she meant herself.

'When are you coming up to Yorkshire, anyway?' Mills asked as they were saying their goodbyes.

'Two weeks on Friday, for the Saturday performance. You will come, won't you?'

'I guess so.' She couldn't say no and it would be interesting to meet this Marianne Fleurot.

*

The school library was off limits to members of the lower sixth while "A" level exams were in progress, so Fran had asked Cecile to meet her in the common room to discuss their response to Dr Sanderson. Mae was the only girl in there when Cecile arrived; she was working on the big central table, which was covered with foliage.

'What's all that?' Cecile asked.

Mae was often seen carrying a sprig of herbs. At first there were pots balanced on the bedroom window-sill but, after objections from both the students and domestic staff, she'd been granted permission to plant a small herb garden at the back of the school house. There was often the smell of drying vegetation coming from the tiny kitchen in the student house and sometimes strange concoctions were brewing on the stove. It was the main source of aggravation between Mae and Madison.

'Rue.' Mae was picking through the pile of leaves, discarding some sprigs to one side. 'But there's other stuff mixed up in it – weeds mainly.'

'I thought they were all weeds,' joked Cecile. 'Isn't that what wild flowers are?'

'Yeah, sort of, I suppose.'

'So what are you making today?' Cecile asked, genuinely interested. 'It smells horrendous.'

Mae's interest was no longer confined to Chinese medicine and the school production of Hamlet seemed to have excited her enthusiasm for the work of mediaeval herbalists.

'I'm going to dry rue and put it in bags to hang round our room; it's supposed to be an insect repellent.'

'I'm not surprised,' Cecile said. 'It doesn't smell very fragrant.'

She went to pick some up but Mae stopped her.

'Don't touch it – it can cause a reaction if you have sensitive skin.'

Her friend held out her hands to show Cecile that she was wearing plastic gloves.

'Where did you get it from?' she asked, stepping back from the table.

'My garden – I grew it from seed. Easy really, it likes lime. I've even seen it growing wild up on the crag when I've been collecting thyme.'

'I bet Madison will complain if you put it in your room.'

Mae laughed. 'It's better than the smell of the stuff she smokes in there! Maybe it will hide her misdeeds.'

'Not all of them,' Cecile replied.

'What do you mean?'

'Her liaison.'

'Which one, there are so many.'

'No, this one is serious, very serious. If anyone finds out…'

Cecile stopped abruptly as the door opened and Fran came in looking flustered.

'Sorry, we had a problem with the sound and they're rehearsing the first act again.'

She stopped abruptly. 'What *is* that smell?'

Mae was putting her plant material into plastic bags and whisking the remaining bits off the table and onto the floor.

'It's all right, I'm going.'

As soon as she was out of the room, Fran turned to Cecile. 'Madison's brother was at the rehearsal.'

'Austin?'

'With his friend.'

'Jules, his name is Jules.'

'Well, Jules was asking where you were. He wants to know if you'll be around later.'

She didn't reply.

'Well?' her friend insisted.

'I don't know.'

'I thought you liked him.'

'I do but – look we ought to get on.'

Fran shrugged and they settled down to amalgamate their ideas in the hope of finding a suitable archaeological site to study in the summer break. Cecile had made a list of castles in the area but her friend had been more ingenious and located the graves of Knights Templars in Wensleydale, which sounded much more interesting.

'That's brilliant,' she said.

'It sounds good but it's going to be difficult to get to.'

'Most of it will be research so we don't need to visit the site much; we won't be allowed to do anything apart from look at it.'

'That's pretty lame then.'

In the end they decided to combine their entries and send their tutor the complete list.

'She seemed nice,' said Cecile. 'She'll sort something out for us, I'm sure.'

Mills was dividing her time between the University of North Yorkshire and Yardley Forensics in Harrogate. Brenda Yardley was recovering well from her chemotherapy but she'd been off sick for such a long time that Mills had become used to managing the laboratory. The staff had grown accustomed to her and even Glyn, the technical manager, was willing to accept her leadership, albeit grudgingly. However, she knew he'd be glad to see Brenda back at the helm. Mills was unsure where that would leave her when she was no longer "in charge".

The drive to Harrogate was carefully planned to avoid the worst of the traffic. It was a sunny morning and Mills arrived at the laboratory relaxed and calm, determined to have a quiet word with Brenda about the future. She had a lecture to give at the university later that afternoon so she'd told Alex she'd be going into Harrogate early and they would have to take separate cars. Actually she wanted the opportunity to speak to her boss before he arrived.

Brenda was already bustling about and although Mills had become accustomed to the dramatic changes in her appearance, it was always a shock to see her looking so skinny. The weight she'd lost had left her gaunt and cheekbones had appeared where there was a friendly chubbiness before. Her hair was growing back snowy white now and wispy. Typically, Brenda hadn't changed her wardrobe but continued to wear her original size clothes, giving her a bizarre appearance. This morning she was in a brightly coloured tunic, tied in the middle with a belt, over a pair of trousers that sagged around her backside. She regularly hauled them up as she stood chatting.

'I've had a meeting with the accountant, Mills. He's made a suggestion but I don't like it. I think we should discuss it as soon as possible.'

'Ok.'

Mills followed her into the inner office. Brenda eased herself gently into the old chair behind the desk and Mills sat opposite her.

'So,' Brenda began. 'He tells me that our outgoings are currently exceeding our income, which is not good apparently.' She smiled.

Mills nodded.

'He insisted we went over our costs item by item. I was getting bored by the end of it, I can tell you.'

Brenda was not the most patient of people and Mills wondered whether the accountant had received the sharp end of her tongue.

'Anyway, the long and the short of it is that our main costs are salaries; fairly obvious really.'

This was her opportunity. 'We did agree that Alex would have to go when you came back.' It felt disloyal.

'I took that as read, dear.' She looked concerned. 'No, I've got to cut back even further or we'll be finished.'

Mills hadn't realised it was so bad; now she *was* worried.

'Have you made any decisions?' she asked tentatively.

'I need you to help me, Mills. I've made a list of all the staff and I want to go through it with you. We must decide who is essential and who we can do without.'

'Shall I make some coffee?' Mills asked, playing for time.

'I wondered where you were,' complained Alex at lunch-time. 'Donna needs a signature and Glyn wanted to ask you about something that's come in.'

'Brenda wanted me to help her.'

Alex looked at her questioningly as he went to bite into his sandwich. 'Must've been important, you were shut away for hours.'

Mills considered her reply. 'She wanted to discuss how to save money on staff.'

'Someone for the chop?'

'Maybe more than one.'

Mills didn't want to be reminded of the conversation that morning. Examining every analyst and technician in turn; evaluating their contribution to the work of the laboratory; discussing which areas the laboratory should be specialising in. One of the most awkward conversations was whether they should continue with digital forensics and, if so, did they need Alex. Brenda said she appreciated how difficult it was for Mills, being personally involved with him. Mills had responded that she just wanted for them to make the best decision for the future of the laboratory. Well, it was true, wasn't it?

'I think she should get rid of the routine stuff like fingerprinting and DNA,' suggested Alex. 'Develop a niche market…'

'Like digital?' Mills asked.

'Yes. Specialise.'

'But the routine stuff is our bread and butter, Alex. How much work have you brought in?'

Mills immediately regretted saying it and began to apologise but Alex was already defending himself.

'It has a huge potential and it's a specialised area. Who else can offer that round here?'

Mills didn't want an argument. 'The fingerprinting and DNA will always be the first requests in a crime.'

'Ok, so get rid of the expensive instrumentation and make more use of the computing power we have.'

'Doing what?'

'We could do more on footwear print identification.'

Mills sighed. 'We can't branch out into new things when we're trying to reduce costs. We have to stick to what we know and what we're good at – like Brenda's textiles expertise and the chemical fingerprinting.'

To her relief, Glyn came into the tea room and they stopped their argument abruptly.

'Can I see you about a phone enquiry that came in early this morning?' he asked. 'They're asking for some additional tests.'

'Of course. Let's go down to your office.'

It didn't take long to discuss the extra analyses and soon Mills was driving out of Harrogate, relieved to be away from the decisions on cuts and the disagreement with Alex over where they should be made. The roof was down and Mills could feel the sun on the back of her neck as she thought about the lecture she had planned for the first year forensics students. She enjoyed teaching, although archaeology was still her favourite subject despite being so heavily involved with present-day forensics. Unfortunately it seemed as if she had left forensic archaeology behind several years ago.

Time was getting on. She left the Mini at a rakish angle in the staff car park, grabbed her briefcase and sprinted into the building.

'Ah, Dr Sanderson!' Professor Cole, Head of Forensics was passing her in the corridor. 'Do you have a moment?'

She stopped briefly to explain she was late but would come to his office after the lecture, then continued on to the large seminar room, where twelve students were already waiting. It was nearly the end of the summer term and any coursework was over because exams were imminent. This was to be a last informal chat before fieldwork started. Most of them were joining second year students who had sites arranged over the summer. One or two were still without a plan and Mills needed to organise them because it was essential they had some practical experience before tackling their own project during the following year. By the end of the session she had sorted out the stragglers and felt able to say goodbye to the class until September.

Professor Cole was in a meeting and Mills was told to return in half an hour. She went in search of Nige to find out if he knew what the Head of Archaeology planned to do about Jake's replacement.

'Sorry, Mills, as far as I know nothing has been decided yet, not until the meeting with the Dean at the end of this week.'

Mills moved a bag of tools and sat down in the corner of his cluttered office.

'Busy?' he asked, peering over a pile of papers. 'You can help me with this marking if you like.'

'No way! I've got my own, thank you.'

She realised she was interrupting his work.

'Want anything from the cafeteria?' she offered.

'Tea, please,' he replied without looking up.

The half an hour was up by the time she'd walked across the campus and back. Depositing Nige's tea on his desk, she dashed along to Professor Cole's office.

'Ah, I see you have a drink. Sit down then, it won't take long.'

His office was spacious and airy with large windows overlooking the lawn and the lake.

Mills sat opposite him clutching the paper cup.

'I know when Professor Green retired we agreed that you would take over any of his forensic work that came along.'

'Yes, but since he left there hasn't been anything, really. I expect after his… after he…'

'Yes, quite.'

Professor Green's methods had been called into question and he had left the university under a cloud.

'Well, now we have been asked by the police to look at a piece of forensic archaeology. Right up your street I imagine, Mills.'

'Yes.' She straightened up and put her cup down carefully on the edge of the desk.

'Human remains found somewhere near Richmond. I don't have any more information but there's the phone number of our contact.'

Mills took the piece of paper, thinking she might recognise the number but no. 'It sounds very interesting.'

'Well, keep me posted and remember the reputation of the university depends on it.'

No pressure then, thought Mills.

It was late but she went back to the office to make the call. To her surprise the phone was answered by DS Fuller. It was a relief that she would be working with someone familiar, even though Hazel could be rather brusque at times.

'Hi Mills, thanks for ringing. We need an archaeologist for this one.'

'Prof Cole said it was the skeleton of a male.'

'Bits of one, yes. We've not found them all and I told them to wait until we could get someone in who knew what they were doing. Can you get over here sharpish?'

'You mean today?' Mills was willing go if needed.

'No, he's not going anywhere, girl. Tomorrow will do.'

Although Mills had no teaching commitments the following day, she had arranged to go over to High Fell School in the afternoon.

'I can be there first thing,' Mills promised. 'Where is it?'

'He's in the middle of a new housing development not far from the A1 near Scotch Corner. I'll email you the directions. Shall I meet you there at eight?'

'Yes, that's fine.'

'I should warn you, the builders are anxious to proceed and they've not been very helpful so far. We can provide a uniformed officer while you're on site but you should be aware that there have been threats made and we suspect someone has been tampering with the site.'

Chapter 3

Mills made a call as soon as she got home. DS Fuller's words had intrigued her and she wanted to find out more from her friend, DS Nina Featherstone. But it was her husband that answered the phone.

'Nige, it's me again. Can I have a word with Nina?'

There was a clonk as the receiver was dropped on a hard surface and she heard Nige calling for her at the top of his voice. Mills had forgotten they would be getting the twins to bed.

'Mills.' Nina's voice was tense.

'Sorry – you must be busy with the kids. Shall I call back later?'

'No it's fine, it's Nige's turn to bath the boys and Rosie is watching a video.'

'I won't take long.'

'Is it about the skeleton?'

'How did you guess?'

'It's a no-brainer. Hazel said you'd called her today and I had a feeling you'd be on to me to find out more.'

'It was when she mentioned threats from the workmen that I was curious,' Mills admitted.

'It's just Hazel being melodramatic. She's rather protective of her "Mr Bones".'

'Is that what she calls him?'

Nina was laughing. 'Yes. But don't worry; I'm sure you'll be fine.'

She wanted to know more but Nige had taken the phone from Nina and was telling Mills that he'd wanted to catch her at the university but he'd had to leave early to pick the boys up from nursery.

'I've been thinking about Jake's post becoming vacant.' It was unusual for Nige to sound so earnest. 'Just a thought, but it could be a good move to suggest a joint post, shared between Forensics and Archaeology. Both sections are trying to save money and you could cover both areas. What d'you think?'

'What? Do two jobs for the price of one?'

'Not exactly, no. They would have to share the hours like. But that's possible, isn't it? If you wanted to work something up, I could put it to the meeting on Friday.'

'Seriously?'

'I think it might solve several problems for the department and you never know, with a shared lectureship you might even be able to teach some forensic archaeology – an added bonus!'

Mills mentioned the idea to Alex when she came off the phone. He encouraged her to think about a proposal to do exactly what Nige had suggested and even helped her draw up a draft. She was grateful for his help but it still irritated her that he was so keen to see her leave Yardley Forensics altogether.

It was a beautiful morning, already warm even though it was only seven o' clock. Mills left Alex sleeping and set off for the estate of new properties in Gilling West, where the skeletal remains had been found. The building site was down a track off the main road but the sales board clearly identified "Swale Heights – a new development of executive four & five bedroom properties."

Mills was early and there was no sign of Hazel Fuller but a couple of workmen were standing beside a small hut, smoking. She parked the car, hoping it wouldn't be in the way and decided to remain listening to the car radio until she saw a familiar face. Five minutes later a car pulled alongside her, Hazel waved and a uniformed officer climbed out of the passenger seat. Mills went to meet her.

'Mills! Thanks for coming. Just wait there while I see if the foreman is about.'

She returned a few minutes later, alone, and with the uniformed constable in tow she led Mills down the side of a half-built house. Behind it was what would eventually be the garden. Currently it was a pile of soil beside a deep ditch.

'There have been no proper controls on the scene,' the uniformed officer said, pulling at a large tarpaulin to expose the site. 'The builders were virtually playing football with the skull until someone thought to contact us.'

Mills peered in. A skull was lying on the ground and there were signs of parts of the skeleton poking out of the soil.

'So what exactly do you want me to do?' Mills asked.

Hazel sighed. 'All we know is that it's a man. Our consultant osteoarchaeologist confirmed it's not a recent burial and so they are deemed "bones of antiquity"; I think that's the term. I've been liaising with the archaeological team in County Hall in Northallerton and they asked if we could get the bones collected, cleaned and passed on to them with all the necessary information on how and where they were found. I think I persuaded them that you would do a good job.'

'Don't they want to supervise the work?'

'We want to get it done quickly to prevent the builders becoming difficult. Nina suggested you could do the collection for us and pass the bones on to them for any further investigation. That way everyone will get what they want without too much delay.' She was beginning to sound irritated.

Mills allowed herself to be talked into taking on the work despite a serious lack of confidence on her part that she had the time to do it. Hazel gave her the details of the team at County Hall and left her to make contact. Finally she introduced the young man in uniform who was waiting sentry-like at the edge of the plot.

'This is Grant,' she explained. 'He's not here all the time but if there's any problem you can ask him to come over and lend a hand.'

Mills agreed to make a start the following day, when she had all the tools and necessary paraphernalia for photographing the site and recording relevant details as she went along. It was an exciting, if daunting, prospect and one that combined forensics and archaeology, just as Nige had said she would be able to if she had a post at the university dividing her time between the two areas.

Mills was still thinking about Nige's idea of a lecturing post divided between the Archaeology and Forensics Departments as she drove across the moors to High Fell School in the afternoon. The sixth-formers had sent her an email asking her advice over their latest ideas for their practical assignment. Frances, who appeared to be the most dynamic of the pair, had produced a list of buildings in the Richmond area that warranted further investigation. The obvious ones: Richmond Castle, the Georgian theatre, Easby Abbey and Middleham Castle were at the top, but further down were some she wasn't so familiar with, such as Culloden Tower, the Friary Tower in

Richmond, and the Marmion Tower and Knights Templars' Chapel in Wensleydale. Initially Mills had been impressed at the speed with which the girls had produced the list but, as Alex had pointed out, it was only a matter of finding the right site on the internet so she was keen to quiz them more about the buildings they had listed.

The girls met Mills at the front of the school, suggesting they sat in the garden again as it was a nice day.

'Otherwise we'd have to be in that tiny room because the library is out of bounds,' Frances explained.

'There's still revision going on for the "A" level exams,' Cecile added.

Frances was carrying a brightly coloured ring binder and an iPad, which she set up on the table nearest the pool. Cecile, who was empty-handed, sat down and waited.

'I've got the list on here,' Frances said, fiddling with the iPad.

'It's in the folder, Fran.' Cecile picked it up and turned the pages until she found what she was looking for.

'Right,' said Mills. 'Let's go through them in turn and see what you've got.'

They started at the top of the list with the well-known sites.

'There's a mass of information about them on the internet,' Frances said.

'But your assignment must include an independent investigation; you can't just look things up.'

'But isn't that research?' Cecile argued.

'Well, yes – and no. I sent you a copy of the specification; did you read it?'

'I did,' said Cecile. 'It said the title must be in the form of a question.'

'And it says you can take part in an excavation but then it says you have to be supervised, so that's not going to happen.' Frances looked at Mills as if she was judging her reaction.

Mills responded by tapping the list. 'Let's go on and see which things on the list might fit the requirements.'

She could see they were losing interest as the possibilities diminished.

'What is the Culloden Tower?' she asked. 'I've not heard about that.'

They explained to her that it was built in 1746 to celebrate the defeat of the Jacobites in the Battle of Culloden.

'But why is it in Richmond?' asked Mills. 'The Battle of Culloden took place a long way away.'

The girls looked glum and shook their heads.

'What state is the tower in now?' she continued,

'It's let as a holiday cottage,' said Frances.

'So it's been kept in good repair,' said Mills.

Cecile perked up. 'There was a tower there before it was built, a pele tower.'

'Do you know what that is?' Mills asked.

The girls shook their heads again.

'A watchtower,' she informed them. 'Presumably to keep an eye out for invaders from Scotland. Perhaps there is something left of that original tower of interest. That is if you can get access to the site.'

Neither girl looked optimistic. Mills checked her watch, their hour was nearly up.

'I suggest you look into the possibility of visiting the Culloden Tower and find out more about the pele tower that was there before, when it was built and when it was in use.' She took a deep breath. 'There is an excavation I'm going to work on that you *may* be able to come just to see. It will at least give you the opportunity to see how the work is carried out.'

Suddenly the girls were interested.

'Is it a *very* old building?' Cecile asked.

'Not a building,' replied Mills. 'Old bones.'

It was a relief to have the skeleton to work on; the meeting about the university post was three days away and Mills could think of nothing else. Alex was full of optimism and insisted she would "walk it". She was less sure, knowing how research groups disliked sharing anything, even though technically they were part of the same department. Much would depend on the Dean and how well Nige put her case. He was encouraging, praising the supporting case she'd put together and insisting it would be the best outcome for everyone involved.

Her meeting with the archaeological team in County Hall had gone surprisingly well and they appeared to have full confidence in her ability to present them with the bones in a timely manner with the information they required. The consultant osteoarchaeologist who had examined the site was happy for the university to do the work of collecting the bones. Mills confirmed she would be taking photographs at every stage and was pleased to let them tell her exactly how they wanted the bones labelled. Finally, they reassured her by saying that it was all quite a routine procedure but someone would probably come down to monitor progress. When Mills mentioned that she wanted to bring a couple of students to the site, they had no objections, mistakenly assuming they were from the university.

In fact they were pleased she would have trained help. She didn't enlighten them but felt guilty afterwards and decided to wait until she'd made a good start on the site before letting Frances and Cecile visit.

The weather was perfect and Mills was able to crack on with the photography during her first day on site. The workmen took little notice of her when she arrived and the foreman seemed happy for her to begin, once she'd introduced herself.

'Is that copper coming back or is it the last we'll see of 'im?' he asked.

Mills didn't know but believed that he would continue to keep an eye on the place.

'What will you do with 'im?' he asked, waving a thumb towards the site.

'I'll be taking the… er, parts… away with me each day,' she explained.

The foreman was anxious to know when she'd be done and she assured him that she would finish as soon as she could.

The building site was noisy but she was able to work in the area behind the house undisturbed. Wagons were rumbling back and forth outside, men shouting to each other in the distance, the clank of metal scaffolding poles and the drone of pneumatic drills. When silence fell she could hear a radio playing eighties music. She worked systematically, taking shots from every angle, both near and from some distance away. She recorded the relevant information in her notebook and by the time she stopped for lunch she was happy that she was ready to begin exposing the remains.

A shadow fell across her notebook as she sat finishing her sandwiches. She looked up at the workman standing in front, slightly too close for comfort.

'How do,' he said quietly.

Mills stood up and moved away from him.

'How's it going?' he asked, indicating the exposed patch of ground where she was working.

'Fine,' she answered, picking up her lunch box and stuffing it in her rucksack.

He stood looking at what there was to see of the skeleton. Mills felt inexplicably protective of "Mr Bones" and muttered that she had to get on.

'You'll be finished soon I expect,' he said, making no attempt to move.

'It'll take as long as it takes,' she replied.

There was no way she would be hurried by any threats from the builders on site.

He turned to leave and she could hardly catch what he was saying but it sounded like she should get a move on if she knew what was good for her.

Progress was slow in the afternoon. The sun was hot and the ground was baked hard. She had only partially exposed the rest of the skeleton by the time the foreman came over to tell her that the builders were leaving for the day and he wanted to lock the gates. Reluctantly, she pulled the tarpaulin over the area and left but not before asking for a key so she could work at the weekend.

The last exam was over and there was a party atmosphere in the student house. Bottles appeared in the bedrooms: cider, wine and even spirits. Music was being played loudly for the first time in weeks and girls were shouting through open windows to friends below. The excitement was heightened by the fact that there was a rehearsal of Hamlet planned for the evening, to test the lighting and it would be the first time that Mrs James was allowing the sound system to be used at full volume.

'I hope you're using plenty of that insect repellent,' remarked Madison as she watched Mae helping her friend Sofia cover her bare arms with liquid from a small green bottle.

'Sage, rosemary, lavender, thyme and mint,' Mae recited.

'It smells lovely,' said Sofia, rubbing it on her face. 'Better than the rue,' she added with a laugh.

'You may mock but those bags have kept the room free of bugs, haven't they?'

'But when you were boiling it up the other night it stank the place out,' said Madison.

'That was for the tincture,' said Mae, indignantly. 'Some people are grateful for it.'

'Who?' demanded Madison.

'Anyone with painful periods,' said Mae airily.

'You're kidding!'

'No,' said Sofia. 'I've tried it. It really works.'

The American girl pulled a face and stood up. 'I'll see you down at the rehearsal; I want to catch my brother.'

Madison slipped on her flip-flops as Mae replaced the green bottle carefully in her bedside locker.

'I'm off to find Austin,' she told no-one in particular as she wandered down the corridor.

The student house was buzzing with excitement and Madison had to push through the crowded hall before making her way outside, where she found Austin with Jules. She knew her brother's friend pretty well from the visits he'd made during vacation times and hailed the two boys in her usual manner.

'Hi gravediggers!'

'Look what the cat's brought in,' responded Austin, dodging a slap from his sister.

'How's it going?' she asked.

Madison had chosen not to take an acting part in the production but had begun to hang around backstage, helping with the scenery and offering to join the make-up team for the dress rehearsal.

'We're not on until the fifth act, dummy.' Austin said, moving away in case another slap was aimed in his direction.

But Madison had lost interest in her brother and his friend. She'd spotted Jeremy standing in front of the stage, alone. She went over slowly and tapped him on the shoulder. He turned with a smile that disappeared when he saw it was her.

'Don't look so pleased to see me,' she said with a laugh.

He turned back to face the stage. 'I'm busy.'

'I'll catch you later then, Jeremy. What time are you finishing?'

'Not until about eight.'

'That's ok. I can wait.'

'I'll be going straight home. I told you, I've got a family to consider.'

'Didn't worry you before.'

His shoulders stiffened and he looked back at her. 'Go away, Madison. I mean it. This has got to stop.'

She turned to walk off and almost bumped into Leanne.

'Why don't you look where you're going!' she shouted at the startled girl before storming off towards the drive.

There was nowhere to go in flip-flops and after a few minutes Madison returned to a group of girls on the front lawn, flinging herself on the ground to watch the rehearsals from a distance. Soon she was drinking from the bottle that was being passed round and sharing a roll-up with a couple of the older girls.

'Smoke is supposed to get rid of mosquitoes,' someone complained. 'But I'm being bitten to death.'

Madison said, 'You need my room-mate's patent medicine.'

'What's that?' another girl asked.

'Dunno,' answered Madison. 'Some herbal stuff in a green bottle.'

'Where's it come from?'

'She makes it. Brews it up in our kitchen. Stinks the place out. Her locker's full of the stuff. Hang on – here come the gravediggers. You must watch this bit, it's such a laugh. The skull is so gross!'

Secretly she was impressed with her brother and his friend. Their scene was one of the highlights of the play, everyone said so. Of course, she'd never tell Austin that. Even posh little Cecile, who Jules was mad about, had agreed.

It had been a really tiring day at the building site for Mills, working through the intense heat at midday and into the long afternoon. She was making good progress while the fine weather lasted but had missed lunch and was beginning to feel quite sick and faint at the end of the day. But before she could go home she had to put her first batch of bones in store at the university, ready to be washed.

The departmental car park was nearly empty and a cleaner was already working down the corridor. There was no-one around so she collected the key from her office and went to the large walk-in cupboard that served as a store room. It was packed with boxes, bags, sacks and bottles: a jumble of samples that had built up over the years. Mills rearranged a shelf on the back wall and placed the two cardboard boxes neatly one on top of the other. It was hot and stuffy in the cramped place and it was a relief to get out and slam the heavy door behind her.

Soon she was back in the traffic heading for Swaledale. She enjoyed driving with the hood down when the weather permitted although the cool breeze did nothing to relieve the headache that had settled on her forehead. Once she was on the road to Reeth she could feel herself winding down a little; after all she had made a good start on the site. The forecast was fine for the next few days which meant she could keep up progress if she worked over the weekend.

She'd anticipated that Alex would be preparing something to eat but to her surprise the cottage was empty. When he did eventually appear, she was resting in the garden with a large glass of water.

'What's for tea?' he called from the kitchen.

She didn't answer.

He came to the back door and repeated his question.

Mills snapped, 'I don't know. Is there something in the freezer?'

He disappeared inside and returned a minute later.

'There's ice-cream or a microwaveable curry for one.'

'I really don't care,' said Mills. 'I'll have a piece of cheese.'

He went in, leaving Mills wishing she didn't find him so irritating at times. When the smell of cooking was too much for her curiosity, she went to the door and watched him preparing a large omelette. Before she could enquire whether it was all for him, he was dividing it onto two plates and following her back out to the table in the garden.

'Do I detect that you had a bad day?' he asked as he sat down opposite her.

'No, it was fine,' she said absently. 'I just had too much sun.'

'Lucky you. I've been indoors all day surrounded by people who think they're going to lose their jobs.'

'Has Brenda said something?' Mills was suddenly listening. 'She hasn't told them?'

'Nothing. It's time she bit the bullet and got on with it.'

'How do they know she's considering it?'

'Search me.'

He shrugged, looking down at his food. Mills wondered if he'd said something to the others himself. She could believe he might have done.

'Brenda's expecting you in tomorrow, by the way.'

'I'm working at the building site.'

'But she wants to talk with us about the cuts before Monday. She's keen to make an announcement next week.'

'I must get on while the weather holds.'

Privately she'd prefer that Brenda delayed her decision until the university had decided what was happening to Jake's post.

Alex seemed to read her mind 'When will you hear about your job?'

She didn't know. 'Next week, maybe.'

She knew he assumed if she went to work full-time at the university, his job would be secure. But that wouldn't be the best outcome for Brenda.

'We'll just have to wait and see, won't we,' she added.

Chapter 4

Technical rehearsals were scheduled every day leading up to the dress rehearsal, and today was the first time there would be a full run through. The performers and older girls, who had missed all the excitement of the production, now hung around watching the final preparations. Girls came and went but there was always a small audience gathered on the grass in front of the big stage. Leanne, still dressed as Hamlet, came over to join Mae, who was sitting in the group.

'You were brilliant!' Mae told Leanne as she made space beside her.

'It wasn't that good. I feel awful today.' She was holding her stomach as she sat down with a groan. 'It's that time of the month and the cramps are really bad.'

'Have you taken something?'

'No. Why? Can you make me one of your potions?'

Mae hesitated. 'Actually, I have one that will help. I've made a tincture of rue. It helps with menstrual problems. You can try it if you like.'

She stood up and offered her friend a hand. 'Come on, there's plenty of time before they need you again. It's nearly lunch time.'

As they picked their way through the seated figures there was a yell.

'Hey Mae! Come and have a drink!'

Madison was waving a wine bottle at them.

'No thanks!' called Mae and pulled Leanne along.

But Madison persisted. 'Come here and tell them about your insect repellent stuff.'

She turned to speak to her friends seated beside her and they all laughed.

'She'll be in trouble if Mr Young sees her,' Mae said when they were clear of the group.

Leanne agreed. 'She's already in trouble with him.'

'Why?'

'I heard him telling her off.'

'What did he say?'

'Something about it having to stop. He said: *This has got to stop*. He was really angry. What d'you think he meant?'

'Take your pick,' said Mae. 'The drinking, the drugs, the boys.'

'She'd better watch it or she'll be thrown out.'

When they reached her room, Mae took a key from under her pillow, opened the locker beside her bed and sorted through the bottles.

'How do you know which one is which?' asked Leanne. 'There are hundreds in there.'

'Not hundreds,' her friend corrected her. 'And they're categorised.'

She pulled out a small green bottle and showed her friend the label.

Leanne examined it and said, 'I don't read Chinese.'

'It's a good thing I do then.'

Mae took a spoon and poured out the yellowish liquid. She balanced the spoon on the locker while she rifled in the cupboard again. This time she produced a small white paper bag.

'Mints,' she said. 'It will take the taste away.'

Leanne opened her mouth obediently, pulled a face and swallowed, grabbing a mint and pushing it in her mouth.

'Arrgh. That was so gross. Are you sure it's safe to drink?'

'It's fine – unless you're pregnant.'

Leanne laughed. 'No problem then.'

Mae looked up as there was a movement at the door and Sofia came into the room.

'Am I disturbing something?' she asked awkwardly. 'I just wanted to get changed.'

Leanne laughed. 'Don't worry, I was just getting some medicine from Doctor Mae. She said I couldn't have it if I was pregnant. No chance of that!'

Sofia smiled and went to her wardrobe.

'It's not just because it's a medicine,' Mae explained. 'It acts as a… I think the word is abortificant or something like that. No, wait.'

She grabbed a notebook from her desk and flicked the pages until she found what she wanted.

'Abortifacient. That means it can cause miscarriage if used in pregnancy.'

'You never know,' said Sofia as she pulled on her running shorts. 'Some of the girls round here might be glad of your medicine.'

Leanne nodded in the direction of Madison's bed and raised her eyebrows.

'What?' asked Mae.

She shook her head. 'I'm saying nothing but she'd better be careful, that's all.'

Alex had been eating his cereal when Mills left for the building site.

'I'll see you at the lab later,' he called as she picked up her keys.

At first she didn't reply.

'Mills?'

'Probably.'

She left before he could pursue it. She wanted to get as much work done as possible but she was also aware that the meeting about Jake's post was being held at the university and if she went over there early enough, she could catch Nige to find out how her proposal had been received.

She found the skeleton easier to deal with now that the skull had been carefully packed away in the storeroom. Today was about getting as many layers of soil away as possible but it was going to be difficult with the ground becoming so very hard after the heat of the past few days. When she walked across the site the mud had turned to rock and the ground around the remaining bones was like concrete. It made uncovering the large bones difficult but the smaller ones impossible. By lunch-time she'd collected the humerus on one side and worked down the radius until she'd exposed the left wrist.

It was mid-afternoon and she had almost given up trying to expose the fingers when she detected a change in the surface of the bone and discovered signs of a metallic artefact. After careful work and several photographs later, she'd cleaned the soil from thick links of a gold coloured chain wrapped around the wrist and partially exposed. The ends of the fingers were embedded deep into the ground and, by the rate she'd been working, she knew it would be hours before she could free them. Reluctantly, she took a number of photos of the chain and called it a day. She dragged the tarpaulin back over the site, wishing she could leave it open for any rain to soften the ground.

She reached the university just in time. Nige was coming out of the building and heading for his car.

'What have you got there?' he asked, pointing at the box she was unloading from her car.

'Just bones,' she said. 'But they belonged to someone once,' she added, aware that they should be shown respect.

'Sounds interesting.'

'Nige, how did the meeting go?'

'Meeting?'

'The meeting… my proposal…'

'Ok, only joking. It went fine. They liked what you suggested.'

'So?'

'So they will consider it. There's a Faculty meeting next week. The Dean will decide then.'

He was smiling.

'So you think they might…?'

'Don't know. Can't say but they're taking it seriously. It will depend on finances I guess.'

She watched him drive off to collect the children and sighed. The waiting was unbearable and she didn't even know if she wanted the job anyway. It was fun to be flitting from one part-time role to another with no serious responsibility to either. Maybe she had commitment issues as they called it – Alex seemed to think so.

She carried the box to the storeroom and placed it beside the first two. It was pretty depressing that progress had halved in one day. As she straightened the boxes into a neat row she wondered how many there would be eventually and how long it would take to clean all the bones. She had the distinct feeling that she'd taken on too big a task and couldn't ask for help. As she drove home she thought about the schoolgirls. She would be meeting them again next week and had wanted them to see the excavation. The task had turned out harder than she'd expected and she couldn't see how they could be involved, except perhaps with the cleaning part. Perhaps the schoolgirls could help her with that particular job.

Alex was waiting for her, ready to start the moment she'd got through the door.

'Brenda wanted to know where you were,' he reprimanded her. 'She came in especially to discuss the cuts.'

'I'll ring her.'

'Too late. She's made her decision without you.'

Mills was shocked and nervous of the outcome.

'What's she decided?'

'She wouldn't tell me. She's announcing it on Monday.'

'But she can't. I won't know about the decision on my post by then.'

'Tough. You should've been there.'

Mills went to the phone and dialled Brenda's number.

'What happened to you?' she asked as soon as she knew Mills was calling. 'I wanted to talk over the plans.'

Mills apologised and mumbled an excuse about the excavation work she was doing.

'Alex told me about that. He said how you prefer to be doing the archaeology. I can understand that. After all, it's what you were trained for.'

Mills was speechless.

Brenda went on, 'I heard about the job going at the university as well. It sounds perfect, although I hope you'd still be able to act as a consultant for Yardley Forensics in future.'

'Brenda, there's no promise of a job. It's all up in the air. And anyway, I don't know that I'd take it.'

Now it was Brenda's turn to fall silent.

'Brenda?'

'We'll talk about it on Monday, dear, after I've made the announcement.'

'But, Brenda…'

'Have a nice weekend, pet.' She put the receiver down.

Mills was stunned. Alex wanted to keep his job, so clearly he'd given the impression that she would be leaving to work full-time at the university, when she didn't even have an offer and now she wasn't sure she wanted it. She was too hurt to be angry.

'I'm going for a walk,' she said and left.

She went where she always went when she was upset: up to the track through the heather and along the tops. From there she could look down on the river. When it was dry she could sit on a stone or lie back on the heather and look at the sky. At times like this she would think about her mother, always wishing she was alive to help her with grown-up advice. She could ask her father but what did he know? He'd married someone half his age who was more interested in shoes than career choices.

'Fiona rang,' Alex called when she returned. 'She was dashing out to some expensive restaurant but said to tell you they would see you at the school. Apparently she's booked into the spa for most of tomorrow.'

Despite the fact she had no desire to entertain her stepmother, Mills was annoyed that Fiona hadn't made the effort to come over to see her.

'Well, you didn't go to see her,' Alex pointed out, unnecessarily. 'It's disappointing that I won't be meeting her, she's a fun stepmother.'

He knew she disliked him referring to Fiona as her stepmother. Ignoring him she went upstairs for a bath.

The party atmosphere continued into the evening at High Fell School. Because it was difficult to time when the dress rehearsal would finish, a barbecue had been planned instead of supper. It was getting dusk and the smell of grilled meat was drifting across the lawn. Moths were beating against the spotlights casting eerie shadows on the grass. The rehearsal had finished but the technical team were still fiddling with the effects; lowering and raising the lighting levels at shouted orders from Mr Young. From her position in a group of girls and boys lounging close to the stage, Madison was watching the English master, waiting for an opportunity to get him alone.

'Did you tell Cecile?' Her brother was speaking in a low voice.

'Tell her what?'

Someone had started playing music through the big speakers on the stage and she could hardly hear him.

'That Jules fancies her.'

'Jules fancies Cecile?'

She shouted to get herself heard above the music but at that moment it stopped and everyone was laughing. Austin glared at his sister and she shrugged.

'You were supposed to keep it quiet,' he said through gritted teeth. 'You were supposed to only tell her.'

Madison was watching Jeremy as he walked slowly away from the stage and towards his car.

'I will!' she called as she jumped up, still clutching her wine bottle, to follow him.

She waited until she was close enough to call him without attracting attention.

'Jeremy, hang on. I just wanted to say something.'

He turned and waited. She fixed a smile and slowed to a walking pace. She thought he looked anxious.

'Don't worry, it's nothing serious. I just wanted to talk.'

She was in front of him now, holding the bottle behind her back.

'I've been thinking,' she began. 'We can still be friends, can't we? After all, there's nothing wrong with friendship is there?'

'You've been drinking. I've got to get home.'

'No, wait.' She had hold of his sleeve.

'Let go, Madison. I'm warning you. You've gone too far.'

'*I've* gone too far? I think it's *you*, Mr Teacher, that's gone too far.'

She was keeping it amicable. She was staying calm. She took a swig from the bottle and offered it to him. He responded by opening the car door.

'Going home to your wife, Mr Young?'

He didn't answer but stood holding the door handle, looking round nervously.

'Worried someone might see? I don't care if they do.'

She stepped forward and tried to kiss him. He pushed her away.

'Worried what your wife would say?' She taunted him. 'Perhaps I should have a chat with her. Is she coming to the performance, Jeremy? Eh?'

He climbed into the car and slammed the door.

She leaned on the bonnet and peered at him through the windscreen.

'I'd like to meet her. Tell her how fond we all are of you. How good you've been to us – especially me. Shall I tell her how good you are to me?'

The engine turned and the car edged forward very slowly. Madison jumped off in surprise and the car shot away at speed up the drive. She leaned against the wall, finishing the bottle while she watched a group of girls dancing on the stage. Eventually a gong sounded and there was a rush towards the barbecue. Dropping the empty bottle in a flower bed, she wandered over to join her friends, cutting into the queue amidst shouts of protest.

'Typical of Mad to jump the queue!'

Madison recognised Fran's voice and turned to gesticulate at her. 'Where's your French friend?' she called back. 'I've got a message for her!'

'What is it?'

'I can't say, it's a secret.' She put a finger to her lips.

'I'll find her.'

Madison was sitting on the ground eating a burger when Cecile appeared and stood before her like a naughty child.

'Don't be frightened. I won't bite, mon amie!'

'You have a message for me?'

'My brother tells me that Jules fancies you.'

The girl looked embarrassed but stood motionless. Madison added, 'That was all.'

'I want to ask you something,' Cecile said, looking down. 'Something difficile, I mean difficult.'

'What is it, sweetie?'

'Promise you won't say anything to anyone?'

Madison was intrigued. 'Promise.'

'Because it is very secret and I don't know who else to speak to who may help me.' And she began to cry.

Mills left Alex in bed next morning, complaining that it was the weekend and he thought they would do something together for a change.

'Sorry, I've got to get on with the excavation. It's the play tonight. Why won't you come, if you want us to do something together?'

'Shakespeare? With a female Hamlet? Really?'

He'd been quite adamant about it when she'd suggested he accompanied her before.

'I thought you wanted to see Fiona.'

'I do... but in the dark, being bitten by midges?'

'Don't you think it might just be worth it?'

'I don't understand...'

If he didn't understand, Mills wasn't going to explain and she slammed the door hard as she left.

She drove too fast with the radio on full blast until the hands-free rang.

'Mills? It's Nina. I wondered how you were getting on with "Mr Bones"?'

'Slowly. The ground's very hard.'

'Alex told me you're working on it today so I thought I might pop over. Have a look. Is that all right?'

Pleased, Mills explained where the site was and said she'd be glad to see her. Her friend was the next best thing to her Mum. She was in a better frame of mind for the rest of the journey and felt quite buoyed up by the time she reached "Swale Heights".

It was the first time Mills had seen the building site deserted. Equipment stood motionless and there was no sound except for a thrush singing in the distance.

She was surprised the gates across the entrance were unlocked. Pushing them aside, she drove her Mini into a space in front of the foreman's shed and collected her tool bag from the boot.

There was still some dew on the tarpaulin and Mills let it run onto the ground as she rolled it back, in the hope it might soften the soil. It wouldn't be good practice to soak the ground with a hose but a bit of dew wouldn't hurt. It wasn't until she folded the tarpaulin and unpacked her tools that she looked at the finger bones protruding from the ground. She'd begun working on the left hand before she realised what was wrong with the third finger. Instead of disappearing into the ground, it was now exposed and the gold bracelet had vanished.

Chapter 5

Mills was still staring at the skeletal finger when she heard a car pulling into the site. She went over to fetch Nina and led her behind the half-built house.

'Hazel said the builders wanted "Mr Bones" taken away pronto,' said Nina. 'I can see why now. It must be holding up the work.'

'She told me they were getting quite threatening about it.'

'Pushing a bit too hard, yes.'

'Do you think they might have interfered with this?' Mills asked.

Nina stared down at the rectangle of soil pegged out in front of them.

'Do you?' she asked.

Mills sighed. 'There was a thick gold bracelet on the body yesterday. I should have removed it but the bone was fixed solid and I didn't want to break it. It was covered up with that tarpaulin and now it's gone.'

'Was it valuable?'

Mills shrugged. 'No idea. It looked fairly ordinary.'

'Gold?' Nina raised her eyebrows.

'I guess.'

'Hmm. You can't trust anyone – believe me, I'm a copper so I know.'

'Should I let the PC know?'

She repeated what Hazel had told her to do: ring the uniformed officer if she needed help. But when she rang, it went straight to voicemail.

'It is the weekend,' said Nina.

She called headquarters and asked them to ensure that someone kept an eye overnight.

'You'll just have to report it when you hand over the bones. Where are they, by the way?'

'Safely locked up in the storeroom at the university.'

'Well that's a relief.'

Mills knelt down. 'D'you mind if I get on?'

'No, go ahead. I'll just watch. I'm interested to see how it's done. You'd think I'd have seen it all before being married to Nige but he never does the dirty work, does he?'

'No, he's much more into the instrumentation side of archaeology, isn't he?'

'You mean he's a nerd.'

The time passed quickly while they chatted and Mills kept working at the soil round the fingers. After an hour, Nina fetched a flask from the car and Mills stopped for a coffee before resuming work until it was time for lunch. To her amazement Nina then produced a complete picnic, including sandwiches, cake and fruit.

'You know, that bracelet might have helped identify "Mr Bones",' Nina said as they sat side by side with their backs against the wall of the house. 'Otherwise there's nothing.'

'You're right. But no-one cares really do they? Just a "Mr Bones" of antiquity.'

'I guess so but it seems to me that my Hindu relatives would feel that this man's soul can't be released while he remains in this state.'

Mills had been trying not to think too much about who these bones belonged to. They were old bones, too old to be of consequence to the police and not so old that they were of interest to archaeologists.

When she expressed this to her friend, Nina asked how she knew they weren't Roman or Viking or something significant.

'The osteoarchaeologist should have examined them for physical and chemical changes. If you look closely they haven't been in the ground long enough to have any significant changes to their structure.'

'Clever people these osteoarchaeologists. Wasn't your Phil one?'

'Yes, he was.'

They fell silent. Mills was thinking about Phil and the first time she worked with him.

'Must be five years ago now,' Nina said and Mills knew she was thinking of when Nige had been attacked and left unconscious in the snow to die if Phil hadn't found him.

She was saved further recollections by a call on her mobile from Michael, the uniformed officer assigned to the site.

'Is there a problem?' he asked.

When Mills explained, he was puzzled.

'We were assured the site would be padlocked out of hours.'

'No, the gate was closed but it was not padlocked.'

'D'you want me to come over?'

'No, there's no need. DS Featherstone is with me and she's informed her colleagues. They said they would arrange to keep an eye.'

Mills thought he would be pleased to be let off the hook but he sounded put out and said he would contact headquarters himself.

'Oh dear, I hope we haven't got him into trouble,' Mills said to Nina.

Her friend laughed. 'It's no big deal. Perhaps he was hoping to impress someone with his diligence and failed.'

She went off to look at the gate to discover if the site had been broken into or the builders had failed to lock it when they left. She reported back that there was no sign of a padlock anywhere and she suspected they had simply forgotten to secure the site.

'Should we tie the gates up somehow?' Mills asked when it was time to pack up. She'd spotted some long plastic cable tie lying around.

Nina agreed that even if the plastic ties were easily broken, Mills would be able to tell if they had been tampered with when she returned in the morning. She held the cardboard box containing the finger bones and three ribs, while Mills made sure the ties were tight.

'You're not going back to the university this evening?' Nina asked as Mills packed her car.

'No. They're coming home with me. I'm off to a play at the school where I'm tutoring and Fiona wants me to be there early.'

'Fiona?' Nina sounded surprised.

Mills explained that her stepmother was vaguely related to one of the girls. Adding that she was relieved Alex hadn't wanted to come and join them at the play.

Nina smiled and gave Mills a hug.

'One day you'll be glad she's around – and your little stepsister.'

'Flora? She'll grow up to be a spoiled brat!'

Mills thanked her friend for her company and sent her love to Nige.

As they drove away from the site, a patrol car was coming quietly down the track. When it passed, Mills could see Nina slowing down and stopping to speak to the driver. Hopefully no-one would be interfering with "Mr Bones" overnight.

The performance wasn't due to begin until seven but Fiona had implored Mills to get there early. The seats were not allocated so there was a desire to get a position near the front but also she wanted to introduce her to Mrs Fleurot. There had been little time to get changed and Mills grabbed her only decent summer dress, knowing that Fiona would be dolled up as usual. To her relief, Alex hadn't arrived home yet, so she ate a quick snack and stepped outside. The sun had gone and the evening was beginning to feel cool. By nine or ten it could be pretty chilly.

The spaces in front of the school were filled by large expensive cars when Mills arrived at six-thirty so she was directed to an overflow car park behind the building by a pair of giggling girls. It was a short walk back across the gardens, and through the shrubbery she could see the pool where she'd sat with Cecile and Frances discussing their work. There was no sign of Fiona; in fact the seating by the stage was completely empty.

'Are you here for the drinks?' asked one of the girls who'd told her where to park.

'They're all in there.' The other girl pointed to the school entrance.

Mills followed the sound of raised voices into the hallway and along to the music room where it reached a crescendo. The posh voices and a faint scent of expensive perfume made Mills want to turn and run.

'Over here!' a familiar voice called from the other side of the room.

Mills squeezed and apologised her way across to where Fiona was standing beside a tall, slim woman dressed in a simple linen suit. When Fiona kissed her, Mills noted it was unusually on both cheeks. She half expected her to speak to her in French.

'Mills, darling, this is Marianne. She's Cecile's mother. And this is my step-daughter.' Fiona giggled.

'I'm very pleased to meet you.' Madame Fleurot spoke in impeccable English but with a very attractive French accent. 'And thank you for helping Cecile with her work. My husband and I are very grateful.'

'Monsieur Fleurot is busy on government business,' explained Fiona. She was obviously enjoying moving in diplomatic circles.

Mills enquired what Fiona had been up to during her stay in Yorkshire and was given a detailed description of the spa treatments she had undergone. The headmistress interrupted their conversation, taking Madame Fleurot to meet another mother and they were left alone.

'Did you see the car outside?' asked Fiona excitedly, as soon as they were alone.

'Which one?'

'The big black one.'

'There are several.'

'The one with the chauffeur? We came all the way from London in it and we've been driven around like royalty!'

'How's Dad?'

'He's fine. Sends his love, of course.'

'And Flora?'

'Yes, she's fine too. You should have come to see the hotel. We had a suite each! Nothing was too much trouble.'

Mills was saved any further details by a call for them to drink up and take their seats. She'd been worrying about how cold it was outside and took the opportunity to pop back to the car where she knew she had an old sweater in the boot.

'Hello Dr Sanderson!'

She pulled the sweater over her head and turned to see two figures through the shrubbery. One was in costume: a long white dress and a wreath of flowers in her hair.

'Cecile?'

The girl waved and turned away, followed by her companion, who was dressed in jeans and T-shirt. Mills didn't recognise her.

Back at the stage, Fiona and her friend had taken seats in the front row. They had sensibly brought rugs to keep warm.

'What have you got on?' muttered Fiona when Mills sat down.

'It's all I had with me.'

'You do know there is a hole in the sleeve!'

Mills ignored her and read the programme she'd found on the seat. Frances was listed under lighting but Cecile's name wasn't in the cast list and Fiona wanted to know why.

'I suppose it's because she doesn't have a speaking part,' Mills suggested.

'What is she, then?' Fiona whispered.

'She has a very important role.' Cecile's mother was leaning across. 'She plays Ophelia in the drowning scene.'

That's shut her up, Mills thought. It was obvious to her that Fiona was not familiar with the play.

'I understand she's a really good swimmer,' said Mills.

'Indeed. She has her eye on the 2020 Olympics.'

Suddenly the spotlights went up then down again as the actors playing the watchmen marched onto the stage. The first act had begun. Mills had not had high expectations but was engrossed in the action and at the interval remarked on the quality of the acting.

'I couldn't imagine Hamlet played by a woman but it is quite remarkable.' Marianne Fleurot also seemed enthralled by the play. 'They are all very good but *she* is outstanding.'

Fiona's comments were confined to the costumes and how pretty the girl playing Hamlet's girlfriend was.

More wine was served in the music room until it was time to return to their seats. Mills was waiting to see how Cecile was going to represent Ophelia's death. It wasn't until the end of the fourth act that it happened. Before the Queen appeared and began the speech that Mills knew almost by heart, the lights went off and everyone's eyes were drawn to a bright spotlight beyond the stage to the right of the school building: in the distance was a small figure hanging from a branch. It was Cecile in her white gown and floral head-dress. She remained suspended for perhaps thirty seconds then dropped out of sight. The audience gasped audibly as the sound of a loud splash came from the loudspeakers. Fiona had grabbed Marianne's arm.

'It's all right,' Mills reassured her. 'It's supposed to be like that.'

The spotlights returned to the stage, where the Queen informed Laertes that his sister had drowned.

There is a willow grows aslant a brook,
That shows his hoar leaves in the glassy stream;
There with fantastic garlands did she come
Of crow-flowers, nettles, daisies, and long purples
That liberal shepherds give a grosser name,
But our cold maids do dead men's fingers call
them:
There, on the pendent boughs her coronet weeds
Clambering to hang, an envious sliver broke;
When down her weedy trophies and herself
Fell in the weeping brook. Her clothes spread
wide;
And, mermaid-like, awhile they bore her up:
Which time she chanted snatches of old tunes;
As one incapable of her own distress,
Or like a creature native and indued
Unto that element: but long it could not be
Till that her garments, heavy with their drink,
Pull'd the poor wretch from her melodious lay
To muddy death.'

It was a speech that Mills had learnt at school and it never failed to make her shiver inside.

The churchyard scene at the beginning of the last act took on a strange air for Mills after spending the day removing bones from the soil and set her wondering who indeed was "Mr Bones" and would he have a decent burial in the end? The sword fight between Laertes and Hamlet was an accomplished piece of choreography between the two girls playing the characters but the audience was beginning to be distracted by a few drops of rain. By the time the play reached its sombre end, there was a fine drizzle and the applause was curtailed by the headmistress insisting everyone run inside.

It was ten-thirty and Mills was keen to leave but as they hurriedly left their seats, Fiona insisted she accompany her to the house.

'We haven't had a chance to chat and I want to meet Cecile.'

'Marianne can introduce you.'

'She's meeting some friends. Please, Mills.'

She followed Fiona obediently, helping herself to a glass of wine from the tray as she entered the music room. It soon filled up with the same smart ladies and distinguished men whose children were lucky enough to attend the school.

'Hello Dr Sanderson, did you enjoy the play?' It was Frances, handing round nibbles.

Mills assured her that she'd loved every minute and explained to Fiona that the girl was one of her tutees.

'So where is Cecile?' Fiona asked.

'She'll be down soon I'm sure. She wants to see her mother before she goes. She might be helping get our house party ready.'

'House party?' Mills asked.

'It was Madison's idea. We're having an after-party. I think that's what you call it.'

'I didn't see Madison in the play,' Mills said.

'No. She didn't want to be in it but she's good at organising parties.'

I bet she is, thought Mills.

Frances stood and chatted awkwardly until they were interrupted by the young man that Mills recognised as one of the gravediggers. He touched Frances on the shoulder and she spun round.

'Where's Cecile?' he asked anxiously.

'I don't know. In the student house probably, helping Madison.'

'No, she's not.'

'Maybe she's drying her hair.'

He turned and moved quickly away, almost bumping into a tall man who was making a beeline for Frances.

'I'm sorry to interrupt,' he said, with a smile at Mills and Fiona. 'I've got to take this young lady away. The rain is getting heavier and we need to make sure all the electrics are safe. Sorry.'

'Mr Young is our producer,' Frances explained.

'I thought the play was marvellous.' Fiona was giving him her pouty smile.

'Thanks. Now Fran, please.'

The girl gave them an apologetic look and left with him.

Mills suggested it was time for her to leave as well but Fiona insisted on her staying until Marianne Fleurot finally reappeared.

'I have been looking for my daughter but she's nowhere to be found. Mrs James has sent one of the girls to look for her.'

They stood awkwardly as the crowd dwindled until only a dozen people were left, perhaps also waiting for their offspring. Mrs James appeared with a Chinese girl in tow. Her hair was plastered round her face which was shiny with damp.

'Mae has come from Cecile's student house but she hasn't seen her. Stay here Mae while I phone the other houses. Would you like to come to my office Madame Fleurot?'

Marianne followed her obediently and they were left with an uncomfortable looking Mae.

'You should go and get dry,' suggested Fiona. 'You'll catch cold.'

'It's ok,' the girl replied. 'I take ginger every day; I don't get colds.'

Mills said she hoped they find Cecile soon because she ought to be getting home.

'She's probably making herself scarce,' Mae said. 'But don't tell Mrs James. Her mother wants her to go home with her for the summer but Cecile wants to stay here.'

'To do her archaeology project with Frances,' suggested Mills.

'Perhaps but also to see Jules, I think.' Mae grinned.

Fiona had seated herself on a sofa, apparently having resigned herself to a long wait.

'D'you mind if I go?' Mills asked. 'It's after eleven and I've got an early start. We'll catch up tomorrow evening in Harrogate before you go home, promise.'

'No, it's fine. Go.' She waved wanly and lay back with her eyes closed.

Mills left Mae with Fiona and went outside into the pouring rain. She was about to climb into her car when she was frozen by a piercing scream. The shrubbery was suddenly illuminated and people were running and shouting. Mills hurried through to where figures were bent over the side of the pool and at the centre of the group, someone was helping Frances pull something heavy out of the water. Mills caught a glimpse of a white gown, then the fragile arms and legs as they laid the body on the edge of the pool.

Chapter 6

Alex was already in bed when Mills finally got back to the cottage.

'Had a good evening?' he asked drowsily from under the duvet.

'There was an accident.'

'Are you ok?'

'Not me – at the school. A girl drowned. I knew her.'

There was no response.

'Yes, I knew her,' she repeated.

She lay looking at the ceiling. 'Not well, I didn't know her well but I'd met her and talked to her. I was tutoring her.'

The tears welled up and she sobbed silently as she recalled the limp body dripping from the pool. The tears tracked down onto the pillow and she lay for a long time before she fell into a restless sleep.

Alex was already up when she was woken by the phone ringing. It was seven-thirty and much later than she'd intended.

'Why didn't you wake me?' she demanded as she ran downstairs half-dressed.

'You had a late night and I thought you were tired. Here's your tea, I was going to bring it up to you.'

She took it graciously and waited for the toast he was buttering.

'Who was that on the phone?' she asked.

'Fiona. She sounded a bit vague.' He passed her the marmalade. 'So what went on last night?'

'Didn't Fiona say?'

'No. She wanted you to know she was back in the hotel and she would try to sleep for an hour or two but can you ring her after that?'

Mills explained how she had watched the girls pulling Cecile from the pool.

'I left Fiona with Cecile's mother in the end. She was waiting with her until her husband arrived from London. Then the police came and there was nothing else I could do.'

'Sounds like she fell in and drowned,' he said glibly.

'But that's the point – she's a brilliant swimmer and she was meant to fall in, it was part of the play.'

'In that case she must've hit her head.'

Everything was black and white with Alex. He always knew best and that was that.

'The post-mortem will establish the cause,' she said as she left to finish dressing. 'I'll be seeing Fiona later so I don't know when I'll be back.'

'You're not going to Harrogate today?'

'Only to meet Fiona. I've got to get on with the disinterment.'

He shrugged but said nothing.

The dull drizzle matched the mood in the student house that morning. Few of the girls had slept at all and some had become quite hysterical and had to be transferred to the staff house where the nurse could keep an eye on them. Mrs James had made the decision not to call the school together to explain what had happened but instead she was moving through the student houses, speaking quietly to the girls in their rooms. Mae and Sofia had brought Fran into their room and she'd taken Madison's bed since there was no sign of their room-mate. Mrs James told them the police would be along in the afternoon to speak to Fran and the others who discovered Cecile's body. There had been a few more tears when she offered to contact the girls' parents if they wanted to go home immediately instead of waiting for the start of the summer break. Sofia said she would call her mother straight away but Fran was adamant she would remain to carry out her archaeology project. After their headmistress had left, Mae insisted that she too would stay with her friend, at least until the end of term.

'I'll make us some camomile tea,' she said as Fran went off to get showered and dressed.

Madison had arrived back when Mae returned from the kitchen.

'Has someone been sleeping in my bed?' she demanded.

'Fran came in with us last night. We couldn't leave her down in her and Cecile's room, not after what happened.'

'Well, you might have asked!' She ranted on for a bit then stopped suddenly. 'What happened that was so important anyway?'

'You don't know about Cecile? Where have you been?'

'Don't ask. It was a blast but now I feel…'

'Cecile is dead, Madison. She drowned in the pool last night.'

Mae was busy tidying the bed when Fran returned.

'Madison came back but she's gone off again,' Mae explained. 'She hadn't heard what happened. She was off campus last night.'

'Typical. With that creepy guy in the van, I expect. He's the one that gives her the drugs. I can guess what he gets in return. I don't suppose she cares much about Cecile.'

'I thought she seemed rather disturbed when I told her and after I explained that the police were called and there was going to be a post-mortem she went rushing off.'

'I expect she wanted to let her brother know. His friend Jules was quite keen on Cecile. I liked him.'

'Drink up,' said Mae. 'You can help me with the Californian poppies. I'm experimenting with a tincture to help insomnia and it's nearly ready to bottle up. We could try it out tonight.'

She rifled in her locker, retrieving several small empty glass bottles.

'These will do.' She placed them on her bed and bent down to rummage in the cupboard again. 'It's a mess in here,' she added and began to empty the contents onto the top of her locker.

'Don't you ever label them?' Fran asked. 'How d'you know what's what?'

'The tinctures are different colours and I can tell by the smell and the taste if I forget.'

'So all those green bottles are the same thing?' Fran asked.

'Not necessarily.' She took the lid off one and sniffed, then another. 'Yes, smell this – it's lavender. And this is rosemary.'

Fran sniffed and nodded. 'Yes. But if it was me, I'd have to put labels on them.'

It was difficult to get any sense out of Fiona when Mills rang her later in the day. She'd taken some of her migraine tablets and her voice sounded distant and vague.

'I'll come over now,' said Mills in exasperation and turned her mobile off.

She packed the sample boxes into the car and removed the waterproof trousers and jacket that had protected her clothes from most of the mud. Fiona would have to put up with the fact that she wasn't dressed for a spa hotel. She'd been working on the site all morning in a fine drizzle that never let up. The advantage was that the soil was being softened by the rain and it was becoming easier to release the bones from their grave. Progress was good and she only remembered to call Fiona when she stopped to eat the sandwich she'd prepared for lunch.

Mills checked her reflection in the rear view mirror and rubbed smudges of mud from her cheeks and forehead. Her hair would dry off in the car if she put the heater on full blast and, if necessary, she could have a shower and wash her hair in Fiona's luxury hotel bathroom.

It was a depressing drive through the rain to Harrogate and, despite the short run from the car to the hotel, Mills was conscious of her hair dripping as she stood waiting by the reception desk.

She asked for Fiona's room, thinking how strange it felt to be using the title "Mrs Sanderson" for someone other than her own dead mother. The receptionist rang the room and handed the receiver to Mills.

'Mills? Is that you?' The voice was faint. 'Come up, darling.' The receiver went dead.

'She said to go up,' offered Mills.

The receptionist indicated the lift and directed her to the suite.

The door to Fiona's room was ajar and inside there was an entrance hall which led to a sitting room. But Mills found her stepmother on an enormous four-poster in the bedroom still dressed in her nightwear. There was a tray beside her but it contained only a coffee pot with a cup and saucer.

'Have you eaten yet today?' Mills asked.

Fiona shook her head. 'I couldn't,' she said at last.

'You must. Why don't we go downstairs and have tea. I'm sure they do cucumber sandwiches or things like that.' Mills was feeling hungry again and wondered if spa hotels served cake.

Eventually Fiona was cajoled into getting dressed and quite soon was insisting that Mills tidied herself up. Pleased to see Fiona becoming more like her old self she submitted to having her hair brushed and dried into a smooth bob by her stepmother. Then together they descended to the ground floor where guests were sampling afternoon tea and watching the rain-swept grounds outside.

Slowly Fiona described what had occurred after Mills had left the school. The police had taken control and spoken briefly to the girls who had found Cecile but then sent them to bed. Marianne was in a bad way, of course. Fiona had done her best to help but Mrs James had taken over, to her relief. She was left with nothing to do but drink tea and wait. They had managed to contact Mr Fleurot and he'd left London immediately. Fiona assumed he had flown up. The couple were given a room in the place where the staff lived and at that point she was driven back to Harrogate by the Fleurots' chauffeur. By then it was three in the morning and getting light.

'He was really lovely,' Fiona said. 'He was going straight back to the school to wait for his orders.'

'So what are your plans now?' Mills asked, helping herself to another scone.

Fiona looked vague. 'I'd like to get the train home today but I suppose it's too late now?'

'I doubt it,' said Mills. 'If you get packed and leave after tea, you could be home in just over four hours. We can tell Dad to meet you at King's Cross.'

The police wanted to speak to Fran since she had first spotted Cecile in the water. Adults often commented on how mature she was for her years, possibly because she'd had to be independent from an early age with her parents moving to different countries as their postings changed. She sat facing the officer while Mrs James perched beside her on the sofa in the music room. She began at the beginning and told them everything in detail.

'It was raining quite heavily and Mr Young said we should go and disconnect all the electrics to make them safe – oh, I've just thought, you don't think she could have been electrocuted, do you?'

'Why do you say that?' the man asked.

Fran thought he looked a bit like her dad but was gentler in his manner.

'No reason. I know she drowned but it just made me think…'

'Just tell the officer what you saw, dear,' Mrs James prompted her.

'Mr Young said to check the pool and he went off to do the stage. I ran round to the pool but I had to be careful – it was quite dark because the lights were switched off after the drowning scene.'

A lump rose in her throat as she said it because the scene from the play was being re-enacted in her head and she remembered how Cecile had fallen so elegantly into the water. She'd looked so beautiful as she floated…

'Are you all right, dear?'

Mrs James was peering at her oddly.

'Take your time,' the man said.

She took a sip of the water they offered her and coughed.

'I went to disconnect the lights and accidentally turned them on.' She paused as she saw the white dress floating on the surface. 'It lit the pool and there she was.' The garland of flowers had come off and had drifted away from Cecile. 'She was lying on her front so I couldn't see her face but I knew it was her. I called for help and some people came. I can't remember who, it's a blur really.'

'You helped them fetch her out of the pool,' the officer prompted.

'Did I?' She had felt the cold wet cloth and strands of damp hair but she thought she'd imagined it after short bursts of sleep when the nightmare was repeated.

They let her go. Outside, Mae was waiting for her and accompanied her back to the room they were now sharing.

'Sofia's already packed; her mother is collecting her this evening,' Mae informed her. 'Mrs James says you can move in properly with me and Madison if you like.'

They gathered Fran's belongings and moved them upstairs while Madison watched from her bed.

'I hope you don't snore,' she remarked but her tone was friendly.

In fact the American girl was surprisingly pleasant for the next few days, even taking an interest in Mae's concoctions, Fran noticed. Her friend was trying hard to find things to take their mind off the tragedy and was brewing up all kinds of remedies with the contents of her garden.

Gradually students were leaving for the holidays. Fran watched large black cars sweeping up the drive and out again with the girls as they left one by one. Soon the remaining few were scattered through the campus and Mae, Fran and Madison were the sole occupants of their student house.

Alex tried to converse with Mills as they drove to Harrogate but she let him assume it was just because it was Monday morning that she was so uncommunicative. She simply answered with a yes or no when he asked about Fiona's journey back to London. Eventually he gave up and turned on the radio.

The atmosphere in the laboratory was equally subdued. It seemed the staff had somehow learned that an announcement on cuts was due. Only Glyn was looking relaxed, presumably confident that his role as Technical Manager was secure. Timothy and Donna were seated in the office while the three junior analysts were in a huddle in the corridor when Brenda summoned everyone to the outer office that Mills and Alex shared.

'Thank you for coming,' Brenda began.

Her unnaturally formal manner caused everyone to shuffle and glance at each other.

She went on, 'I've had to make some difficult decisions since I returned to the laboratory. Mills and Alex have helped me, of course.'

Five faces turned to look at them; only Glyn stared rigidly ahead. Mills sensed he felt snubbed by Brenda's failure to mention his assistance in the decisions she'd made.

'Times are hard for everyone and we've had our share of knocks. Like everything else, less money is being spent on forensic support and we've got to tighten our belts.' She looked round the room with a serious expression. 'I've got to let two members of staff go.'

The gasp from Donna was audible. Mills wondered how Brenda was going to divulge who was to go. Surely she wouldn't announce the names publicly, not in front of them all?

Brenda was beginning to look uncomfortable. 'I think the best way to do this is if I see each of you in alphabetical order, so…' She stopped and turned to go back into the inner office. 'You can sort that out Mills.' The door closed behind her.

Mills quickly scribbled a list of their eight names and stuck it on the door of the outer office. One of the junior analysts was top of the list and Mills indicated for him to go in. He tapped nervously on the door and a faint voice told him to enter. Mills sat at her desk, prepared to fetch each member of staff in turn, wishing that she and Alex weren't the last two names to be called.

It was impossible to tell the outcome of the discussion when the first analyst came back out of Brenda's office. He looked shocked but whether it was because he had lost his job or kept it was uncertain. Mills didn't like to ask.

'Tell Donna to come in next, please,' she asked.

She gave the girl an encouraging smile when she appeared, sure that Brenda wouldn't wish to lose such a valuable scientist. But Donna was just as enigmatic when she left; her eyes were bright but whether it was tears or excitement was impossible to tell. Had Brenda sworn them not to discuss the outcome of their talks? Glyn came through the door with a grin on his face which had not disappeared when he emerged ten minutes later.

'Very interesting,' he remarked as he left the office.

It was coffee time when it was finally her own turn to see Brenda, so she carried two mugs into the office and handed one to her boss.

'Sit down Mills, dear.' She sipped the black coffee and sighed. 'I need this. It's been a horrid morning.'

'Does that mean…'

Brenda held up her hand. 'Don't read anything into that, please.' She leaned back and sipped the hot liquid. 'I want to tell you about it all *after* I've seen everyone else. Just sit and enjoy your coffee while we have a break.'

Sometimes Brenda could be exasperating.

'I wanted to tell you about the university job that's going, before you made any decisions,' Mills said.

'I know. In fact I do know all about it because Alex told me.'

'I hope you don't think there's anything definite because there isn't! I could be without anything…'

Brenda stopped her. 'Just wait a few minutes. We can talk after I've seen Alex. He'll be waiting.'

Mills picked up her mug and left the office. Alex was standing outside ready, brushing past her in his haste to get in. He was in there exactly twelve minutes and she could hear that it was not going smoothly. He came out, red-faced, slamming the door behind him and went straight through their office without a word. It was a long time before Brenda opened her door and invited Mills in.

'Right, girl. Here's the deal – as they say.' Brenda was almost like her old self: decisive and energetic. 'I had to lose one of the juniors so I'm afraid it was a matter of last in, first out.'

'Ashley?'

'Sorry.'

'No, it makes sense, I guess.'

Ashley had been taken on to help specifically with routine fingerprinting work that Donna could easily cover.

'Then I had to lose one more post. Frankly I couldn't see how we could manage without Glyn, Donna or Tim and we need the two juniors for all the routine work – Donna can't take on any more.'

That meant Alex, thought Mills. Or did it?

'So I decided to ask Alex what he would do. I said that I would have to lose him or you.'

Brenda was scrutinising Mills across the table.

'You asked him to choose between his job and mine?' Mills asked.

'I asked if he could do your job.'

'So are you asking if I can do his job?' Mills was confused.

Brenda laughed. 'No, of course not! You can do your job *and* my job; you've demonstrated that in my absence. I think we can carry on without his expertise. It's a loss but needs must. He doesn't have your practical analytical skills, does he?'

'No.'

'So even if you were working at the university, we'd still need you to pop over and help us out, wouldn't we?'

Mills was busy thinking how this would affect Alex, and their relationship.

'Don't worry, Mills. Alex is very clever in his field; he'll get another post just like that.' She clicked her fingers. 'Oh, it's nearly lunch-time,' she announced despite the fact it was only eleven-thirty by her wall clock. 'I think I've had enough for today.'

Mills took the hint and left, full of foreboding about what she might expect to find out in the laboratory. But she needn't have worried – Alex had left the building and no-one knew where he'd gone.

Chapter 7

It was a relief to leave Yardley Forensics and head off to the university. Everyone wanted to speak to Mills about the changes, particularly to find out who had been given "the push", as Glyn had put it so elegantly. He'd guessed that Alex was to go by the way he'd stormed out immediately after he'd seen Brenda. The laboratory manager expressed sympathy but Mills knew he'd never liked Alex and had always resented his presence.

The dull drizzle suited her mood. There was no point going to the site until she'd sorted out all the samples already stacked up in the store. She needed a reliable postgraduate to take on the work, and wanted Nige's assistance to find one. But when she arrived, the office was empty and the departmental administrator informed her that Dr Featherstone had taken the second-years on a field trip and wouldn't be back until later. Desperate for help of some sort, she went to the postgraduate office to see who was about but it seemed they too were involved in the field trip.

She had decided to make a start on the cleaning process herself when a call came through on her mobile. Thinking it must be Alex, she grabbed it but the number was not one she recognised.

'Dr Sanderson? It's Fran. I wanted to check you are coming to school tomorrow?'

Mills hesitated while she gathered her thoughts.

'Yes, of course. I'll be there as usual in the afternoon.' Then a thought occurred. 'If you like we can visit my excavation site and we could see if we can find you some work associated with it.'

The girl sounded excited at the prospect and thanked her profusely. Now she had someone who might be pleased to help her clean the bones as part of her experience of archaeological work. After all, not all aspects of the subject involved exciting discoveries and she might let Frances help her excavate the last few remaining bones if she proved to be a good student.

Feeling a little more encouraged, Mills made a start on the first set of bones, carefully removing them from their box and laying them out on a tray before labelling them and transferring them back into store so they would be ready when she brought Frances over the next day. Satisfied there was nothing more she could do that day, she left the building and walked quickly across the car park in the pouring rain.

Outside, Nige was unloading the departmental minibus and handing bits of equipment to the waiting students.

'Hi Mills. Have you got a minute?'

He waited until they were alone before he got to the point. 'The meeting to decide isn't until Wednesday but I was talking to the finance guys and they think the idea of splitting Jake's post between the two sections makes a lot of sense. Forensics has more money and students than we do. I think we might have ourselves a successful arrangement.'

'I hope so, Nige. It would be nice for something to go right for once.'

'How will it work with the lab in Harrogate?' he asked.

'That's the big question.'

She described what had happened in the morning.

'… and I haven't seen Alex since,' she ended.

'That's a downer.' Nige stroked the stubble on his chin. 'Good luck with that.'

'Thank you, Nige. That's a great help – not!'

He grinned sheepishly. 'Nina's better at this sort of thing,' he added.

Mills smiled but inside she was dreading what mood Alex would be in when she returned to pick him up from the laboratory. The journey back to Harrogate took longer than expected in the downpour and she arrived later than she'd said in her text. Alex was waiting in the entrance to the building and ran across to the car with his bag held above his head to keep the rain off.

'Sorry – it took longer…' Mills began.

'Doesn't matter.'

'I went to uni. The traffic was awful. I…'

'It doesn't matter,' he repeated firmly.

They drove in silence except for the sound of the windscreen wipers slapping backwards and forwards. Eventually, Alex put the radio on and leaned back with his eyes closed.

'I'm angry with Brenda for making such a misguided and stupid decision,' he said without moving.

Mills told him how sorry she was about what had happened but he remained silent and motionless until they reached Mossy Bank.

Inside the cottage, a red light was flashing on the phone. Mills listened to the message while Alex thumped about upstairs. Fiona still sounded upset as she thanked Mills for getting her onto the train home to London. She wanted to talk to her about the "dreadful accident".

'Dad?' Her father had answered the phone.

'Millie? Is that you? Are you ok?'

'I'm fine. How's Fiona?'

'Bit shaken up by her trip but she's here – hold on.'

Her father never spoke for more than a few seconds. Soon Fiona was thanking her profusely for looking after her.

'You were so kind to me, Mills. I thought I would never see my Flora again.'

'How is she?'

'Oh she's all right. She's at swimming or something at the moment. It's my "me time" as Hugh calls it.'

'So you got back all right?'

'Yes. I even plucked up the courage to ring my sister to ask how poor Marianne and her husband were. I thought I should send flowers – what do you think? Anyway she said they were absolutely distraught; well you would be, wouldn't you? They seem to think that Cecile might have been unconscious when she entered the water.'

'Has there been a post-mortem already?'

'I don't know. They just said that she'd bumped her head and they thought she might have fallen into the pool.'

'The post-mortem will show if that was the case.'

'Apparently the Fleurots want to take poor Cecile's body back to France as soon as they can.'

'That won't be possible before the results of the autopsy are available,' explained Mills.

'Well, it's all very disturbing. I wish I'd never gone up to see the wretched play. Don't they say it's cursed?'

'That's Macbeth.'

'Well, I told your father it was a bad idea.'

You didn't have to come, thought Mills as Fiona finished their call.

She cooked and they ate in silence except for the occasional polite exchange about the meal. Mills washed up, half-listening to Alex who was chatting with a friend online. He was explaining that his contract was running out at Yardley Forensics and he was looking to see what opportunities were around. It didn't sound hopeful from the responses to his questions. He was on his second call when Mills asked if he wanted coffee.

'No thanks. I might go out for a while.'

When Nina rang, Mills was alone in the cottage.

'Nige told me about Alex's job finishing,' she began. 'Sorry to hear that but I guess he'll find another quite easily. Clever guy like him.'

'Possibly.'

They chatted for a while before it occurred to Mills that her friend might know about what happened to Cecile Fleurot. She asked if her colleagues in police headquarters at Newby Wiske were involved.

'I can find out. How do you spell her name?'

She took the details and promised to get back to her if she heard anything about the incident.

'The PM will identify if the bump on her head occurred before she went into the pool,' Mills added. 'And there'll have to be an inquest if it's true, won't there?'

'Yes. I'll ask about that too.'

Nina told her to wish Alex luck with finding a new position but Mills wasn't sure he would appreciate the gesture. She waited up until eleven but was in bed before Alex returned with beery breath.

'Are you not going in today?' Mills asked Alex as she was leaving.

He shook his head and carried on watching breakfast TV as she picked up her keys and left for Harrogate.

The atmosphere in the laboratory was subdued, with everyone getting on with their work, presumably pleased to have their jobs. Mills concentrated on getting all the paperwork completed for the day before popping her head round the door to Brenda's office.

'I'm off now,' she said.

Brenda looked up from the sandwich she was munching at her desk. 'Fine. And how's Alex?' she called as Mills closed the door behind her.

'Not fine,' Mills muttered as she left.

At least for the rest of the day she could forget the strain of the situation at Yardley Forensics and at home to concentrate on helping a budding archaeologist. She had been in a similar situation herself and wanted to do what she could to ensure that Frances achieved her qualifications.

It was the first time Mills had been back to the school since the evening of the play and it looked strangely abandoned. The stage had gone and no students loitered in the grounds. Exams were over and presumably they'd all gone home. All except girls like Frances whose parents were living and working overseas. Even the entrance hall was deserted and Mills wandered down the corridor looking into rooms, hoping to find someone who would know how to locate her pupil. Finally, she gave up and rang the mobile number Frances had contacted her on.

'I'm coming!' The girl sounded out of breath. 'I'm just by the school house.'

The hall door swung open and she appeared, red in the face and full of apologies. When she'd calmed down, Mills told her about her idea.

'I thought we would visit the site where I've been excavating a skeleton.' Frances was nodding solemnly. 'And then we could go to the university to carry out some cleaning procedures.'

Her face lit up and she couldn't hide her delight.

'Do I need any special clothes or equipment?' she asked, wide-eyed.

'No, you're fine just as you are.'

In the car, Mills explained the background to the building site where the bones were found. Frances was clearly excited by the prospect of seeing a real archaeological site and to get involved in the work. So, when they had arrived on site, Mills was surprised by the girl stepping away as the tarpaulin was removed from the bones remaining in the soil. Puzzled, she asked if there was anything wrong.

'No,' she replied. 'It's just… seeing it lying there… it's silly but…'

Mills had been thoughtless. The girl's friend, who should have been working with her, had been found dead. Frances had discovered Cecile in the pool. No wonder she was affected by the sight of a partial skeleton.

'Take your time,' Mills said. 'It takes a bit of getting used to. I forget because I've been working with bones for so long.'

'It was just the shock of seeing it for the first time,' Frances said slowly. 'I'll be fine now.'

Mills explained how she'd been carefully removing bones one by one and storing them in boxes back at the university.

'Now I need to start cleaning them and that's where you can help me.'

On the way to the university, Fran asked about the background to the burial site.

'What do you mean exactly?'

'What was there before they started building the houses? Were there any buildings there before?'

Mills hadn't been interested in the origins of the site and knew nothing about it.

'I guess you'd have to ask the builders or the planning office if you wanted to know,' she replied.

'If I'm going to write a report on my project I should find out the historical context,' Fran said.

Mills agreed, but she hadn't really meant the girl to focus her project on the site, it was just another bit of work experience.

They drove through the university main gate so Mills could show her student the campus. It was her first visit to the university and she was suitably impressed by its modern buildings and landscaped lawns and lake. They parked close to the department and Mills led Frances to the room where the samples were stored securely.

'Right Frances,' Mills began.

'My friends call me Fran.'

'Fran, then. These bone samples are ready to wash. We'll use water and a small toothbrush. It's important they are cleaned but we don't want to damage them.'

She spent some time demonstrating to Fran how to brush the bones without using excessive pressure. The girl learnt quickly and had a delicate touch which gave Mills confidence she wouldn't damage her precious samples. She kept the skull herself and worked gently using a small scrubbing brush for the larger sections. The skull was already in two pieces and as she rubbed gently she could tell she might have even more if she wasn't very careful. She could sense Fran was looking over every now and again to study the bony head of the skeleton.

'Reminds me of the bit in the play when the gravediggers are speaking,' she said after a while.

'Has everyone gone home now?' asked Mills as she scrubbed.

'Nearly everyone. Mae, that's my friend, she's staying, and Madison is still around.'

'The American girl?'

'Yes. She's a laugh but she can be trouble.'

'Wrong sort of friends, you mean?' said Mills, thinking of the lad she'd seen passing the American girl a small packet in the hallway.

Fran was concentrating on working with her toothbrush.

'Not too much pressure,' Mills warned.

'Mae is into herbal remedies,' offered Fran. 'She made all the bags hanging on the chairs at the performance. They kept the mosquitos away.'

They worked together in silence for a while until Fran finally placed a washed metacarpal with the other bones.

'They say Cecile will be buried in France,' she said, staring at the tray. 'I wanted to go to her funeral.'

Before Mills could think of a reply, the girl continued. 'Mae had chosen some wild flowers we could send in a wreath. We both thought we'd be there.'

'I expect her parents wanted her to be near her family,' Mills suggested.

Fran nodded. Mills could see her eyes were wet with tears.

'Mae knows so much about flowers and plants. She has a garden where she grows herbs and stuff so she can make medicine like her mother uses. She's Chinese.'

Mills recalled the girl she'd seen at the play.

'We thought we could make a wreath, or a posy, with the flowers that she was wearing when... when it happened. Do you think that would seem odd? Madison said it was sick but I don't think it is. She looked so pretty in her head wreath.'

Fran was looking up at her now and Mills nodded in agreement. Encouraged, the girl put down the bone she was working on and twisted round on her chair to face Mills.

'Can I ask you something, Dr Sanderson?'

'Of course.'

'About the post-mortem. I wondered what they look for. She was such a good swimmer, I can't believe she drowned.'

'I think they believe she hit her head.' Mills stopped, unsure how much of what Fiona had told her was true.

'And will they know for sure what caused the accident?'

'Hopefully.'

They resumed their work, stopping only to examine the samples for cleanliness before placing them in the drying tray.

'This is such an interesting project,' Fran remarked as they placed the last two samples into the tray. 'I'm so glad I can do this with you, especially now that I'm working alone.'

'About that...'

'I've been thinking about the background investigation I'll need to do as well.'

'Good.'

'I can get some information about the site before it was sold to the builders and I'll go further back. The skeleton could be quite old, couldn't it?'

Mills was taken aback. 'You mean you'll write about the background to *my* site?'

'Yes. Is that a problem?'

Mills hadn't considered it. There was no requirement on her to delve into the past to find out where the skeleton came from. Therefore there was no reason why she would, but Fran certainly could if she really wanted to.

They'd had a very useful afternoon cleaning the first tray of bones so Mills laid the next boxful out in the store to dry and locked the door before driving Fran back to school. It was in the car that the girl started asking about the post-mortem again.

'Will they just look for bruises or do they test everything, like the blood and the organs? I've seen it on telly and they always cut the body open but sometimes they look for drugs and poisons.'

'I guess it depends what they want to know,' Mills answered. She was deliberately vague, not wishing to encourage Fran to think about her friend on the autopsy table.

'They'd be able to tell what she'd eaten, wouldn't they? And find toxins in her bloodstream. I bet they could even find plant extracts couldn't they?'

Mills was relieved to change the subject as they suddenly hit heavy traffic. It wasn't healthy for the girl to be dwelling on her friend's post mortem. It didn't help that they were working on the skeleton of a dead body for her project.

'I'd better talk to Mrs James about your project before you change direction completely,' Mills warned.

'She won't mind. She doesn't care what we do so long as we get the grades.'

'All the same, I'll have a quick chat if she's around.'

They arrived back at school just before six and Fran rushed off for her evening meal after confirming she would be free to carry on working the following day. Mills was reversing the car when she spotted Mrs James striding round the corner so she stopped and wound down her window.

The headmistress listened distractedly while Mills explained how Fran wanted to work on the background to her investigation site.

'Whatever you think best Dr Sanderson. I'm late for supper, I hope you don't mind.'

'I'll tell her to write a proposal for you, shall I?' Mills called after her.

But Mrs James had disappeared inside the building.

Mills wondered if she was doing the right thing; Fran was vulnerable following her friend's demise. Why was she asking about details of the post mortem and if it would detect plant extract in the dead girl's system? Did Fran know something about how Cecile died?

Chapter 8

Alex was waiting to tell Mills his news that evening. He'd contacted an old colleague from the company he used to work for and learned of a job being advertised, based in London.

'I've sent an application. It's better money and there's potential for career development. I don't have that at Yardley's.'

Mills agreed, reluctantly.

The phone rang and for the rest of the evening she was busy.

'Mills, it's Nige. Just wanted to remind you that the Dean's committee will be making their decision about your post tomorrow.'

'Thanks Nige. I planned to come in with my student to do some more cleaning.'

'I'll see you there then. Here's Nina.'

Mills could hear the boys shouting in the background.

'Stop them, Nige... Hi, Mills. Just a quick one. I wanted to ask you about that play you went to see.'

'Hamlet?'

'That's right, at High Fell School. Did you say your dad's wife knew a girl there?'

Mills explained Fiona's relationship with the dead girl then asked her friend if she knew who was doing the autopsy.

'I can find out.'

'Would you? It's just... well...'

'Now then, Mills. What are you up to?'

'Nothing, honestly. Just interested.'

When the call was over, Alex asked her why she wanted to know the name of the pathologist doing the PM on Cecile Fleurot.

'It's for Fiona. She wanted to know when it might be over so Cecile's parents can take the body back to France. In fact I'll ring her now to see if they've had any news.'

She picked up the phone before Alex could reply and he turned on the television. Mills carried the receiver into the kitchen and leaned on the work surface.

'Dad?' It was unusual for him to answer her calls. 'Where's Fiona?'

He explained she was putting Flora to bed. They spoke for a few minutes but her father was not good at chatting and it was with obvious relief that he handed over to his wife, who made up for both of them. She was clearly back in good spirits but her tone lowered audibly when Mills mentioned Cecile.

'Oh Mills, Marianne is so upset. The post-mortem was due to be held earlier this week but Monsieur Fleurot has insisted on a pathologist coming from France, so now it has been delayed until tomorrow.'

Mills reassured her that it would make no difference to the outcome but confided that she was trying to find out who was carrying out the PM.

'Ah, I can tell you that,' Fiona replied. 'Marianne asked me about him. I have a phone number too.'

Mills was going to assure her that she wouldn't know him but Fiona had disappeared to find the pathologist's name.

'It's Slade,' she said. 'I told Marianne that you might speak to Dr Slade, as you work in that area.'

Mills sighed. Fiona could be exasperating but it was rather flattering that her stepmother thought she could help.

'I'll ring the number you've given me,' she said then deftly changed the subject by asking after Flora.

She was rewarded with a blow by blow account of how the nanny, Agnes, had resigned after a disagreement following Fiona's visit to Harrogate. So now she had to take Flora to the various classes herself. Apparently Flora was signed up for yoga, which had not been as relaxing as Fiona had hoped. This was in addition to a number of other classes for children in Canary Wharf, including gymnastics, swimming and dance. Mills came off the phone an hour later laughing audibly.

'I'm taking the rest of the week off,' Alex announced as they went to bed. 'I'm due leave.'

He seemed to have calmed down since Monday and was obviously considering new opportunities. But London? Although they'd not discussed where he might find a job, he must know she wouldn't consider moving from the dale.

Feeling guilty for spending so little time at Yardley Forensics, Mills called in from the hands-free in the car to explain she had important work to do at the university. Brenda was understanding but pointed out there was a pile of paperwork waiting for her. Mills promised to be there the following day as she turned in to the grounds of High Fell Hall. Having parked at the front of the school building, Mills called the number Fiona had given her and explained to the pathologist that she was representing the family of Cecile Fleurot. Initially he was rather distant but when she explained she was to meet the pathologist sent by the family, he seemed more interested.

'Dr Sanderson, did you say?'

'Yes – from the University of North Yorkshire.'

'I see. I'm expecting Dr Moreau to arrive this morning. The body is at the Harrogate District Hospital mortuary. We'll start at noon. I hope to be finished by three.'

He terminated the call before Mills could thank him. She looked at her watch. There would just be time to get Fran to the university to continue the cleaning work before driving to Harrogate to meet the French pathologist.

'I was looking at the building site on the internet last night,' Fran began as soon as she climbed in the car. 'Did you know you can get all sorts of information from the land registry if you pay them?' She didn't wait for a response. 'Apparently the land used to belong to a big house. It was called "The Waldrens" – isn't that a weird name? I saw it on an out of date map we've got in the library and I can just see it on the satellite map on my computer.'

'Very good. You could try local museums, libraries and council offices for details of the old property.'

'I've found some stuff on the internet already.'

'Just remember you will need to refer to any sources in your report and the internet isn't the only place to look.'

'I know.'

Mills took Fran to the university and set her up with the next box of bones, now dried and laid out ready on their tray. She explained that she was going to the hospital to meet the pathologists who were doing her school friend's post-mortem. She did so for a reason.

'Fran, you asked me something yesterday about the PM: you asked if plant extracts would show up in her system. Why was that?'

The girl looked at the ground. 'I just wondered.'

'Do you think she might have taken something? Drugs maybe?'

'No, it's not that! I just thought… it's probably nothing.' The girl was still looking down, avoiding her gaze.

'So what is it? Is it something to do with Mae's medicines?'

She looked up, startled. 'How did you know that?'

'So you think Mae gave her something that affected her?'

'No! Mae says she definitely didn't give her anything but she says that something has gone missing and it was the same evening when Cecile… when she…'

'So what was it, this medicine?'

'Tincture of rue.'

'Rue?'

'It was for period pains.'

'And she had taken it?'

'I don't know. I just wondered if they could find out.'

'Is it harmful?'

'I don't think so. I'm sure Mae wouldn't be making it if it was.'

Mills left Fran with enough work to keep her occupied until she returned later in the day. The girl's revelation about the tincture of rue worried Mills as she sped down to Harrogate. It was pure conjecture that Cecile had taken the medicine so to mention it to the pathologists could be a complete red herring. It wasn't her place to tell them what to look for. As she drove, she devised different ways of approaching the subject: the girl's friend dabbles in home remedies and it might be helpful to check for plant toxins? Or maybe: I was told she might be taking tincture of rue for period pains. It's probably irrelevant but... By the time she reached the hospital she was less sure it was sensible or even necessary to mention it.

'Ah, Dr Sanderson, we wondered if you were coming!'

Mills mumbled her excuses, straightened her jacket and swept her fringe out of her eyes. She could feel sweat on her forehead.

'I'm so sorry. There was a horrendous queue into town.'

The pathologist ignored her and turned to the woman standing beside him. Dr Moreau was beautifully dressed in a smart navy suit, her glossy hair swept into a chignon at her neck. Mills was admiring her gorgeously arched eyebrows and subtle make-up as the Frenchwoman offered an elegant hand.

'Dr Sanderson. A pleasure to meet you.'

Her hand was cool, in contrast to her own sticky palm.

'We'd better get on, then,' her English counterpart muttered, leading the way through the door marked "Private".

Mills had not expected to be directly involved in the post-mortem. Her impression was that the Fleurots wanted her to speak to Dr Moreau when it was over, to find out whether she was happy with the local pathologist's findings. She was surprised to be ushered into the mortuary. Everyone was assuming she would watch the entire procedure.

Mills was fairly comfortable with skeletal remains and was used to handling parts of bodies in varying states of decay. She had seen dead bodies and had been able to cope with them all – except for Mum, of course. She'd even watched autopsies on video as part of her background training in forensics but she'd never been present at an actual post-mortem. She felt she should make this clear but it was becoming more embarrassing to do so by the minute. Now she was being gowned up before being led to a position on one side of the gurney in order to observe. She just hoped she wasn't expected to take part.

The technical aspects of the procedure were so fascinating that Mills wasn't affected at first. The body lying on the gurney was so white and motionless it could have been a dummy. She held onto this thought but gradually the vision of the schoolgirl floating on the surface of the pool began to take over. She dug her nails into her palms and pressed her lips together. No-one was looking at her and she was able to wipe away the tear that had collected in the corner of her left eye. She concentrated on the idea that this cutting and sawing was being done to help Cecile – to discover why she died so young. She wiped another tear away and swallowed hard. The pathologist was recording audio notes and she listened carefully, waiting for the opportunity to mention the herbal medicine. His monologue went on throughout except when he directed the assistant to do this or that.

Eventually, during a pause in the proceedings, Mills tried to tell him about the herbal medicine but he wasn't really listening and suddenly there was a change of pace. Ignoring her, he stopped what he was doing and called sharply to his assistant to take photographs. Dr Moreau was leaning in with a surprised expression and the two medics went quiet as they looked over at Mills.

Something was removed and placed in a bowl. More photographs were taken and the pathologists turned their backs to her while they conferred with one another.

Mills listened carefully but she could only pick up a few words and couldn't tell what had excited them.

As anticipated, the autopsy was over before three o' clock. Dr Slade left immediately, promising to send his report to Dr Moreau as soon as possible. Mills was left alone with her as they removed their lab coats.

'Were you able to follow what was happening?' she asked as they washed their hands.

'Bits,' Mills admitted.

They were in the corridor leading to the main hospital entrance. It was now or never.

'You found something?' she asked.

'I would like something to drink,' Dr Moreau said, without comment. 'Shall we?'

She followed her companion to the cafeteria, where she insisted on buying Mills a cup of tea.

'I'm only in England for a few hours but I must have a proper cup of tea.'

'I'm not sure this is a good example of our English tea,' Mills remarked.

'So, I will wait for Dr Slade to send me a copy of the report he prepares for the coroner and then I will correspond with Madame et Monsieur Fleurot. It will probably be many weeks before that happens.'

'Right.' Mills paused. 'Will you be writing a separate report?'

'Not unless there is a difference of opinion, which I doubt. It is protocol that I should let your pathologist take the lead. My presence is really unnecessary to be honest.'

'I suppose the Fleurots feel more comfortable with a pathologist from their own country.'

The woman's demeanour changed suddenly. 'Dr Sanderson, I must ask you not to speak about what has occurred here this afternoon. Everything is confidential.'

Mills shook her head. 'Of course I won't,' she promised.

'Not even to the Fleurots. The information is confidential before it is released by your coroner. It is the law, yes?'

'Yes.'

They drank their tea in silence for a while and Mills checked her phone. There was a text from Nige: *where ru? they made the decision I said you'd be here at 4.*

'I heard what you said about the plant extract. It is probably not important but please will you let me know if you receive any further information about this?'

'Of course. But I thought…'

'It would have been rather difficult to raise issues with a pathologist during a post mortem but small things can sometimes be important.'

'Ok.'

It was already three-fifteen. Mills apologised for rushing off to the university, wishing she could spend longer, but the Frenchwoman shrugged.

'Yes, I heard you worked there. I was talking to a friend of yours.'

'Really?'

'Dr Freedman. I think you know him?'

Mills sat back down in her seat. 'How do you know Phil?' she asked, hoping she didn't sound too excited by the news.

'I've been doing some work at the site where the German plane crashed in Switzerland. It has been a major identification task, as you can imagine. Phil has been giving us the benefit of his expertise. You know he was working on the mass graves in Colombia?'

Oh yes, Mills knew that. Their relationship ended when he went over there and it had been her fault.

'I have to leave now anyway,' Dr Moreau said, looking at her watch.

Mills was disappointed. She wanted to find out what Phil had been doing since he left. 'Please say hello, when you see him,' Mills said, gathering her jacket from the back of the chair and picking up her bag.

'Of course. He said to ask how you are.'

They walked down the corridor together and shook hands before Dr Moreau rushed off to get her train. Mills turned away reluctantly; her mind still absorbed in the time five years earlier when she was helping Phil Freedman, much in the way Fran was helping her now. She unlocked the car and sat for several minutes, lost in her thoughts, until another text from Nige reminded her that she had just thirty minutes to get to the university. She replied that she was on her way back from a post-mortem but she knew it was inevitable she'd be late. She arrived long after the committee had gone home, Nige having given them the impression that Mills was carrying out an autopsy. She rushed in to find Nige sitting opposite the Head of Department chatting about football. He quickly put her in the picture.

'...so, to cut to the chase, we feel this is an excellent opportunity to co-ordinate our skills in both archaeology and forensics.'

Professor Cole was leaning back in his chair beaming at her. 'I assume you will accept?' the Head of Forensics was asking.

Mills knew he expected her to jump at the offer and it would be wrong to prevaricate. There were questions about the contract and the salary but she'd be mad not to take it. She should be biting his hand off.

'Of course.' She smiled at him and then at Nige. 'It's a really exciting opportunity.'

It was left that she'd receive a formal offer letter in a couple of days, outlining the details of the appointment. The Head seemed keen to get away and Nige had to pick up the boys so Mills went down to the laboratory to find Fran and apologise for keeping her hanging on. She found the girl sitting beside a neat tray of prepared bones. The rest of the bench was clean and tidy.

'Wow, you have been busy.'

'They're all done.'

Mills inspected them. She needn't have worried: they were pristine.

'Good for you. They look perfect.'

She carried the tray into the store and locked up.

'We'll soon have them finished at this rate,' she observed.

Fran looked pleased.

Neither of them mentioned the autopsy on the way back to the school but confined their discussion to "The Waldrens".

'I'm going to do some more background on the use of the site,' Fran said.

'I spoke to Mrs James but she didn't have much time...'

'Don't worry. I told her what I'm doing and she's very happy with it all.'

I know, thought Mills, but she won't be marking your work, will she?

They agreed to meet up again at the end of the week to finish the disinterment of "Mr Bones" and Mills drove home wondering how to tell Alex that she had a full-time job at the university.

To her surprise he was cooking already and had bought a bottle of wine. Mills waited as he poured two glasses.

'I'm celebrating,' he announced. 'I've got a job interview!'

Chapter 9

'Anyone fancy coming into town?'

Madison was lying on the lawn outside the student house. She was concentrating on painting the nails of her left hand. No-one answered.

'Mae?'

'What?' She had feigned sleep to stop the American teasing her about her gardening activities.

'Coming for a drink? I've booked a cab.'

Fran looked at her watch and shook her head. She'd planned to spend some more time on the internet.

'D'you want to help me with my research?' she asked Mae, knowing her friend would jump at the excuse.

They went off to the library leaving Madison by herself. She didn't want to be drinking alone and immediately sent a text to Herbie, asking him to meet her in "The Fleece" then called the taxi firm to send the cab earlier. She had just enough time to get ready before it was due.

A night out with Herbie was usually fun, although she really wanted to be with the friends who had left for the vacation. Even Austin had elected to head for the States with Jules in tow, leaving her back in England trying to find a way of continuing her relationship with Jeremy. She was sure if she stayed in the area and was free all summer, he was bound to see her occasionally.

She recognised the vehicle as it drew up in front of the school. She'd seen the driver a few times since the end of term when she'd started her regular trips into town. He was an unpleasant guy with long greasy hair and a nasty grin that gave her the creeps.

'Hello, darling!' he called. 'Off on the town again are we?'

'Yep.'

She climbed in the back of the car. She wasn't going to make the mistake of sitting beside him again. The memory of his hand on her bare thigh made her shudder.

'Come and sit up front,' he called.

'No way!'

He shrugged and reversed out, swinging the car round and speeding up the drive.

'On your own tonight?'

'Yep.'

'Where's that French girl? She not with you this time? She's a looker and no mistake.'

Madison ignored him.

'The usual place?' he asked once they were on the road.

'Yep.'

'I finish at ten – I'll be down later.'

She ignored him.

'I said, I'll come down and we can have a few bevvies.'

'I'll be with a friend,' she said.

'That low-life? You can do better than him.'

The fact he knew Herbie made Madison uncomfortable.

'You need a mature man in your life.'

Madison smiled. She had a mature man in her life. If only he knew.

He shut up until he stopped outside the pub.

'So I'll come down then,' he tried again.

She paid him with a note.

'Here you are, Gramps. Now push off back to the care home!'

The bar was empty and Madison found Herbie playing pool with two guys she'd seen around. She bought herself a drink and stood watching until eventually he came over.

'Hi. Get me a pint and I'll see what I've got for you.'

'I don't need anything,' she replied. 'But I'll get you one anyway.'

She wanted to keep a clear head. She'd had an idea, a plan that had been forming over the last couple of days.

She carried the lager back to the pool room and stood quietly watching the guys play. On another occasion she'd be bugging them for a game and when Herbie came over to collect his drink, he asked her what was wrong.

'Aw, nothing. I just want to keep myself together for once.'

He looked quizzically at her, then led her outside where he produced a bag of pills and popped one in his mouth before lighting up two cigarettes and handing her one. Before long he'd persuaded her to take a tablet and when they went back inside she began ordering shots.

'That's more like it,' he said and told her to "get them in" for his friends too.

After that it was a bit of a blur until the pub was closing and Herbie was walking her to where the taxis waited. As they approached, one drove off, leaving a single car behind.

'No!' Madison said, stumbling on the cobbles and grabbing Herbie's arm. 'Not that one. He's a creep!'

'No choice.'

'I'm not going with him and that's it. I'll wait here all night if I have to.' She was tired and just wanted to sleep.

'Don't be daft.'

'I'm not going in his cab on my own – no way! You'll have to come with me.'

She knew she could persuade him and after a few minutes discussion with raised voices and Madison threatening to lie down in the market square, Herbie agreed to escort her in the taxi if she paid the fare for him to get home.

The taxi driver was asleep, resting back in his seat with his mouth open. He looked confused when Herbie banged on the window. When he realised it was Madison he initially refused to take her, complaining she'd been abusive. But learning that he was to do a round trip delivering Herbie back on the other side of Richmond, he changed his mind.

'How does he know you?' Madison asked in a loud whisper when they set off.

'He doesn't – I don't know him anyway.'

'You said you knew Herbie!' she shouted at the driver.

He looked at her in his mirror.

'He's a druggie,' he said. 'We all know him in town.'

Herbie grinned. 'It's nice to be noticed.'

Madison didn't care what Herbie was, he was a good mate. She leaned against his shoulder and closed her eyes.

When she opened them again she was alone in the taxi. They were moving slowly along a dark road but it wasn't the way back to school. She sat still, fumbling in her bag for her phone. If necessary she would call the cops. Meanwhile she'd wait. She stayed in position, looking out of the window, thinking the driver wouldn't notice she'd woken up.

They reached a junction and the car slowed sufficiently for her to read the signpost. They were turning in the direction of Scorton, three miles away. It must be fate, meant to be. She knew all about Scorton. It was where Jeremy lived with his pregnant wife in a cosy little house. She'd seen it on the internet. You could look up anywhere and their house was there: a tiny terraced cottage on the main street. They were going to be driving past his house in Scorton very soon and she needed to get out.

'Where's Herbie?' she shouted.

'He went,' the driver called back. 'He needed a leak.'

'You left him?'

'I wasn't waiting.'

They were approaching some lights and she guessed it was time to do it. She reached for the handle and pushed at the door.

'What are you doing?'

The driver slowed the car and turned.

'I'm getting out of here,' she shouted, feeling the adrenalin rush.

The car stopped suddenly and she half-fell onto the road. The driver door opened. Madison stood up, pulling her shoe back on.

'Go away or I'll call the cops!' she shrieked.

He made to come towards her and she bawled at him to "piss off".

A door opened and a man peered out, pulling a dressing gown on.

'What's going on?'

The driver jumped into his car and drove off with a squeal of tyres, leaving Madison screaming after him.

A woman joined the man in the doorway.

'Are you all right, love?' she asked.

Madison was too angry to respond at first but after being asked twice she assured the couple she was "fine and dandy".

'I just need to get home,' she said, wishing they'd stop interfering.

'Can we help?' the man asked, stepping onto the pavement outside his house.

'Should we ring the police?' the woman called.

Madison pulled the hem of her skirt down and drew her cardigan round her.

'No thanks. I have a friend here.' She looked up and down the street. 'He lives in the village: Jeremy Young.'

'Oh, that's Diane's husband, he's a teacher,' the woman said to her husband. 'I don't know the number but it's just down there on the other side of the road. With the green front door.'

Madison assured the husband she didn't need an escort but she knew they were watching her as she made her way unsteadily down the pavement and across the road. It wasn't easy to discern the colour of the doors but she recognised the cottage from the internet. It was in darkness. Feeling a little less confident than she'd been a few minutes earlier but determined to go through with it she rang the bell and waited.

She looked round to see if the couple were still watching her and rang the bell for longer this time. She was still staring back up the road when the path was illuminated from the cottage door.

'Hello?' It was a woman's voice.

Madison froze. She'd expected it to be Jeremy. Where was he? She waited, hoping he'd appear.

'Can I help you?'

It was Jeremy's wife, Diane, peering round the door. Madison hadn't anticipated that. She turned to look at her. They stared at each other until Madison found her voice.

'Sorry it's late. I'm at the school. I know Mr Young, he's our drama teacher.'

Immediately Diane invited Madison in, sat her down and prepared her a hot drink. Madison kept staring at her pregnant bump. Diane – she insisted she called her Diane – asked her what had happened and listened while Madison told her about the taxi driver. Then she asked her if she would like to stay.

'I can make up a bed on the sofa, it's quite comfy.'

'No really, I can't.'

'I would offer to take you back to your school but I don't have a car. My husband's visiting his mother overnight. I could call a taxi but I imagine you might not…'

She went up the stairs, reappearing with a pillow and duvet. Madison was simply too exhausted to argue and lay down on the sofa, allowing Diane to arrange the soft duvet over her. It smelt nice and she was reminded of home as she drifted off to sleep.

'I was thinking last night that I should have informed the school you were here,' said Diane, offering a mug of coffee.

Madison struggled out of the duvet and swung her feet onto the floor. She must look a sight. She pushed her hair out of her eyes and tried to smooth down her creased T-shirt. Her head was throbbing – whatever Herbie had given her, it had not been good stuff.

'No problem, I'll be back as soon as I get a cab.'

'I was wondering,' Diane began. 'You didn't have anything with you last night?'

Madison looked round for her Hermes handbag.

'I thought it odd you didn't have a bag.'

Madison sighed. Most likely she'd left it in the cab, unless Herbie had run off with it. She told Diane it was the taxi driver.

'What's the name of the company?' she asked before marching out of the room.

Madison could hear her raised voice, demanding to speak to the manager. This was followed by a long pause and then an even longer conversation. Madison couldn't hear what was said but when Diane returned she was looking irritated.

'They deny all knowledge of it. I told them exactly where he dropped you off, so they have no excuse. They can easily identify who was driving.'

'I know the guy, he's a creep.'

'You must report it to the police.'

'I will, as soon as I get back to school.'

She couldn't remember much about the evening before so was unsure whether Herbie had sold her anything or not. If he had it would be in her bag and if that came to light she'd be expelled – again. She'd have to tackle the taxi driver herself.

'Well, let me make you some toast before you go and I'll ring a different firm to get you safely back to school.'

'Madison didn't come back last night,' Fran told her friend at breakfast.

'Not the first time,' Mae replied, taking another spoonful of cornflakes.

'She was on her own this time though.'

Madison had been in the habit of selecting a few of the girls to accompany her on her clandestine nights out. Mae had never been asked such was the girl's animosity towards her.

'She can look after herself. She's a tough cookie.'

Fran grinned at her friend's attempt at an impersonation of the American girl. 'But she knows all the pubs in Richmond. She sees lots of boys down there.'

'How do you know?' Mae asked sharply.

'I only went once. I didn't go again.'

'What about Cecile?'

'She came too. I told her I didn't like it but she went with her a few times after that.'

'Did she take drugs too?'

'I don't know. She wouldn't tell me. But she stopped going after a while. She wouldn't say why.'

'She was stupid if she let Madison give her drugs,' said Mae, helping herself to a piece of toast.

'You can talk!' Fran laughed. 'All the concoctions you make up.'

'They're old remedies from natural sources, not a mixture of chemicals.'

'I suppose. Has that missing bottle turned up yet?'

'No and I'm really cross about it.'

'Perhaps Madison wanted to experiment with something more natural?' suggested Fran.

'I doubt that, more likely to wind me up!'

Fran went off to refill her coffee cup before asking her friend to help her carry on with her research.

Mae groaned. 'Not another day in the library? Look outside, it's hot and sunny. Why don't you help me in the garden?'

'No, listen. I thought we could go to the place where the bones come from. I want to get some background on the site and someone around must know what was there before they built the houses.'

'I'd like to see the bones,' agreed Mae. 'Will we be able to do any digging?'

'Not without Dr Sanderson but I can show you where they are.'

They checked the bus timetable pinned to the board in the hallway. There was plenty of time to get organised before it was due and they walked slowly back to the student house, stopping while Mae examined a weed growing out of the paving.

'It's hot out here, Mae, you'll need some of your homemade sunscreen,' Fran said.

They spotted Madison getting out of a taxi and waited until she was within earshot.

'You're up early,' Mae said.

'Oh, sorry,' she called, sarcastically. 'Did you need a cab?'

'No,' replied Mae stonily. 'Some of us can't afford them.'

'What's up with her?' Fran asked as they walked away.

'Don't ask,' said her friend. 'She's probably lacking sleep, if you know what I mean. At least he's sent her home in a taxi,' she added.

'Who?'

Mae laughed. 'That's the question, isn't it? Who does she know that would stretch to a taxi?'

'What are you saying?'

'Nothing.'

They walked back to the student house in silence.

Madison was sitting on the edge of her bed, fiddling with her hair.

'Hey Mae, I need to use your phone.'

'What's the matter with yours?' asked Mae. 'Run out of minutes?'

'I have not! I've lost my bag. My phone was in it.'

'Where? Have you rung the police?' Fran sat beside her on the bed.

'Don't fuss. I left it in the taxi. I just need to call them.'

'Here!' Fran said, giving Madison her mobile.

Mae sighed loudly. As soon as Madison had left the room she admonished her friend for falling for her tricks.

'I think she was telling the truth,' her friend argued.

'There's one way to find out.'

Mae led her friend down the corridor. The signal was best in their bedroom and the only other good reception was beside the kitchen window. They could hear Madison shouting as soon as they were outside the door.

'Listen, you pervert, I want it back. You can bring it to school right now or I'll call the cops.'

There was a long pause before she spoke again and this time the pitch was higher and louder.

'You have no right to open it. Whatever I have in there is no business of yours!'

Another pause.

'If you do that I will personally come down to the office and cut your balls off!'

Fran looked at Mae, who was grinning.

'How dare you blackmail me! Two can play at that game. I have witnesses that you tried to abduct me last night… Ok, ok. Good. Then just get down here now!'

The girls moved swiftly away from the kitchen door and walked casually down the corridor as Madison reappeared.

'Can I have my phone back?' Fran asked innocently.

'Sure.' The girl threw it across to her and marched off.

'Here.' Mae grabbed the phone and checked the number Madison had called. It was the taxi service recommended by the school but not the one that she'd arrived in.

'I guess she must've left it in a taxi,' Mae said. 'You were right.'

'But she said he'd tried to abduct her. She should tell someone.'

'You think so? I feel sorry for her,' said Fran. 'She gets herself in all sorts of trouble and there's no-one to look after her.'

'I think she can handle herself perfectly well, thank you.' Mae's voice was uncharacteristically hard. 'She's a self-centred bitch as far as I can see and she gets everything she deserves.'

Chapter 10

On the bus to Richmond, Fran asked Mae what she'd meant about Madison being sent home in a taxi.

Her friend seemed to be deciding whether to say anything or not.

'It's just that Leanne told me about hearing Madison and Mr Young having a row. Leanne thought he was telling her off but I've watched how Madison acts around him and I wonder…'

'You wonder what?'

'That he might be…'

'No! Not Mr Young. That's impossible – he's married!'

'You are such an innocent, Fran.'

'Are you sure?'

'No, not sure. Just like I'm not sure she is or at least was, pregnant.'

'Pregnant?'

'It makes sense. Madison was asking me about the rue tincture for period pains. When I told her that a really large dose could cause abortion she seemed even more interested in it, not less.'

'You think she's pregnant?'

'Maybe she *was*.'

Fran was still digesting the information when they arrived in Richmond market square.

'You think she took your bottle of rue?' Fran asked as they climbed off the bus.

'I'm just saying she was mighty interested in it.'

There was time to grab a snack for their lunch before catching the bus that went all the way to

Barnard Castle. Fran, anxious not to miss their stop, followed the route carefully on her map until they reached Gilling West. They were the only people to descend into the bright sunshine.

'We mustn't miss the bus back this afternoon,' warned Fran, as Mae followed her down the deserted street.

It was the hottest part of the day and it was a relief to turn down the shady lane leading to the construction site. A large advertising board announced there would be a new development of four and five-bedroomed homes. Dust from the building work covering the road was stirred up by a lorry as it came towards them. The driver shouted and they pressed themselves against the wall as the vehicle went by.

'Are you sure it's all right to go in?' Mae asked when they reached the entrance to the site. 'It says "No admittance to unauthorised personnel" on the gate.'

Fran hesitated. It had been different when they'd arrived in Dr Sanderson's car.

'I don't know.'

Mae sighed. 'Let's go back down the road and decide what to do.'

They retraced their steps as far as a low wall where they sat and ate the pastries they'd bought in town. Fran was regretting her idea and apologised to her friend. 'It was stupid to come here to research the place when we can't even go in.'

'No problem. It's fun and anyway, we can ask this lady if you like.'

She indicated a woman who had come out into her front garden which ended at the wall they were perched on. They immediately jumped up, brushing crumbs from their clothes. Fran took her bag off the wall and examined the map studiously.

'You girls look as though you're lost,' the woman remarked as she drew closer.

Fran looked up. The woman was old, older than her grandmother and *she* was sixty-eight. She was quite well dressed for an old person but was wearing a beige cardigan even though it was really hot in the sun.

Mae gave Fran a look that said *she* would handle it.

'Actually we were looking for "The Waldrens" but it seems to be a building site.'

The woman laughed. 'It's gone I'm afraid. You've missed it. They flattened it last summer. Did you know someone who was staying there?'

Mae told her they were doing a project on the site but didn't mention the bones – in case, she explained to Fran later, it upset her. She asked if the old lady had known the house.

'It was a residential home when I moved here,' she explained. 'For elderly people who couldn't manage on their own. It was big too. They had a job finding places for everyone when they moved out. I got to know a few of the more mobile ones, they'd be out in the grounds in the good weather and we'd pass the time of day. Apparently it had been an approved school before that.'

'An approved school?' Mae repeated. 'What's that?'

'Like a borstal.' She smiled at their blank faces. 'A place for young offenders they'd call it now.'

'Prison!' exclaimed Fran.

'Well, you could call it that but it was for youngsters so it wasn't a prison.' She paused.

'Although from what my friend tells me, it *was* like a prison – horrible.'

A lorry came past, making it impossible to converse.

'Noisy things! I'll be glad when it's all over. When I came here it was just a quiet lane with the building at the end of a long drive. Not very pretty of course, a Victorian brick monstrosity that looked like something out of Dickens.'

'Do you know if it was called "The Waldrens" when it was a young offenders place?' asked Mae.

'I doubt it. Somebody will know. There are people in the village who worked there before it became a care home. I think it changed in the seventies.'

'They must be really old,' said Fran, calculating the years.

'Don't you go saying that to Mr Thomas!' She laughed. 'He wouldn't be pleased, oh no.'

Her neighbour, it seemed, lived in a house on the green and had done so all his life.

'I wonder if he'd talk to us about it,' said Fran, turning to Mae.

Her friend smiled at the old lady. 'Would you be able to introduce us to Mr Thomas?'

She looked surprised. 'What? Now?'

Fran went to contradict her but her friend jumped in.

'Yes please. It is really important we do this today. We may not get another chance.'

And so they followed her down the narrow brick path through her neat garden. It was cool inside the tiny cottage and it took a minute or two to grow accustomed to darkness. She pushed a cat off the sofa and ordered them to sit down while she rang her neighbour.

'It's Eileen,' she began before inviting him over.

He arrived before they'd finished the orange squash she served them in fancy green glasses.

They sat for over an hour while he described what life was like for the borstal boys.

'My father worked there as a prison officer, several of the men in the village did. He was a hard man and many a time he gave me a belting. He used to take me into the prison when I was small just to show me what it would be like if I misbehaved. It scared me I can tell you.'

Mr Thomas was a diminutive man with bright blue eyes and a mop of white hair. He was very old and a little deaf so Mae had to raise her voice to ask the question.

'Was it really like a prison?'

'They called it an approved school in those days but it was prison. It was a tough regime – supposed to be the best way in them days. The inmates certainly didn't want to return. But it broke some of them. They were lads of my age and I knew some of them quite well. They would come and do our garden and I'd give them food when my dad wasn't looking. The things they were there for, it was extreme punishment. That was the worst time.'

It sounded like a dreadful place to Fran and she asked him lots of questions about the boys' schooling and whether they saw their parents regularly. The old man shook his head slowly.

'When my father was working there they weren't very interested in educating the lads. They gave them work to keep them in check. Dad left at the end of the sixties but there were some evil men working alongside my father – fellow officers. He admitted that when he retired. One was even suspended for excessive punishment.'

'So when did it become a care home?' Eileen asked. 'It must have been a while ago because some of the residents had been there for years.'

'Mid-seventies.'

'And just think, now it will be houses for young families, oblivious of everything that went on there,' she said.

Brenda was in her office when Mills checked. But her door was closed, which meant she did not want to be interrupted. How she would react when Mills disturbed her would depend on her mood. Sometimes she would be happy to be distracted from the task in hand but, if she didn't want to see anyone, it could turn nasty. She tapped gingerly on her door and opened it.

'Mills! Come in! You can help me with this.'

'What is it?'

'I've been asked for a reference for Alex. He's applied for a job.'

'Yes, he's got an interview next week.'

'Yes, it says so here. It's a big step moving into banking.'

Banking? Mills realised he'd never actually said what the job was and she'd simply assumed it would be along the same lines as the work he'd been doing at Yardley. She was puzzled.

'Yes. I expect they need digital forensics,' Mills muttered.

Brenda was scrutinising the letter through her half glasses.

'No. It sounds more like a financial adviser role.'

'It must be a mistake.'

'It sounds like a graduate scheme to me. When is he going to London?'

'London?'

'For the interview.'

Mills apologised. 'Next week. I'm sorry Brenda, I haven't really been paying attention.'

Alex hadn't told her much about the interview and she'd been so busy. Was it actually for the job in London? He had told her about it but she hadn't really believed he was serious.

Brenda wanted her help in preparing a glowing reference for Alex. Her boss said it would be an excellent opportunity for him to progress. Mills thought the tone of the reference they devised together was over the top but agreed they should give him as much support as they could.

'And if he is offered this before the end of his contract, I won't have to pay him any redundancy money,' Brenda said with a grin.

She really was incorrigible.

'Now what did *you* want, pet?'

Mills had nearly forgotten to ask her boss about the bracelet. She had a photo on her phone and transferred it to Brenda's computer so they could view it on the large monitor.

'You say it's on skeletal remains of antiquity?'

'That's what they called it. It looked like gold and, from the few links I could see, it was quite chunky.'

'Well I'm no expert but it looks rather modern to me.' She zoomed in to get a closer look. 'In fact it reminds me of those identity bracelets that were all the rage in the sixties.' She peered at the screen. 'You won't remember them, dear. They were chunky... silver... or gold... with a piece where you put your name. We used to swap them when I was at school, between boyfriend and girlfriend.'

'You mean like medical ID bracelets.'

'Exactly.'

'People still wear ID bracelets but this body is really old. I'm sure it's been carbon-dated.'

'Has it indeed? And what date was it?'

Mills didn't know. Stupidly she'd not asked the simple question.

Brenda removed her glasses and leaned back in her chair. 'You'd best get an expert to have a look then but I'm willing to bet it's younger than that. D'you want me to send this to a couple of people I know?' She indicated the picture on her screen.

Mills agreed and went off to find out how the age of the skeleton had been established. It took just one email back from County Hall to confirm that the bones had been carbon-dated. The report did not give a single date but a range because of the uncertainty of the analysis. Mills took a copy of the report to show Brenda.

'There it is. 1550 plus or minus a hundred years.' Mills placed the page on the desk in front of her.

Brenda's expression gave no clues to what she was thinking. She removed the brightly coloured scarf and ran her fingers through her sparse hair.

'Hmmm. 1650.'

'Pre-1650,' Mills corrected her.

'1550 plus one hundred was 1650 when I was at school, pet.'

Mills felt hot. 1650 was a significant date in carbon-dating. Anything before that date could be confidently dated but after that it became problematical until 1950 when bomb testing so affected the carbon-14 in the environment that it was obvious. There was a period of real uncertainty between 1650 and 1950 for carbon-dating.

'I had a similar case over a rug a few years ago,' Brenda said, tying her scarf back on her head carefully, knotting it at the nape of her scrawny neck. 'It was a double-niche Anatolian carpet in an American museum. The suggested age was similar and it caused such a dispute. In that case if it turned out it was not made in 1650 the alternative date would have been 1960!'

Mills was momentarily distracted by her deep throated laugh. She hadn't heard that for a while, she thought.

'So you are saying that my skeleton could have died in 1960?' Mills was shocked.

'Who did this work?' Brenda demanded, peering at the page again. She tut-tutted loudly. 'They should have pointed this out, they know the issues.'

'To be fair they may not have known the context,' Mills offered.

'You'd better inform the police.'

'It doesn't mean it was 1960,' objected Mills.

Brenda was busy studying her computer monitor.

'All right I'll call Nina.' Mills sighed. 'She'll know what to do. Anyway it should be easy to see the difference between a body from 1550 and 1960.'

Brenda raised her eyebrows again. 'So you're sure we're talking 1550, plus or minus?'

'Yes.' But now she had nagging doubts.

'The reason I ask is because one of my contacts, a professor from Scotland, has just come back to say the gold links from that bracelet look decidedly modern. I'll get back to her and give her the options: 1550 or 1960. That should nail it.'

There was no response before it was time for Mills to go home. She'd spent the rest of the day trying to concentrate on the growing pile of paperwork but she was in a state. She picked at the sandwich she'd brought for lunch and spent her break on the internet looking at cases where carbon-dating had got it wrong.

'D'you think the osteoarchaeologist could have been mistaken too?' she asked Brenda before leaving.

'Difficult to judge how long bones have been in the ground – you know that better than me, Mills.'

'Which is why they did the radiocarbon-dating.'

'Exactly. And since that isn't conclusive either, let's wait for my professor to get back to me, eh?'

She smiled at Mills. 'So get yourself off home and tell Alex what a spectacular reference we gave him today.'

Madison had collected her bag from the taxi firm in the afternoon. She opened it up and checked everything was there, her purse, her makeup bag, her phone, before leaving.

The woman in the office, who manned the phones, gave her a sympathetic smile.

'Everything all right, love?' she asked. 'Only, I had a call from someone who said they'd seen you in Scorton last night.'

'I'm good,' Madison replied.

'If you wanted to complete a complaint form…' she was reaching under her desk.

'No! No I don't. Thank you.'

Madison knew what would happen if she reported the old man; he'd tell the school that she had drugs in her bag when he found it. Not any more, they'd gone, but that's what he said he'd do and she'd have to go along with it.

She walked along the street to the pub and looked for Herbie but the pool room was empty. She took a cab back to school and went through her phone on the way. There were three missed calls from Jeremy. At last she had his attention. She'd catch him at the end of the day before he left to go back to his bulbous wife.

'I've changed my mind,' she told the driver and gave him the address of her brother's school.

It wasn't quite as grand as hers but it was in pleasant wooded grounds and the modern student houses were more suitable than her dated accommodation. They had a really good gym and the pool was enormous. Like High Fell, there would be few pupils remaining in residence. Her brother was due to go back to the States at the end of the week and she sometimes wished she was going too, despite wanting to see Jeremy so badly. But it wasn't just that: Herbie needed her and she needed him too.

She could see Jeremy's car so she paid the cabbie and let him drive away. She would wait in the staff car park for however long it took for her lover to appear. She sat on the warm tarmac by his car and lit a cigarette. All in all it was a very satisfactory end to a pretty horrible day.

The sun had gone in and it was beginning to feel chilly when Jeremy finally emerged. She could see him walking toward the car carrying a pile of folders and his old battered briefcase. She watched him fondly as he struggled to extract the car keys from his pocket, nearly dropping his papers in the process.

'Hi Jeremy.' She jumped up and threw her cigarette end on the ground.

'You've been trying to get hold of me, so to speak.' She'd rehearsed the line and went up close to him as she recited it.

He recoiled a little, looking round to see who might be watching.

She waited. 'You've been calling me, Jeremy.'

He unlocked the car and opened his door. Madison jumped into the passenger seat.

'I need a lift back to the school,' she said. 'We can talk on the way.'

'Get out!' he shouted, leaning into the car.

She thought he was going to come round and drag her out but she remained where she was.

'What were doing at my house last night?' he demanded. 'I told you to stay away.'

'I couldn't. I wanted to see you.'

'You were drunk. You arrived on my doorstep, God knows what for. What were you thinking?'

'I was thinking it would be nice to see you. But you weren't there. That's all.'

He climbed into the driver's seat. 'Well you've seen me now. Get out.'

'I didn't say anything to her, you know.'

He didn't reply.

'I could've done.'

Nothing.

'Perhaps I will... next time.'

He turned to look at her, his face was stony hard.

'You will not.'

'How will you stop me, eh? If you're so clever Mr Young, tell me, how are you going to stop me?'

'Put your seatbelt on.'

He drove her the three miles to the gates of High Fell School.

'Get out,' he said without looking at her. His voice was calm now.

'When will I see you again?'

'Never.'

'You don't mean that.'

No answer.

'Okay. Until I'm passing Scorton again then?' She climbed out and walked through the gates without looking back. She didn't want him to see the mascara running down her face.

Chapter 11

Mills had been expecting the call from Fiona. She was surprised it hadn't come sooner and was actually pleased with the interruption. Her discussion with Alex about his job interview had degenerated into an argument around who had a greater degree of commitment to their relationship and it was doomed to end in tears.

'Fiona! Lovely to hear from you.' Mills knew her heartiness sounded false.

'You sound chirpy, darling.'

'How's Flora? And Dad?'

'They're fine. Look, I rang to see how the post mortem went. Was it awful?'

'No.' That sounded wrong. 'Well, yes of course,' she added.

'Poor you. Marianne asked me if you heard anything... anything unusual.'

'No.'

It was true. She didn't know what had caused the two pathologists to go into a huddle.

'Poor Marianne wants to take Cecile's body back to France for the funeral but they haven't released it yet. We thought you might know why.'

'Sorry, I don't. I suppose they want to be sure that it was an accident.'

'What else could it be?'

Mills had already been wondering if Cecile might have taken her own life. She knew that suicide was a main cause of death in teenage girls and the French girl had seemed to be quiet and withdrawn compared to her school friends.

'Don't know. Look, I'll see if I can find out anything and get back to you.'

'How's Alex?'

It was as if Fiona had detected something was wrong.

'He's fine. He's got an interview down in London next week.'

It was the trigger for Fiona to try, once more, to drag them both down to stay. Mills had no intention of accompanying Alex and told her so. She could see he was listening and when she came off the phone another argument ensued.

'We don't have to stay with them,' he argued. 'The company is booking a room for me in a hotel right in the middle of town. We can do something…'

'Like what?'

'Go to a show or something.'

'They'll expect us to go and spend time with them. You don't know her. She'll plan our every move. There's no point.'

Mills picked Fran up from school early the next morning so they could finish clearing the skeleton from its grave on the building site. As they stood together regarding the few remaining bones, Mills tried to decide how they could possibly be from the 1960s. The workman who'd shown interest in the remains and tried to hurry her up was standing at the edge of the plot watching. She shifted round so she shielded the ground and ordered Fran to wait. The girl had collected the tools and was about to begin work but Mills was wary now there was a chance, however small, that the body was not "of antiquity". It was possible that this would become a police matter, however innocent the cause of death might be. Mills didn't want to mention it to Fran so she suggested that she tried her hand at writing the notes instead.

'Hopefully this will be our last visit to the site, so you should make some sketches and describe the environment as clearly and in as much detail as possible,' she instructed her.

Conscious that the man was still observing her, Mills began to work fast, digging at the ground more roughly than she should and risking damage to the remaining bones. She'd been doing some homework since Brenda told her about the likely age of the ID bracelet. She thought there would be a significant height difference between people born in the 16th and 20th centuries but apparently that was not as significant as one might believe. She examined everything she removed from the dry soil but nothing helped. There could be clues she could look for in the teeth but that would have to wait until she got to the university and could examine the skull. She was no expert and it would have to be handed over to someone who was.

When the depression in the ground was empty, Mills stepped back to take a final photograph. Fran showed her the sketches she'd made, far superior to anything Mills would have produced. She praised her and the girl blushed. She left Fran to load up the car while she ventured into the wooden hut that served as the site office. She assumed it was their lunch break because there was a group of men sitting round eating and drinking. She sought out the foreman, who was reading his paper.

'I just wanted to let you know we've finished,' she told him.

'Oh ay?'

There was nothing more to say. With five pairs of eyes on her she handed over her key and stepped self-consciously out into the sunshine.

'Shall I finish cleaning the bones today?' Fran asked as they sped along the main road to the university.

'Yes. I need to make some calls about the remains.'

Her reticence in letting Fran handle the bones was overwhelmed by the desire to get the matter sorted. She would ring Nina to establish the procedure but first she wanted to look at the skull again.

After lunch while Fran scrubbed gently at the fibula with a toothbrush, Mills took the jaw bone from the store and examined it closely. Did the teeth look worn? They would be worn down in the middle-ages because of the diet but how worn down? These teeth were yellowing, chipped and two were missing but she was none the wiser. At least there was no sign of any modern dentistry which would have proved she had definitely been mistaken.

She went to the office she shared with Nige, to call Nina. He was working with his headphones on and he looked up in surprise when she waved across at him.

'Hello stranger,' he said, pulling the headset off. 'I've got a message for you and the Head wants to see you.'

'It's been hectic,' she said, grabbing the phone. 'I've got to ring Nina.'

He grinned. 'Tell her to get some milk.'

'I will not. You can ask her yourself when I've finished.'

When her friend answered, Mills told her about the confusion over the dating of the skeleton. It came out as a garbled story and Mills had to repeat it again slowly while Nina listened patiently. As usual, she was a calming influence.

'Don't worry, Mills. It's clearly not your fault.'

'I'm not an expert, Nina.'

'I know. We'll have to arrange for someone to have a look at the remains in more detail. It's good you photographed the bracelet because that is probably the best bit of intel we have.'

'I shouldn't have left it there overnight.'

'Don't beat yourself up about it. Where are the remains now?'

'Here at the university under lock and key.'

'Leave them there until I get back to you. Oh – and can you email me that photo of the bracelet?'

'Of course and I'll find out who Brenda asked to provenance it.'

When the conversation was over she handed the receiver to Nige.

'Hang on,' he said. 'Mills, your dad's wife is trying to get hold of you.'

She indicated that she'd heard him and rushed back to see Fran.

'I've finished, Dr Sanderson.'

The remainder of the bones were lined up neatly on the tray.

'We'll put them in the storeroom to dry,' Mills said.

After locking them away, she went back to the office to send the photograph of the bracelet to Nina, leaving Fran to work on her report in the library. Mills took the opportunity to call Fiona.

'It's about Cecile: Marianne and her husband have been asking to take her body back to France but now they are saying that to get permission there will have to be a hearing. Marianne says she can't face it; she's been in a terrible state ever since it happened.'

'What about her husband?'

'Yes, he'll be there but I thought it would help if you could go?'

'Me?'

'Yes. You're familiar with the ins and outs of these things. You could help me with the technical things.'

Mills sighed. Fiona had no idea.

'When is it?'

'Not for a while; next month I think. I'll find out and get back to you.'

'Ok.'

It was possible she wouldn't be allowed to attend anyway, since she had no official reason to be there unless, of course, the family requested it.

Mills collected Fran from the library and drove her back to school. During the journey the girl told Mills what she had discovered about the building site: how there had been a big house that had been used as a residential home for the elderly. Mills was tempted to tell her about the possible confusion over the dating of the body but decided she should be discreet until she knew the outcome.

'For a long time?' she asked casually.

'Since the mid-seventies, the old lady said. Before that it was an approved school.'

Mills pondered on the implications if the dating proved to be wrong and it was from the sixties. Both of them were quiet for the rest of the journey until they turned through the gates to High Fell Hall when suddenly Fran said she wanted to ask Mills something.

'What is it?' Mills had slowed to avoid the American girl, who was walking up the drive looking at her mobile, apparently oblivious of them.

'Mrs James rang me this afternoon about Cecile. She said there was going to be a sort of inquest but not a proper one.'

'A pre-inquest hearing?'

'Yes… I think she called it that.'

'Sounds right.'

'She said I'd have to go.'

Mills parked the car outside the school house. 'I suppose they want you to describe what you saw,' she said gently.

'Will you be there?' The girl was looking at her.

'I don't know. Probably not but I'm sure Mrs James will be there for you.'

'She said I should ask my mother but she's abroad and anyway she'd just fuss. I told the Head you'd probably be there so it would be ok.'

Mills felt some sympathy for the girl. She wasn't a child and would cope perfectly well; she just needed a little support. It seemed everyone wanted her to attend.

'I'll see what I can do but it will depend on the coroner,' she warned.

Fran gave her a broad smile and jumped out of the car. 'I'll tell Mrs James it's all right then,' she called as she ran into the school.

As she turned out onto the main road, Mills spotted Madison standing by the bus stop. She almost stopped to offer her a lift but thought better of it. The girl was busy on her phone and didn't even notice her as she drove past.

Alex was waiting for her when she arrived home.

'Nina called. Can you ring her back?'

She obeyed immediately, dreading what her friend had to report.

'There's no doubt, Mills. They were straight back confirming Brenda's view – it's a 20th century identity bracelet. Are you still there?' Nina asked.

Mills was already envisaging the consequences of the news.

'So are there any bones left at the site?' Her friend persisted with her questions.

'No. Sorry, I'm just trying to take it in.'

'Well at least they're safe. We'll need them for forensic investigations.'

Mills could feel the sweat collecting on her forehead.

'They've been cleaned.'

There was silence. 'Well never mind, Mills. I'm sure you'll be able to do something with them – DNA or whatever.'

'Will they come to us?'

'Probably. You know Yardley is one of our preferred laboratories.'

This was one occasion when Mills wished they weren't. She apologised once again and Nina repeated that it wasn't her fault: the consultant osteoarchaeologist was to blame.

Mills was still thinking about carbon-dating.

'Nina. If the bones aren't 17th century, they must date back to after the fifties, probably the sixties but they can be dated quite accurately now we know they're from the 20th century. It would be worth looking back at the report and talking to the laboratory that did the work.'

'Would you do that for me if I send the report across?'

Mills began work as soon as Nina's email arrived. She took figures from the internet and concluded that the man must have died after 1955 and no later than 1965. She stared at the computer monitor, considering what this meant. There was nothing to indicate the site had been a burial ground and Fran had told her it was an approved school before the seventies. It was beginning to look as though she might have been unearthing a crime scene.

'Oh no.' She groaned and Alex looked up.

'Problem?'

She explained what she'd been doing and what she'd discovered.

'So I've been clomping all over it with my big boots.'

'You made notes, I assume? And taken photographs?'

'Of course.'

'Well then…'

'You think that's it? Alex, I've scrubbed and washed the bones.'

'So? What evidence would there have been on the bones? Eh?'

'And the bracelet was stolen!'

She told him about the missing bracelet. It could have identified the body. Now it was gone.

'It's late, Mills. Let's get some sleep; things will look better in the morning.'

Madison was sending her fifth text to Jeremy, asking him to meet her in town. She planned to keep bombarding him with messages until he replied and was threatening to come to the house again if he didn't get back to her. Another text arrived from her father just as the bus appeared in the distance. He'd been insisting she travel back to the USA with Austin at the end of the week and had stopped sending any more money, thinking that would mean she had to come home. He didn't know she could depend on Herbie to help so she could stay in England with Jeremy. Even Austin had started asking her to be sensible and return home for the summer – like she ever would. She stubbed out her cigarette and climbed on the bus.

Herbie was playing pool as usual and she hung out with him and his mates until closing time. She waited for a message from Jeremy but there was nothing and by the time they left the pub she was in a pretty depressed state. Herbie suggested going on to a mate's flat to find something to cheer her up and she agreed, reluctantly. They drove in the back of the dilapidated van that belonged to Rick with the shaved head and all the way Herbie's mate with the tattooed neck was touching her up. She kicked him but Herbie told her quietly not to make a fuss – they were his mates. He was always telling her to behave with his friends but she didn't always feel like being nice to them.

The flat smelt of damp. The bare bulb dangling precariously from the patchy ceiling illuminated a room with little furniture apart from a filthy mattress on the floor and a pile of clothes in one corner. Rick passed round a bottle of vodka and Herbie opened a packet of "Clockwork Orange". Another bottle of spirits appeared and someone had turned the music up. Two more men arrived who seemed to know Herbie. Madison could hear her mobile but she ignored it as she took a drag and passed it on. Soon all the pain she felt over Jeremy's rejection was forgotten.

'C'mon where's that bottle?' she shouted before slumping down on the mattress, disregarding the rank smell that greeted her.

Chapter 12

Mills hadn't slept much and when she did she dreamed she was in court being reprimanded for ruining a police investigation. She dragged herself out of bed at seven and sat in the garden, drinking tea. The sun was already warm and, as Alex had promised, things didn't seem quite as bad as they had the night before. He appeared an hour later and they shared an early breakfast outside. It was almost like it had been before he announced he was looking for jobs elsewhere, away from Swaledale.

'I thought we could do something today,' he suggested, coming out of the house with another mug of tea for her.

'Such as what?'

'Shopping. Or we could go for a long walk,' he added, seeing her look of disapproval at his first suggestion. 'We haven't done that for ages.'

'Maybe later.'

'What do *you* want to do then?' he asked irritably.

Mills couldn't bear the idea of idling away the weekend, she needed to be doing something to resolve the muddle she was in over the skeleton.

'Since you ask, what I'd really like to do is go and see Nina about those bones.'

He sighed and folded his arms. 'Ok. Do you want me to come?'

'No, it's fine. We can go for a walk when I get back.'

So they went their separate ways. She called Nina and arranged to be over with her mid-morning. Alex said he would get some shopping and see her back at the cottage later. She felt better as soon as she was on the move. Her friend would know what had to be done and Mills could help the police by offering to analyse the bones at Yardley Forensics. As she drove she considered how DNA might help them to discover who the skeleton belonged to. He'd died before DNA testing was in use so the possibility of being able to identify him using it was slim at best. But if the site was an approved school, there was a chance that the body belonged to one of the inmates or someone who worked there, which would help narrow the list.

Nina was giving the children a snack when Mills arrived.

'Sorry about the mess,' she said. 'I thought if Nige takes the boys out, we can have a chat in peace.' She turned to her daughter. 'And you want to do some drawing, don't you Rosie?'

Her daughter nodded and helped her mother clear the table so she could spread out her paper and colouring pencils. Nina ordered the boys to wash their hands and called her husband to help her get them organised. Finally, Nige took them off to the park and Nina made coffee. She suggested they went into the tiny backyard, where they sat side by side on an old wooden bench.

'So, what's the problem?' Nina asked. 'I assume it's about the remains?'

'Yes, of course. I spent ages on the report you sent and it looks pretty positive that the man died in 1960 plus or minus five years.' Her friend's expression remained calm, so she went on. 'The fact is you confirmed Brenda's view that the identity bracelet was not old, which ties in with the later date.'

Nina said nothing and Mills continued. 'And if we had the bracelet it would have identified the person.'

'Not necessarily. People exchange them. I wouldn't beat yourself up about it.'

'Someone would have been able to tell us who he is from that bracelet, I know they would.'

'Well, maybe a DNA test will give us something to work on.'

'Why? He died before testing was introduced – even if he had a record.'

'You told me the site had been an approved school. Maybe he was an offender, so perhaps there is a relative alive who we can trace through the DNA, another member of his family with a criminal record.'

'It would have to be a close relative to give any conclusive information.'

'True. The parents are presumably dead by now but there may be brothers or sisters somewhere; it's possible.'

Mills sighed and leaned her head against the wall and let the sun warm her face. Then she opened her eyes to look at Nina again.

'Can you get a list of boys in the approved school at the time?' she asked. 'And the names of the staff working there?'

Her friend looked slightly amused. 'And what would you do with those?'

'There might be photographs,' she suggested. 'You could look for the identity bracelet.'

'I could? Mills, do you realise how busy we are at the moment. We do have a team looking at cold cases but they mean ten or twenty years old not fifty! There's cold and then there's frozen!'

Nina picked up their empty mugs and went inside to refill them. Mills shut her eyes again and cursed.

'Do you mean there won't be an investigation into how the man died?' Mills asked when Nina reappeared.

'Not unless there's a chance of finding out. It'll depend on the bosses but I wouldn't think so.' She paused. 'Does that worry you?'

Mills was surprised by the question and had to think before answering.

'I feel I've let him down by assuming he was unimportant. I suppose the fact I thought the skeleton was hundreds of years old made it disconnected with a real person. Knowing it belongs to a man who was alive in the sixties and even knowing that he was at an approved school makes him three dimensional. I feel I treated him badly. It makes it worse to think he may have living relatives.'

'You don't know that but it is something we might be able to check if they reported him missing at the time. Would that make you feel better?'

Mills grinned. 'Yes. Thank you.'

'Good. I'll initiate the DNA test, so you can take the bones directly to the laboratory. I'll let the council know what has happened and ask them which osteoarchaeologist they hired to do the assessment because he or she should be crossed off their list.'

Mills drank her coffee while Nina chatted about the children. Rosie was enjoying school and her brothers would soon be joining the reception class.

'But what about you, Mills. How are you and Alex getting on?'

She deliberately dodged the loaded question. 'Alex is fine, although he thought he was getting a cold last week.'

'You know what I mean. How are things between you now?'

Her friend knew things were getting difficult.

'Alex has an interview for a job in London.' There she'd said it.

'Oh.'

'He knows I won't move from the Dales.'

'Can't he find something up here?'

'Apparently not.'

Mills had looked and she knew for a fact there were opportunities but they weren't very exciting. She couldn't blame him for wanting a demanding job and she told Nina so.

'I suppose Nige and I have been lucky. We're both doing what we want in one place.'

'It might have been different if I hadn't got the university post,' said Mills. 'Perhaps we should blame Nige for our predicament!'

'Don't be silly, he didn't do anything apart from suggest your name.'

'Well, I'm very grateful. I wouldn't want to live anywhere else.'

Rosie came out to show them her pictures and gave Mills a perfect drawing of a dog. Soon Nige was back from the park and Mills took some photos of Rosie, Owen and Tomos on her phone. She would have liked to stay longer but felt obliged to get back. She made Nige laugh when she told them Alex was keen for them to spend some "quality time" together but Nina said it was sweet that he wanted to.

'Before I go, Nina, I wanted to ask you – have you attended an inquest?' Mills asked.

'It's one of the roles of a family liaison officer.'

'Of course. So you know what happens.'

'Why? Are you required to appear at one?'

'No. It's just that I was asked by Marianne Fleurot if I would go to her daughter's inquest.'

'Don't worry,' Nina told her. 'A coroner's court is very different to the crown court you gave evidence in last year. It is not adversarial. I'm sure you'll find it interesting, Mills.'

It wasn't unusual now for Madison to be out all night at the weekend so Mae wasn't surprised to see the American had finally returned while she was at lunch.

'I can get you something to eat if you like,' she offered mischievously, knowing Madison wouldn't be able to face anything for hours.

There was a groan from under the duvet.

'A coffee, then?'

No answer.

'You know it will be damaging your immune system, all the alcohol and... other stuff.' Mae began tidying her locker, removing the bottles and replacing them in neat rows. 'I can make you something up to help boost it. My mum uses ginseng but there's Echinacea or garlic. Would you like me to prepare some ginseng tea?'

Madison pulled herself into a sitting position, throwing back the covers. She was still in her clothes and when she pushed the hair from her face, Mae saw her eyes were smudged with mascara.

'Will you shut it, motor mouth?' she demanded weakly, throwing a pillow in Mae's direction.

It fell ineffectually on the floor between them.

Mae, having gained a response from her room-mate, proceeded to look for the ginseng amongst the packets of teas at the back of the locker.

'I'll make it quite weak,' she said, holding up the box of green tea with ginseng.

Madison groaned as she climbed out of bed.

'I'm taking a shower. Just back off, why don't you?'

Mae shrugged. 'I'm having some. It's good for stress.'

Madison steadied herself on the end of the bed before sitting back down suddenly.

'Are you ok?' Mae asked.

The girl was pale, her eyes vacant. 'It's cool, I just need to sit.'

Mae went across to her; the aroma of smoke and alcohol almost made her recoil. She saw bruising and scratches on Madison's arms and moved closer. The American grabbed the duvet and wrapped herself in it.

It was Mae's opportunity to speak her mind; a chance to say something to her room-mate. Something she'd wanted to say for a long time. 'Why do you hang around with them?' she asked. 'Don't you see it's doing you harm?'

'Butt out, Mae.' The voice was muffled by the duvet. 'You know nothing about it.'

'But I do.'

Fran had told Mae about Herbie and the others. She'd been to one of the parties but soon escaped. That was the word she'd used – escaped.

'I know what they're like.'

'You don't!' she shouted back at her.

'Fran told me about them. I know what they do, Madison. You need to get out.'

She was leaning towards the shrouded figure as the shouting from the bedclothes became louder and Fran burst in. Mae stood up and shrugged.

'She doesn't want to get up,' she said, moving back to her locker. 'Ginseng tea, Fran?'

As soon as they were in the kitchen, Fran asked Mae what had been going on.

'It was nothing.'

'Are you sure? It sounded like something to me. What's she been doing now? Taking more of your medicines?'

'Look, I don't know she took the rue. I just said she might have, ok?'

As soon as they'd drunk the tea, Mae said she was off to her garden; she needed to get out in the fresh air, away from that American druggie she had to share a room with. She had a good mind to tell Mrs James about her, she told her friend.

Fran didn't ask to accompany her. Mae could be quite abrasive, particularly with Madison, and she felt she had more empathy. She thought she might be able to have a quiet word to see what was upsetting her. She made a black coffee in the American girl's favourite mug and carried it back to their room.

Madison was at the open window, cigarette in one hand, mobile phone in the other. Fran watched her as she held it to her ear.

'Are you there?'

Fran observed Madison staring at the phone before trying again, waiting in silence before speaking again, more urgently this time.

'I know you're there. Listen, I need to see you.'

This time the person at the other end seemed to be responding.

'Really? That's so cool.'

A long pause.

'No, I won't tell anyone.'

A shorter pause.

'Yes, yes!' She sounded excited, happy. 'The usual place – tomorrow. I'll be there.'

Fran didn't move as Madison returned the phone to her pocket and turned away from the window.

'What d'you want?' she asked, sharply but not angrily. Fran had clearly startled her.

'I brought you some coffee. I thought you might need it. Long night?'

'You bet.'

She took the mug and perched on Fran's bed.

'Want one?' she asked, indicating the cigarette in her hand.

'No thanks.'

Fran had never smoked and Madison knew it but she acknowledged her offer for what it was – a gesture of friendship.

'Mae doesn't mean to wind you up, it's just her way,' Fran began.

'Really?'

'Yes. She's worried about you. We all are.'

'All?'

'Herbie and his mates, they're dangerous…'

'Don't you start!'

'Sorry. But you should be careful, Mad.'

'I know what I'm doing.' She got up and threw the cigarette butt out of the window. 'Anyway, I'm heading off next week.'

'Going home?'

'Not exactly.'

'Mad, where are you going?'

'On vacation with a friend.'

Despite all her questions, Madison would not say who she was going with but began gathering her things to take a shower.

Fran persisted. 'Does Mrs James know? When are you going? Is it somewhere hot?'

'I'm not saying anything. Perhaps I'll tell my folks I'm going with you.'

'What?'

But Madison had disappeared down the corridor and Fran heard the bolt slide across the bathroom door.

Fran wasn't sure about telling Mae but she had no-one else. She wandered to the back of the school house that afternoon, where her friend was crouched on her plot, almost hidden by tall fern-like foliage.

'You mean she's going away with a man without her parents knowing?' Her friend was shocked.

'I don't know, she won't tell me. But what if she says she's going away with me?'

'We must tell the Head.'

'No!'

'What if it's Mr Young?' Mae stood up and pulled off her gloves. 'We should tell her at once.'

'We might get him into trouble.'

'So?'

'It may be a joke, I don't think we should rush to report it, do you?'

Mae considered for a moment. 'You're right. She's probably winding you up.'

She picked up a hoe and began jabbing at the ground animatedly.

Fran wandered through the garden and paused in the dappled shade staring at the empty pool. She'd come here several times in the past few days, trying to remember the night she'd found her friend, her white dress forming a frame around the frail figure suspended in the water. Now she'd received the letter about the hearing, she was trying to recall every detail but it seemed less real as time passed and was becoming a blur if she didn't concentrate. She'd dreamt of finding the body and had woken up crying but last night it wasn't Cecile's face she saw – she was watching herself disappearing under the leafy surface.

Chapter 13

Madison selected her clothes carefully, her new skinny jeans with the silky blouse in shocking pink, matching her newly-painted nails. She fiddled with her hair before deciding to leave it loose – he liked to run his hand through it when he kissed her. She applied her makeup carefully, not overdoing the eye shadow. He'd said he liked her because she was so natural. She wiped off the red lipstick and chose a soft pink.

'Going somewhere nice, love?'

The janitor had come in, dragging the vacuum cleaner behind her.

Madison blushed. 'Yes, I'm meeting my boyfriend.'

'Oh, how lovely! I wish I was your age again.'

She switched the machine on and drowned Madison's reply.

The choice of shoes was more difficult because she had to manage the rough track to the moor. She pulled her best trainers from the wardrobe, hoping the ground would be dry. There was no need for a jacket because it was another burning hot day but she hoped he would bring something for them to lie on.

Madison walked slowly across the lawn and took the track up onto the open ground. She was early but would be happy to wait in their secret spot where it was protected from the wind and prying eyes. She automatically searched for her cigarettes as soon as she left the school premises but now she hesitated then placed the packet back in her bag. Jeremy didn't like her smoking. Her head felt clearer than it had for weeks and she breathed in the warm air as she strolled, checking behind her occasionally to ensure no-one was following.

To her surprise he was waiting for her at the top of the track. She went forward to give him a hug but he turned and led the way to the outcrop of rocks that was their secret rendezvous.

'You're early,' she called.

He leaned against the largest stone and waited for her to join him.

'I came because of Diane,' he said.

He looked drawn and Madison immediately wanted to comfort him but his demeanour stopped her from approaching.

'Has she had it yet?'

'If by "it" you mean our baby, no. She has been asking about you.'

'She knows about us?'

Madison was at once excited and scared. She'd wanted his wife to find out about their relationship – now it was out in the open they could be together properly.

'She's met you, remember? She's worried about you. She wants to invite you round, would you believe!' He gave a laugh.

Madison couldn't interpret his mood. She laughed. He glared.

'It's not funny. She asked me to invite you to dinner of all things. I've told her you've gone back to the States so I'm telling you to keep out of our lives, ok?'

Madison sat down on the prickly heather. It wasn't what she had been expecting to hear.

'You said she was going away.' Her voice sounded small.

'She's visiting her mother next week before the baby… *our* baby is born.'

'I thought we could hang out.'

He looked at his watch. 'I've got to go. I told you before, I can't…'

He began walking down the track, Madison followed, calling him back and begging him to stay just for a little while. Eventually he stopped, turning round as she caught up with him, throwing herself at him. He took her wrists and stared at her, inches from her face.

'I told you to leave me alone,' he shouted, tightening his grip then letting go.

She stood trembling as he disappeared down towards the public footpath that went round the edge of the school grounds. Then she reached for the cigarette packet.

Madison was unaware of the figure to her right and behind her. Mae, who was picking bilberries, had straightened up just in time to see Madison and the teacher arguing before he strode off down the track. She lowered herself back into the heather and waited until the American girl finished her cigarette before following her back to school.

'Been out for a walk?' Mae called, as she closed the gate from the footpath into the grounds.

Madison turned round slowly. 'Oh it's the wicked witch of the East!' she exclaimed. 'Have you been following me?'

'Of course not. I've been collecting berries.'

'Not more of your concoctions.'

They were walking side by side towards the student house.

'Speaking of my medicines,' said Mae, 'did you take my tincture of rue? I can understand if you took it but you should have asked first. I just want it back.'

At first she denied it but Mae could be very persistent and eventually Madison was exasperated.

'What if I did take it? You can make some more.'

'It *was* you! I knew it.'

They'd reached the room they shared and Madison threw herself on her bed.

Mae stood over her. 'So, tell me, what did you take it for?'

'What you said: period pains.'

'Really? Are you sure? Nothing more serious?'

'No. Will you leave me alone?'

'Not until you give me back the bottle.'

'I can't. I don't have it. I gave it to a friend. Ok?'

Mae went over to the window, deciding how to proceed. Then she turned to face Madison.

'I saw you with Mr Young this afternoon.'

She waited to see what her reaction would be.

'So what?'

'So, if you don't tell me what happened to my bottle of rue, I may have to speak to Mrs James.'

Madison seemed to be weighing up her options before finally responding. 'I guess it doesn't matter now anyways. I gave it to Cecile – she asked for my help.'

'What help?'

'Her period was late, she asked my advice. I said the herbal stuff was good for that sort of thing. *She* had your stupid bottle.'

The pre-inquest hearing was to be held at Harrogate Magistrates Court at the end of the week. Mills received the phone call from Fiona, giving her the perfect excuse for not accompanying Alex to London.

'Poor Marianne won't be there but Cecile's father will want to speak to you, Mills. They are so anxious to get her back to France, you must help them,' her stepmother begged.

Mills explained there was nothing she could do but Fiona was adamant she was going to be a real support for the dead girl's parents. She also insisted that Alex drop in for a meal while he was in town for his interview. Mills quickly finished the call and emailed Fran, reassuring her that she would be in the court when she gave her evidence. She hesitated before pressing "send", wondering if she should tell the girl that the skeleton was not "of antiquity". She was unsure what her headmistress might feel about one of her charges working on a body that had only been dead for around fifty years. She decided to wait until she could tell Fran in person.

Alex was upstairs packing. He was making an early start the next day, driving down to Gloucester to spend a couple of days with his parents then on to a "college mate" in Milton Keynes, where he was going to leave the car.

'There's no way I'm driving into London,' he said.

He was carefully folding his best shirt before placing it in a small case. A suit carrier hung from the door. Mills watched him select a tie then change his mind.

'Take them both,' suggested Mills, before going back downstairs.

Alex had given no indication of who this "college mate" was so she wasn't going to ask. Clearly he didn't want her to know and she didn't care whether it was a male or female friend anyway.

She found a pizza in the freezer and gave it half an hour in the oven before calling Alex down for dinner. He looked at his plate before asking if there was any salad.

'No.'

She was sawing at the hard pizza crust underneath the dried out topping. Alex knew better than to protest but fetched himself a beer and offered her one.

'No thanks.'

They ate in silence until finally Alex asked about Fiona's phone call.

'The hearing on Cecile Fleurot is on Friday.'

'I was thinking I could pop in to see your father and Fiona, to say hello.'

Mills paused while she chose her words. 'I think she said they were busy this week.'

Alex was looking at her. 'Really?'

She stared back defiantly. 'Yes.'

Alex was still packing his car when Mills left for the university in the morning. She had to see three students about their summer projects but, more importantly, she was to collect all the boxes of bones and deliver them to Yardley Forensics, according to Nina's instructions. The analyst would only require a small sample but it would give Donna the opportunity to select the most appropriate part of the body – apparently the long bones were best: the humerus and femur – or teeth. She would know what to do.

The meeting with the students was brief; one hadn't turned up and the others were keen to get away. The boxes were neatly stacked and labelled in the store, exactly as Fran had left them. It took three journeys to pack them all in her car but she worked quickly and left without meeting anyone to detain her. In less than an hour she was unpacking them at the other end.

She was removing the last box from her car when Brenda arrived, insisting on opening the doors for her.

'Are you moving in, pet?' she asked with a grin.

Mills explained what the boxes contained before spending the next hour completing the paperwork. Then she had a conversation with Glyn and Donna about the requirement for DNA on the bones and teeth. As usual, the laboratory manager complained about the workload but said he would get it done as soon as possible. Donna listened without comment then suggested where they might sample, what might be provided in the way of evidence and how long it would take.

'So can we expect the results by the end of the week?' Mills asked.

'I don't see why not,' said Donna.

Her boss disagreed. 'Maybe.'

Glyn was irascible, although possibly a little easier now Alex was going.

Mills left them to it, returning to the office.

'Was that your skeleton of unknown provenance?' Brenda asked.

'Yes, although now we're pretty sure he died in the mid-sixties.'

'Ah, so my colleague was right about the bracelet?'

'We think so.'

'We?'

'I spoke to Nina and her people have confirmed it.'

Brenda beamed. She loved winning any kind of difference of opinion.

'By the way, I've been asked for another reference,' she offered. 'For Alex.'

'Oh yes?' Mills didn't know he'd applied for anything else.

'The Home Office, eh?' Brenda was watching her.

'Yes.' Mills fiddled with the stapler on her desk.

'Digital forensics in security, that'll be more interesting than a bank, don't you think?'

Mills thought so. Maybe he couldn't tell her about it because it involved national security.

'I'll make sure my reference is even better than the last one,' Brenda said, laughing as she disappeared into her office.

Mills settled down to work through the pile of papers on her desk, determined not to leave that evening until it was cleared.

It was raining heavily so Fran was able to persuade Mae to stay indoors and help her with her project.

'I found some articles about the approved school in the "Northern Echo".' She reached for her iPad. 'There are a few references to boys who ran away during the sixties but look at this.'

She showed Mae the photograph of a man in a white short-sleeved shirt. He had grey stubble and dark glaring eyes.

'Not a very flattering shot,' Mae commented as she glanced over.

'He's an officer at the approved school who was suspended for "excessive punishment" in 1964.'

'I wonder what *excessive* meant.'

'I've been looking. It says they were allowed to be caned up to eight times on their backsides. It doesn't say what's excessive but I guess more than that.'

'That still happens in schools in China.'

'You're kidding.'

'In the countryside. I read about it.'

'Well, this guy was excessive.'

'Let me see.' She peered at the screen. 'He looks a bit like that old man we spoke to in Gilling West. D'you think it could be his dad?'

Fran couldn't see a resemblance and shook her head.

'He's called Porter so he can't be Mr Thomas's father.'

'Well, it shows what it was like in those days if they were metering out excessive punishments.'

Fran nodded. Mae always liked to have the last word. Her friend went to the window and looked out.

'It's still raining.' She looked back at Fran. 'Anyway, what's all this got to do with archaeology?'

'Nothing really. I just thought I should provide details of the location of the site and there isn't much about the place on the internet before it became an approved school.'

'I think you should be visiting libraries and museums, not sitting on your computer all day.'

'You sound like my mother. I did find one thing about Gilling West though. This boy – he was only nine – he found this sword and it's in a museum in York. Apparently it's amazing and he got a Blue Peter badge for finding it!'

Her friend was laughing.

'Will you come to town with me tomorrow to visit the museums and libraries then?' Fran asked.

'I might.'

A door slammed in the distance and Mae grimaced.

'Madison's out of the shower.'

The American appeared wrapped in a towel, scowling at the girls as she entered the room before making for her wardrobe. They watched as she dried herself and dressed, exchanging glances as Madison selected her shortest skirt and highest heels. There was a single mirror in the room, above the old fireplace and they watched her arrange her makeup along the narrow mantelpiece.

'Don't you have something better to do than watch me?' she demanded staring at them from the mirror.

'No, it is *so* entertaining,' Mae retorted.

Madison was applying mascara with intense concentration but when she'd finished to her satisfaction, she stepped back, sweeping the cosmetics into her bag.

'You do what you like,' she said. 'I have to go out.'

'Anywhere nice?' Fran asked, trying to neutralise Mae's sourness.

Madison turned. 'I am going to visit Diane Young,' she announced as if she expected them to be impressed.

'Who's she?' Mae asked.

'You mean Mr Young's wife?' Fran asked.

'That's correct.'

The American grabbed her bag and made for the door, where she turned, hanging on to the handle.

'She's invited me for lunch.'

She slammed the door behind her before either girl could respond.

'Oh my goodness – did you hear that?' Fran had grabbed Mae's arm.

'She's lying,' said Mae. 'There's no way Mrs Young would invite her round. You saw how she got dressed up. I haven't seen that top before. It's new. More likely she's seeing *Mr* Young.'

'D'you think that's who she's planning to go away with?'

'She makes half of it up. I wouldn't take any notice.'

Fran caught the sound of a car engine and ran to the window.

'There's a taxi.' Sure enough, she spotted Madison running through the rain holding her jacket above her head. She jumped in and slammed the door before it drove off. 'D'you still think she took your bottle of rue to get rid of… you know…'

'I asked her,' said Mae. 'I got it out of her in the end. She told me she'd taken it.'

'So she was… you know…'

'No – it wasn't for her. It was for Cecile.'

'Cecile? Why would Cecile…'

'Apparently her period was late and she asked Madison for help.'

Fran let the information sink in, trying to work out why Cecile could possibly have thought she was pregnant. 'I don't understand. She didn't even have a boyfriend.'

'What about Madison's friends?'

'But she'd stopped hanging out with them ages ago, not long after we warned her.'

'Had she?' Mae asked. 'You can't know who she was with all the time. And she was always very secretive about Jules.'

Chapter 14

Diane Young had looked surprised when she saw Madison but opened the door wider and invited her in.

'Is it still raining?' she asked, as she took her jacket and hung it on a peg in the narrow hallway. 'Come in and sit down. Would you like tea or I could probably find a fizzy drink if you'd prefer.'

Madison hesitated. She didn't want to stay long.

'Tea, please.' Asking for a soda sounded juvenile.

She followed Diane to the kitchen and watched her fill the kettle from the tap.

'My husband's teaching this afternoon,' she said, taking two cups from the dishwasher.

'I know,' Madison said. 'I came to see *you*.'

'Well, that's nice.'

She didn't sound pleased, thought Madison.

'But it was about him… why I came.'

'Oh, yes?' Diane turned to face her. 'What is it, Madison?'

It wasn't the right moment. 'Can I carry anything?' she asked.

'No, you go and sit down. I'll be in in a minute.'

Madison went back to the sitting room and sat waiting, going over what she'd planned to say. *It's about Jeremy – Jeremy and me.* His wife would look confused and then angry as she registered that he was in love with another woman. *How long has this been going on?* she would ask. *Fifteen months and three weeks*, she would reply. Diane would cry and Madison would leave, saying *I'm sorry but we can't help loving each other.*

'So how can I help you, Madison?' Diane was in the doorway holding a tray. She set it on a low table and passed her a cup and saucer. 'I hope you take milk?'

'Thank you.'

Diane began settling herself down on the sofa.

'It's about Jeremy and me,' Madison began.

'Go on,' she said calmly, leaning awkwardly across for her cup of tea.

'I'm sorry but we can't help loving each other,' she blurted out.

She looked amused, sitting there with her big belly. She was actually smiling in a patronising sort of way.

'How old are you, Madison?'

'Sixteen.'

'I remember what it was like to be your age. It's not so many years ago that I don't know how you feel – all those hormones racing about. I remember having a crush on my gym teacher.'

Madison looked across and actually felt sorry for the woman. She didn't understand.

'You don't understand. We're in love. It's been going on for fifteen months – longer.'

Diane was looking at her with her head on one side.

'Are you making this up?'

'No, honestly. Ask Jeremy.'

'I will.' She glanced at a clock on the mantelpiece. 'He'll be here in exactly twenty minutes. We can ask him.'

We can ask him? Was she serious? Did she expect her to stay? 'I should leave.'

'No, Madison, I think we should sort this out as soon as Jeremy gets in. Drink your tea. I'll fetch some biscuits.'

When she returned, she acted as if nothing had occurred.

'So, how are your studies going? What "A" levels are you taking?'

She chattered on about how she was a teacher at the boys' school; that was where she'd met her husband. That's how she referred to him: *my husband*. She taught biology and loved every minute. Madison didn't need to say a word except to answer yes or no to her questions about the girls' school. It was slow torture and several times Madison threatened to leave but Diane ordered her to stay seated and she obeyed, like one of her pupils.

Suddenly, unexpectedly, the door opened and Jeremy was standing there. His smile vanished as he looked at Madison and then his wife.

'Hello, darling. Look who's here.' Diane was attempting a cheerful note.

'Oh, hello there.' His nonchalance didn't fool anyone.

'Madison came to tell me about her relationship with you.'

'Relationship? What d'you mean?'

Diane looked at Madison and smiled. 'Go on.'

She cleared her throat. 'I've told her about us. Everything.'

Diane looked at Jeremy and raised an eyebrow.

Jeremy shrugged. 'I don't know what she means.'

'She says that she's in love with you…'

'Oh well…' He looked relieved, was smiling.

'…and that you are in love with her.'

He gave a loud, forced laugh. 'Oh dear!'

There was an awkward pause while Diane struggled to get off the sofa. He went over to help her and they stood holding hands.

'Jeremy, tell her…' Madison called as they left the room together. She felt defeated. He would deny it and his stupid wife would accept his side of the story.

She could hear them in the hall whispering about her until Diane's voice suddenly became louder and she heard her telling him to be kind in case she told the same story to her headmistress or, worse still, to *his* school head.

Madison jumped up and opened the door.

'I'm going. Maybe you don't believe me but the school might be more interested.'

'Wait, Madison.' It was Diane. 'I understand how you must feel. Why don't you let Jeremy give you a lift back? They must be wondering where you are.'

Jeremy refused at first but Madison needed to speak to him alone and he was eventually cajoled by Diane into taking her.

He started as soon as they were in the car, calling her a little bitch. How dare she come to *his* house and speak to *his* wife like that. It hurt so much; he could have been stabbing her with something sharp. He cursed. In front of them was the Darlington bus on its way back to Richmond. He swung the car out to pass as they left the village.

'Drop me at the next stop,' she insisted. 'I don't want to stay in this car with you. Let me out.'

'With pleasure.'

He accelerated and they were very quickly in Brompton on Swale.

'Here! Now!'

She slammed the door hard without looking round and heard him roar off towards Richmond. In a few minutes she was on the bus, looking out of the window to hide her tears.

*

The coroner made it clear that the purpose of the hearing was to decide whether an inquest was required, following the post-mortem. After all, there had been no reason to suspect that Cecile's death was either violent or unnatural. Mills was keen to hear the findings of the post-mortem and hoped to discover what had so interested the two pathologists and caused Dr Moreau to be so defensive. The fact there was a hearing at all convinced her that Cecile may have taken her own life.

Fran had sought her out as soon as Mills arrived at the Magistrates court. She was pale and nervous, asking Mills questions about the procedure that she couldn't answer readily. Eventually Mills told her to stay seated while she went to find Cecile's father among the small group of people hovering by the door of the courtroom. It wasn't difficult to detect the French accent of the well-dressed man talking to another. She made herself known to Monsieur Fleurot and he introduced her to his lawyer, who was there to help the family arrange for the body to be taken back to France.

Fran watched as, one by one, people drifted into their places. Everyone had dressed very formally and she tugged at her skirt in an attempt to hide her knees. Dr Sanderson was talking to Cecile's dad; Mrs James had tried to catch their attention but failed and settled on a chair at the front. Fran didn't want to have to speak to her headmistress, not after yesterday's confrontation. It was stupid of Mae to tell on Madison in the first place. It wasn't like she'd never been out overnight before.

Someone was closing the door and those still standing looked for a seat. Fran took her bag off the chair next to her, Dr Sanderson sat down and the room fell silent. First the coroner gave a long speech about why they were there, as if they didn't know. He told them what would happen. He didn't say in what order the witnesses would be called so she had no idea how long before her ordeal would be over.

No-one moved and there was no sound except for the occasional cough. The atmosphere reminded Fran of her grandfather's funeral and she wondered if she would be able to go to Cecile's. She had talked to Mae about it but her friend simply dismissed the possibility because it would be in France. She hadn't mentioned it to her mother; it would even be awkward if Mum found out she'd attended the hearing without telling her.

The man with Cecile's father was talking to the coroner about Cecile going home to France – or at least that's what it sounded as though it was about. The coroner said he would come to that at the end. So the witnesses were being called and Fran's heart began to beat a bit faster. But it was ok; the police were giving their statements first. She looked at Dr Sanderson, who turned and smiled at her in an encouraging sort of way. The police officer read his report in a very formal manner followed by questions to clarify when and where it happened. Somehow it made it easier that they didn't seem to be talking about her friend at all.

Mrs James was wearing a dark suit, appropriately subdued compared to her usual preference for red jackets. She looked older than ever and Fran wondered if it was caused by the strain of the hearing or worry over Madison going missing. As Mae had said, it wasn't fair – they were in more trouble with the Head for not telling her earlier than Madison was for staying out. It was complicated by Madison saying she was going on holiday, so they didn't know if she was in town somewhere or far away. They hadn't told Mrs James that though. They'd decided to tell her as little as possible: just that Madison had not come home for two nights, which was unusual. That was a mistake. *Unusual? What do you mean "unusual"?*

'Frances?'

Dr Sanderson was tapping her arm. She looked up and found herself the centre of attention.

'Frances? Would you like to come forward?' The coroner was smiling at her.

Her face felt hot as she stumbled past the chairs and made her way to the front. She hoped no-one could see how much she was shaking inside. She went through the procedure as if in a dream. She described the picture when she reached the pool – she'd been over it a hundred times and every time she was reduced to tears. But today, in the court, surrounded by men in suits and police in uniform, with Mrs James staring at her from the front row, she felt nothing. The room was silent when she finished.

Then the coroner asked the same question he'd posed to Mrs James. *Did your friend seem unhappy?* She answered that Cecile had seemed fine – and she had. Fran wasn't to know she was worried about her period being late. There were no further questions and the coroner said she could go back to her seat. Only when she was beside Dr Sanderson did a few tears fall silently down her face.

Finally it was the turn of the pathologist to present his findings. Suddenly everyone was straightening up and paying attention, particularly Mills. The assumption was that Cecile had drowned and the pathologist said that there were signs of trauma but confirmed that the cause of death was consistent with drowning. When pushed to elaborate, he described a blow to the skull which suggested she had fallen, caught her head on the side of the pool and been unconscious when she entered the water. It seemed that Cecile was a strong swimmer and had rehearsed the scene many times but on this occasion things had gone horribly wrong. Mills thought he had finished, as did the coroner, but the pathologist asked to continue with his report.

'She was very fit for a girl of her age and had no health issues as far as I could detect but there is something I should report…'

The coroner stopped him. 'Yes, quite. We should record it but I suggest we break here and clear the court of everyone except the immediate family.'

He told them to return after lunch and they made for the door obediently. Mills could hear Mr Fleurot telling his lawyer to remain.

'Do we have to stay?' Fran asked her when they were outside.

'No. The coroner will want to give his opinion on the hearing and whether he has decided to hold a full inquest. Why? Do you want to go back to school?'

'Not really. I've been told I can't leave the grounds without permission from now on.'

'Why's that?'

The girl shook her head, muttering something inaudible. So Mills, thinking a walk would do them good, suggested they find a sandwich. It was a dull day with drizzle in the air as they made for a coffee shop Mills knew, a couple of streets away. It was busy but they found a table in the corner and Mills let Fran choose something to eat before going up to order. When she sat down again she pressed Fran on why she was grounded.

'It's about Madison,' she said irritably. 'It's always about her.'

'The American girl?'

'Yes. She's stayed out for a couple of nights and Mrs James is furious.'

'Well, she would be. She's *in loco parentis*.'

'Right. It's just... she's always staying out at night. It's what she does.'

'Surely that isn't allowed?'

'No, but you try to stop her.'

'Is it a boyfriend?'

Fran shrugged.

'So where does she go?'

'Into town usually. House parties. Drinking. Smoking.'

'Drugs?'

'Nothing illegal.'

Mills knew what that meant – she'd heard it several times before from students at the university. But things had changed earlier in the year and now there was no such thing as a "legal high".

'So how long does she normally stay out for?'

'Just overnight. She comes back to sleep it off.'

Their food arrived and the conversation waned for a while.

'Why were we sent out for a break?' Fran asked.

She'd eaten half of the cheese toastie before pushing the plate aside and starting on her hot chocolate.

'I expect the coroner thought we needed some lunch,' Mills lied.

'No. He said he wanted just the family there. Why do they do that?'

'Perhaps he wanted to speak to them alone, you know, personally.'

Mills didn't believe it herself. There was something he didn't want the pathologist to share with them all; something he didn't want the media getting hold of maybe?

The drizzle had turned to heavy rain and they hurried back to The Court House under Fran's umbrella. As they waited to be allowed back into hearing, Mrs James tapped Mills on the shoulder and asked if she could have a quiet word, looking meaningfully at Fran. She led the way down the corridor until they were out of earshot.

'For reasons I shan't go into,' the headmistress began, 'Frances is not allowed outside school unaccompanied by an adult. I thought I should tell you, in case you are expecting her to carry out any work on her own.'

Mills thought about it. 'No, I don't think that will be a problem.'

No, the problem was that neither Frances nor Mrs James knew that the body she'd been working on was of a man who died in the sixties. It wasn't really the place to raise the subject now.

'Good. It's most unfortunate but there it is.'

'She did explain,' Mills said.

'Oh, did she?' Her face took on a strained expression as she leaned towards Mills. 'I am becoming most anxious about Madison. I've spoken to the police about it and they are optimistic that she'll return but I have to inform her parents and they'll be worried sick, I should imagine.'

Clearly it would reflect badly on the school if anything happened to the girl, thought Mills.

The courtroom had been re-opened and people were taking their seats once more. She could see Fran was still waiting outside.

'Perhaps we'd better…' Mills indicated the open door.

'Yes, of course.'

Fran joined them as they found their way to their seats. Mills had wanted to speak to Monsieur Fleurot before the hearing re-convened, hoping to find out what only the family was allowed to hear. His demeanour provided no clues.

The coroner summarised the key points of what had occurred during the morning without referring to the private session. Then he said he would draw his conclusions.

'We have heard today about the tragic events that led to the death of a talented young woman. Cecile Fleurot was a clever scholar with exceptional athletic ability. It is all the more terrible that this very talented young swimmer should have drowned accidentally while playing Ophelia in a production of Hamlet, a part that is one of Shakespeare's most tragic female characters.'

The coroner paused; the room was silent.

'Understandably, her parents wish to take their daughter back to France for a family funeral and there is no reason why this need be delayed any longer.'

After a series of formalities, it was all over and they were moving slowly into the hallway. Fran headed for the ladies cloakroom as Mrs James approached.

'Do you mind if *I* drive Frances back?' Mills asked. 'I need to discuss a few things with her and I promised to show her round the forensics laboratory as she's here.'

The headmistress seemed relieved and waited only until Fran reappeared to remind her of the rules about not being out alone, before going off in the direction of the shops.

'I wondered if you'd like to look round the lab I work with?' Mills had decided it was time to tell Fran about the provenance of the bones she'd been working on and a visit to Yardley Forensics seemed the perfect opportunity.

'Great.'

'I just need to say goodbye to… oh, here he is!'

Monsieur Fleurot was heading towards them.

'Dr Sanderson, may I speak with you?'

'Of course.' She looked round to see where they might talk privately.

'Shall we?' He indicated the door into the street and she followed.

It was still raining so he stopped at the entrance and shrugged.

'I travel back tonight, so I apologise to make this brief. First, I thank you for the help with the post mortem.'

She tried to tell him that she'd done nothing but he held up his hand to stop her.

'But I must ask you not to mention the baby.'

He used the French word, bébé, for baby but it was unmistakable.

'Baby?'

'Oui, yes – you know she was enceinte – pregnant, you say in English?'

He must have guessed from her puzzled expression that she did not know. She shook her head. It explained the whispered discussions at the autopsy and the private session for family only this morning.

He was rubbing his forehead with his hand.

'Mon Dieu, it is such a catastrophe!' he pronounced it the French way – as if there was no "e" at the end. 'I want to tell you not to say anything about this pregnancy to anyone. My wife does not need to know about it, it would destroy her. She has no need to know. As far as she is concerned there was never a baby!'

The poor man was distraught.

'Does Mrs James know about Cecile's…'

'No! You must tell no-one, do you understand?'

Mills could see Fran move into view.

'Of course.' Presumably the coroner saw no connection between Cecile's condition and her death; otherwise he would be calling for a full inquest.

They shook hands and he went back inside as Fran emerged from the doorway.

Mills took a deep breath. 'Right then, let's go.'

Chapter 15

The laboratory was only a short drive from the Court House. On the way, Mills gave Fran a brief description of its main business: DNA testing, fingerprints and chemical analysis. When they arrived, she introduced her to Glyn and checked it was all right to show her round. There was no sign of Brenda.

'So this is where Donna does the DNA testing,' Mills explained as they peered into one of the labs. She took a deep breath. 'Do you recognise those boxes on the bench in the corner?'

'Are they…?'

'Yes. The bones you cleaned for me. They're examining them for DNA.'

Fran appeared to be considering the information.

'Will they find DNA after all that time?'

'Not after centuries but it appears these bones are perhaps not, after all, centuries old.'

No response, so Mills continued. 'The skeleton has been shown to be only fifty years old.'

'Oh.'

Mills couldn't interpret what "Oh" meant.

'So does that mean my project won't…'

'No, it's all right. The work you did still counts as an investigation. I checked.'

'Wow. So the man was buried in the grounds of the approved school.'

Mills hadn't really considered this information before.

'I suppose he must've been.'

'Wow. But what about my report?' Fran asked, still peering at the boxes.

'Have you been investigating earlier uses of the site?'

'Yes but…'

'Well, that's fine then. No need to confuse the examiners with the age of the skeleton.'

Mills wasn't sure about the reliability of her statement but she wanted to reassure the girl – she'd been through enough. It was a good time to call it a day.

On the drive back to the school, Fran talked about the hearing. She'd found it an ordeal but she'd been glad she'd gone, she said.

'I suppose now they'll take her to France and I'll never have the chance to say goodbye properly.'

'It's a long way to go for the funeral,' Mills offered. 'Were you very good friends?'

'I suppose. We hung out and I guess I was the closest friend Cecile had. Now it's just me and Mae.'

'What was she like – Cecile?'

'Quiet. She was really shy, except when she was doing sport, then she could be quite noisy.'

'She was a good swimmer?'

'Good? She was amazing. She was in all sorts of competitions. She went away on training camps abroad and all sorts.'

'Was she a party-goer?'

'Not really.'

'Did she have a boyfriend?'

'No. Madison's brother fancied her but she stayed away from him.'

'No-one special, then?'

'Why are you asking?'

'No reason.'

'Is it because of what her dad said?'

Mills looked at her. 'What d'you mean?'

'He said "baby" didn't he? I heard him. Is that the secret that the coroner told him?'

'I don't know what you mean, Fran.'

'He told you that Cecile was pregnant, or had been, didn't he?'

'What makes you say that?'

'Because Madison told me her period was late.'

'At least let's go to the pub!'

Alex arrived home in jubilant mood. He had apparently been offered his dream job, based in London.

'It's Friday – it'll be packed out.'

'That's why I want to go now,' he insisted.

They drove in silence to "The Farmer's Arms" and Mills grabbed the only free table in the bar while Alex fetched the drinks.

'Here's to a permanent job!' he said, raising his pint glass and taking a long drink.

Mills sighed and sipped her wine.

'So how exactly did you get offered two jobs in one company?' she asked, without admitting she knew he'd had two job interviews. She waited to see how he responded.

'Actually, I had another, at the last minute. I may not have mentioned it in the rush.'

'Another one? In London?'

'Yes. I managed to combine them on the same day, which meant I could compare them. After I'd been to the bank I knew they liked me and they gave me the salary scale I'd start on if I got it, so I was able to ask for more than that at the other interview.'

'So where was that?'

'In the Home Office.'

'Doing financial stuff?'

'No, much more interesting than the bank. They've got this group working on counter-terrorism. They want to build up their expertise in digital forensics. It's vital for them and really exciting.'

'So they offered it to you, there and then?'

'Yep. I haven't heard from the bank yet but they seemed pretty impressed; although I don't want to work for them, even if they say yes. Homeland security is much more fun.'

'I suppose so.'

'Come on, Mills. You of all people should agree on that. You would much rather be doing the forensic investigation stuff than your routine archaeology.'

She knew it was true but said nothing as she studied the "specials" boards hanging on the wall above the fireplace. While Alex went to the bar to order their meal, Mills tried to convince herself that if she found the perfect job, she would want to be off, even if it meant moving to London. Determined to sound more supportive, she encouraged him to tell her about the government post.

'It's the Home Office Centre for Applied Science and Technology,' he explained. 'They do all sorts of things and they're taking on people for cyber work. I think the counter-terrorism stuff might be based outside London, somewhere in the south.'

He looked at her, as if waiting for her to comment on his decision to move away, but she tried to change the subject.

'Mills, we've got to talk about this… this "elephant in the room",' he said in a hushed voice, looking round.

The mention of an "elephant in the room" always made her giggle. She finished her wine. 'Not now. Not here.'

But when they got home, there was a message from Fiona to call her urgently so Mills managed to postpone the conversation until another day.

'Fiona? What's the matter?'

'Darling, it's Marianne: she's beside herself. I could hardly follow what she was saying. Her accent... lots of French words... I did it at school but...'

'Is it about the hearing?'

'Yes. Her husband called her during the day. I suppose he's back home now so he can explain it properly. But what was the problem? I thought you said it would be straightforward.'

It was hardly her fault, Mills thought. 'What did she say?'

'It was all a muddle. Your father wondered if they might decide it was suicide but she didn't mention anything like that. It sounded as though she thought Cecile was pregnant. Does that make any sense?'

'Yes.'

'Yes? What d'you mean by "yes"?'

'I mean she was pregnant.'

'How?'

Mills paused. She was tempted to give a facetious response but...

'Mills, answer me! What did the coroner say?'

'He didn't say anything, Fiona. He took Monsieur Fleurot for a quiet word and told him in private. I only know because he thought I was told at the autopsy – which I wasn't.'

There was silence at the other end.

Mills waited. 'Are you there?' she asked.

'Yes, I was just thinking. Does that mean she killed herself? I mean, if she was pregnant... a good catholic girl...'

'They didn't seem to think so. It was just an unfortunate accident.'

'So who was the father?' Fiona seemed to be sensing a scandal.

'I have no idea.'

'Did she have a boyfriend?'

'I don't know. I only met the girl a couple of times. Presumably she did.'

'I wonder if Marianne met him.'

'You should ask her. Anyway I'll leave you to it. Give my love to Dad.' She put the receiver down abruptly. It was the way she often finished a conversation with Fiona.

Alex looked up and she announced she was off to have a bath. It had been a long day. Perhaps they would talk tomorrow when she wasn't so tired. He shrugged and turned back to the television.

Alex suggested they had breakfast in Leyburn before they did the shopping. Mills agreed willingly and they were lingering over a second cup of coffee when a text message arrived.

'It's Fran, from High Fell School,' she explained. 'She wants to talk.'

'It can wait until Monday.'

Mills was texting back: *Is it urgent?* She knew the hearing had affected the poor girl; presumably she wanted to talk about it.

Alex was paying the bill when the response arrived. *Really sorry but can we talk today?*

Mills was pre-occupied while they went round the supermarket. Unusually, she let Alex make decisions over brands and quantities. She packed absentmindedly and wandered out of the shop almost walking into the path of a slow-moving car.

As soon as they were home she called Fran's number.

'We need your advice, Dr Sanderson,' Fran began.

Mills could hear there was someone with her.

'Mae says we should tell Mrs James but it will get us into big trouble. My parents will go ballistic if I'm excluded.'

'Tell her what, Fran?'

'That Madison was going to lunch with Diane Young when she went missing.'

'Is she not back yet?'

'No, but she said she'd be going away for a bit. That's the other thing we haven't told the Head.'

'So who is this friend Diane?'

'Not a friend: Mr Young's wife, he's a teacher.'

'It sounds as though they should start there then. She might know where Madison has gone.'

Mills assumed it was Mae's voice that was prompting Fran in the background.

'The problem is… we don't want to get him into trouble.'

'Trouble?'

'Madison and Mr Young. We think they were… close.'

Mills was puzzled. 'You should tell Mrs James everything you know about Madison's whereabouts if she's gone missing.'

The two girls were conferring in whispers. Eventually another voice, presumably Mae's, asked the question.

'Would you come with us when we go to see the Head?'

She arranged to drive over to the school that afternoon, assuming that Mrs James was available. The girls assured her that their Head had cancelled everything and was on call all weekend because of Madison's disappearance. Mills explained the situation to Alex, who had no option but to accept that the discussion about their future would have to wait.

Mae stood by the window, watching for Dr Sanderson's Mini. It was just after two o'clock and Mrs James would be waiting. Fran was brushing her hair and tying it back in a ponytail for the third time.

'Here she comes!' called Mae, making for the door.

Fran followed her down the stairs and out onto the drive that led to the School House. Dr Sanderson was parking as they approached and they hurried her to the Head's office. Both women looked apprehensive as they seated themselves round the table that took up most of the room.

'Thank you for seeing us, Mrs James,' Mae began, in her best English. 'I'm sure you are very busy.'

The Head smiled at her without warmth. 'So what did you girls want to tell me?'

Mae could see Fran reddening and knew it would be down to her.

'We're worried about Madison not coming back yet and thought we should tell you absolutely everything we know that is relevant.'

She looked at Dr Sanderson, who nodded and smiled encouragingly.

Mrs James appeared stressed. 'Carry on.'

Mae looked at Fran, who was staring at the table.

'Well, Madison was getting dressed up on Wednesday and she said she was going out for lunch.'

'Where?' demanded Mrs James. 'Where was she going?'

'She said she was going to have lunch with Diane Young.' Fran's voice wavered.

'Jeremy Young's wife?' The Head looked puzzled.

'Yes,' Mae said, looking at Fran. 'She was friendly with them.'

'Then we must contact them at once.'

She went to her computer, typed on the keyboard and checked the monitor before picking up the phone. Clearly no-one answered and she asked them to call her as soon as they received her message.

'I hope they've not gone away,' she said as she returned to her seat.

Mae looked at Fran, who nodded almost imperceptibly, before continuing. 'Actually, Madison did say that she was planning to go away.'

'She didn't inform me!'

Fran spoke up. 'She said she was going on vacation with a friend but she wouldn't say who. She said she wasn't telling her parents. In fact she told me she might say she was staying with me.'

Mrs James sighed. 'Do you think she might be away with Mr and Mrs Young?'

Mae shrugged. More likely with Mr Young, she thought, but said nothing. Fran was looking at the table again.

Dr Sanderson coughed. 'May I suggest that the girls speak to the police? I assume they are handling it as a missing person case?'

To Mae's relief, Mrs James gave her the card of her contact in the police and Dr Sanderson said she would make sure they gave their information to the right officer straight away. The Head seemed relieved that someone was taking over responsibility, expressing the view that she had enough to do communicating with Madison's parents, who were still over in the States.

Within an hour, they were talking to a really nice sergeant who said to tell him everything – even the smallest detail could be relevant. Dr Sanderson had told them to repeat what they'd told Mrs James. They didn't want to get Mr Young into trouble so they didn't say anything about him and Madison. However, they did make it clear that it was not unusual for the American to be out all night before returning to school. This raised eyebrows and they were asked if they knew where Madison went. Mae took great delight in telling them about Herbie and his druggie mates.

When the policeman left, Mae went off to her garden and Fran accompanied Dr Sanderson to the car.

'How are you, Fran? It must have been difficult for you at the hearing yesterday.'

'I've been thinking about Cecile a lot,' the girl replied.

'It's only natural.'

'I was thinking about what Madison said. She told me that Cecile had asked her for help. She told me it was because her period was late.'

'Perhaps she didn't even realise she was pregnant.'

'That's just it. Madison took a bottle of rue from Mae's locker and gave it to Cecile. She knew it was for period problems. I couldn't understand it before because she was a catholic and they don't… Maybe she didn't even know it could cause an abortion.'

'Are you saying that Cecile definitely took medication before she died? Did the coroner know?'

'I doubt it. It was just Mae's tincture of rue. No-one knew except Madison until she told me.'

As soon as Mills was back at the cottage, she looked up the herb rue and its effects. It was clearly not something to be taken without expert advice but could be used for a variety of ailments, such as headaches and abdominal cramps. It was supposed to be good for rheumatic pains if rubbed on the skin. But the phrases that stood out for Mills were: *rue is itself toxic when taken internally in large doses* and *severe cases of poisoning are reported in countries where voluntary abortion is illegal*.

As usual, Mills turned to her friend for advice.

'Nige? Is Nina there? I want to ask her about the girl who drowned at the school production of Hamlet.'

'Of course, what is it? Don't tell me – you suspect foul play!'

'Is that supposed to be a joke?'

'Sorry, I'll get her.'

Nina listened patiently while Mills filled her in on what had happened at the pre-inquest hearing.

'So as far as the coroner is concerned, it was accidental. The pregnancy doesn't affect the parents being able to take her body back to France,' she explained.

'But they don't know about this herbal medicine?' asked Nina.

'No.'

'We won't be able to do anything until Monday but I can let the coroner's office know what you've told me. Can you send me an email with the details?'

'I don't know the dose but it seems she was taking an extract made from the rue plant, which is toxic in large amounts.'

'Not my area either, Mills, but we have an expert, Jo Rhodes, who knows all about these natural herbs and will be able to help us.'

'I wondered if she poisoned herself by overdosing on this plant.'

'Poor girl. I can see she would've been desperate. Has this anything to do with the missing girl – she's from the same school, isn't she?'

'That was worrying me. She's the girl that gave Cecile the rue in the first place. It's rather a coincidence, don't you think?'

Chapter 16

Mills usually looked forward to Sunday mornings: the opportunity for a lie-in, a leisurely breakfast and a walk up onto the fell. The early morning sunshine lit up the bedroom but she dreaded the day ahead. There hadn't been a chance to have a proper discussion about Alex's job offer and she could hear him moving around downstairs already.

There was a mug of tea waiting for her when she came out of the shower and she dressed slowly, delaying the moment when they would be seated together in the kitchen. Alex was putting chairs out in the garden and the smell of bacon drifted through the open window.

'Are you up?' he asked when she finally went downstairs.

Without waiting for an answer he disappeared into the kitchen, reappearing with a plate piled with bacon sandwiches, their usual treat at the weekend. For a while they were too busy eating to converse but eventually Alex broke the silence.

'I've got to give them an answer tomorrow.'

'Have you?' So he was going ahead then.

'We need to at least discuss it, Mills.'

'What is the point? You've already decided.'

'I think it could work out well,' Alex said. 'I'll be able to afford a small flat on a tube line in North London and you can come down or I can come up at weekends. It'll be fun. You're so busy we don't spend much time together in the week now, do we?'

Mills sighed. 'No.'

'So it'll be an adventure.' He went off to fetch more tea.

Mills knew what it would be like. At first they would see each other every weekend but soon the time between visits would lengthen and things would crop up. He would make friends in London and there would be excuses for not being able to come. Eventually they would simply drift apart. Perhaps it was for the best.

'There'll be so much to do in London.' Alex was back, grinning with excitement.

'You mean like football matches?' He was a Spurs supporter.

'No – the theatre, shows, the ballet.'

'The ballet?'

'I thought you liked ballet?'

'I do but…'

'So we can go to Covent Garden or wherever.'

'Sounds fun.'

'You could sound a bit more enthusiastic!'

'Sorry. I am. It will be fun, as you say.'

Alex changed the subject by suggesting a day's walking as they were up so early and the weather was settled. Mills was allowed to choose the route and suggested they went across the top to Gunnerside Gill and then down into the village for lunch at the "King's Head". Then back to Ivelet along the river.

It was a good decision to spend the day walking. It allowed them to talk or not as they wished and when they chatted it was about trivial things until they stopped to rest at the old mine workings on Gunnerside Gill.

'By the way, what happened about your skeleton at the building site?' Alex called, picking his way amongst the old mine tailings.

Mills sat on a large stone. 'Nothing much. The bones are more recent than we expected but there's no-one reported missing from that time.'

'So what happens now?'

'They go back to the police archives.'

'Aren't you going to do any more digging, I mean into the case?'

'Nothing to work on, unless someone from the remand home remembers something or the bracelet turns up.'

It was a pleasant stroll following the gill down to Gunnerside, where the pub was busy with walkers and cyclists. They shared a table outside with a couple from Leeds who were biking the route of the Tour de France and were keen to talk about their progress.

'You two are so lucky to actually live here all the time!' said the young woman.

Mills looked at Alex and raised her eyebrows.

'Yes we are,' was all he said.

They took the way back following the river upstream to Ivelet then cut up to Mossy Bank. It was mid-afternoon and the air was so still that midges were beginning to appear. Alex put the television on and Mills did some marking that was overdue. Soon it would be time to make dinner and the weekend would be over. She considered when she would have to catch the train from London to get back at a reasonable time on a Sunday night after visiting Alex. She imagined a packed compartment, engineering works, the journey from the station, and sighed.

Banks Lane in Scorton is popular with dog walkers. A quiet turning off the main road to Brompton on Swale, it leads to a parking spot where the lane narrows but one can proceed on foot to the gravel quarries. In the winter it can become muddy but on a Sunday morning in July it makes a pleasant stroll if the sun is shining.

Bryan parked carefully before opening the door to let his collies out. They rushed off up the track jumping at each other before darting away. He hung his binoculars on his neck and locked the car, calling for the dogs to wait. He was sure he'd heard a whimbrel on a previous occasion and was still hoping to see it. Lunch wouldn't be ready until one o' clock, so he could spend a good couple of hours, if Charlie and Bennie would keep quiet.

At first he walked quickly to keep up with them but once they'd worked off their initial energy, the collies calmed down, sniffing and marking the hedgerow. Bryan took his usual route to the edge of the quarry and sat in his favourite spot. The sun was warm and he removed his jacket, spreading it out so he could lean back and listen for the whimbrel call.

He must have dozed off because he was woken by loud barking, far off at first, then closer. Concerned that the collies had met an unfriendly dog, he jumped up and ran in the direction of the commotion. Bennie came first, running towards him then turning to race away, leading Bryan to where Charlie was barking.

The dog was at the edge of the lake, standing over someone. He shouted at Charlie to come away, worried the dog had knocked the person over, and ran up apologising to the young woman. But she didn't respond and for a second Bryan thought she was ignoring them. Then he feared that Charlie had really injured her, that he'd knocked her over and she'd hit her head. She looked unconscious and for a moment Bryan stared at the prostrate form, registering her bare feet, the grazes on her legs, her pink blouse and the trickle of blood on her forehead. Horrified at what had happened, he bent down to touch her but quickly pulled back when he realised that the red stain was dry, at the same time registering how cold and floppy she was. He stood up quickly, pulling his mobile phone from his trouser pocket and with shaking hands called the emergency services.

'I've found a girl – I think she must be dead,' he said.

'Her parents are already on their way from the United States,' Hazel explained when she had returned from the briefing.

Nige was away on field work and Nina had arrived late after dropping her children off with her mother.

'The missing American girl?'

'You heard about it? She was a boarder at some expensive posh school near Richmond. Anyway, she's been ID'd by the headmistress, who is now totally hysterical. We can't get much sense out of her. She thinks it's her fault for not keeping an eye on her pupils, which is probably true.'

'Do we know how she died?'

'We think it's trauma to the head but waiting for the report. We'll get a better picture when we have that and whether it was sexually motivated.'

'What was she doing there, I wonder?'

'Teenage girl, country lane. What do you think? Oh, sorry, I forgot about your sheltered upbringing.'

Nina knew that Hazel's jibes at her traditional Hindu family background were made in fun and she usually went along with them, but the situation was not one for humour.

'*You* won't have to tell her parents why their daughter was wandering round country lanes alone and how she was…'

'Hey, come on, I know how it is. I've done the Family Liaison Officer course too you know.'

'And decided it wasn't something you could cope with, Sergeant Fuller.'

'I admit you are much better suited to it than me. And in this case they are going to need that support. Unfortunately I don't suppose they will be able to give us any useful information about her lifestyle while she was over here.'

Hazel handed her a single sheet of A4.

'All we have at the moment is the information given to the local officer by the headmistress, a Mrs James, and some of the girl's friends. She went off on Wednesday and hasn't been seen since. I'm going over there now with Mitch to have a look around.'

'This is the school where that French girl drowned. Mills went to the inquest last week,' Nina said.

'No wonder the headmistress is upset. You know what they say: to lose one is careless but to lose…'

'Hazel! Stop it!'

Sometimes her friend's black humour went too far.

'Ok,' said Hazel. 'I've got to rush anyway.'

She picked up her bag and made for the door.

'By the way,' called Nina. 'The proper line is *To lose one parent may be regarded as a misfortune; to lose both looks like carelessness.* We did it at school.'

The dead girl's parents were due to fly from Gatwick to Leeds that afternoon and would arrive at the hotel in Richmond late evening. Nina had offered to meet them on their arrival but her DCI said she should arrange to pick them up next morning and drive to Newby Wiske, where he would meet them himself.

She read the paperwork Hazel had given her but it said very little, just their names and address, their itinerary with flight times and the name of their hotel. In her role as liaison officer she was not expected to get too involved personally but how could you not be affected? The loss of a child, whatever age, was a terrible burden to bear, whether he or she was the victim of a crime or it was simply an accident. And at this stage it wasn't clear which it was in the case of Madison Roberts.

Nina started going through her emails and found a message from Mills reminding her that she'd promised to contact the coroner's office about the herbal extract that Cecile Fleurot was taking. Before doing so, she looked up the number for Jo Rhodes. She'd approached the homeopath once before when there was a case of poisoning, quite accidental, that had left a small child very poorly. Fortunately in that case the toddler had made a full recovery.

Jo's mobile was switched off.

'It's Nina Featherstone. Can you ring me when you're free? I need to pick your brains about rue – it's a herbal remedy. I wondered if it's toxic, I mean seriously poisonous?'

She turned on her computer, typed in "rue" and spent the next hour trawling websites, becoming increasingly confused by the various complaints that could be improved by the herb, from eyesight to indigestion. It was a relief when Jo Rhodes called back.

'Hi Nina, how can I help you?'

'Thanks for getting back to me, I wanted your advice. I need to know how dangerous it is to consume extract of rue.'

'Rue?' There was a pause. 'It depends what amount you're talking about. It can be taken in small quantities to relieve certain symptoms.'

'So it's not toxic?'

'Not if taken as prescribed but excess would be bad, like most things.'

'We have a case where someone may have been taking it because they were pregnant.'

'No, that wouldn't be good. It could result in a miscarriage.'

'And could she actually poison herself by overdosing on the plant?'

'Maybe but it could be difficult to establish, if that's what you want to know.'

Nina thanked her and replaced the receiver. It was for her to inform the coroner, if she felt it was relevant. Her decision was further complicated by the death of the girl who'd given Cecile the rue. She could wait until they knew the cause of the American girl's death but Nina was wondering if it was a direct consequence of Cecile's demise. Maybe Madison Roberts had felt guilty, or someone else thought she was.

She sent an email to the coroner's office with the information expressed as clearly as she could, although it sounded a bit vague when she read it back: '...it's possible that... it could be the case... I am concerned that...' At least it will be his decision whether to take any action, she thought.

She was no more confident when Hazel arrived back from the school in the afternoon.

'Well, that was a bloody waste of time,' she called, slumping onto her chair and swinging round to face Nina. 'Hysterical teachers and blubbing schoolgirls. It was difficult to get a coherent sentence out of any of them. The headmistress was the worst. I reckon she's shitting herself that the school will be closed after this.'

'Really?'

'Madison Roberts had been missing for days before she was found.'

'She didn't report it?'

'Oh yes, but not until Friday. The girl was gone on Wednesday but no-one bothered to tell her at first. Nice kids, covering for their friend, eh?'

'Did they know where she was going?'

'You tell me. Their stories were all over the place. Mitch has gone back to the quarry hoping to see if they've found any personal effects; so far there's no bag or phone. He's dropping in to see a teacher from the boys' school where her brother is a pupil. He lives in Scorton so it's on his way to the quarry where she was found.'

Hazel turned back to her desk and began tapping her keyboard. 'Aha. Here we go. *At first sight, she appears to have been beaten around the head with a heavy object.* Ok, so it's murder, Nina. The fun begins. I hope you didn't have plans.'

'I'm family liaison for the Roberts, if you remember. It won't be much fun.'

'Sorry, I didn't mean…'

She jumped up and went to the door. 'Tea?'

Wheels were set in motion when Mitch came back from the crime scene. As DCI he automatically took on the role of SIO and began the process by arranging a briefing at short notice. At the time when Nina should have been collecting the children from her mother, she was packed into the conference room with all other available officers.

The meeting was short. There was little information except the statement from the man who'd found the body and what Mitch and Hazel had gleaned at the school. A statement from the girl's friends confirmed she had left school on Wednesday afternoon, saying she was going away and they finally decided to tell their headmistress on Friday. His subsequent conversation with the teacher from the boys' school had provided little help.

'Mr Young is a drama teacher who directed the girls' school productions. He hadn't seen the victim since the night of the play and the brother is back home in the States.'

'Did Madison have a part?' asked Nina, thinking of Cecile drowning like Ophelia.

Mitch gave her an odd look. 'I don't know,' he replied sharply.

The meeting finished with Mitch allocating tasks for that evening and the following day. There were statements to be taken, searches to oversee and CCTV footage to study.

As soon as they were out of the room, Hazel nudged Nina in the ribs.

'What was that about?' she asked with a laugh. 'Asking if she was in the play?'

'Nothing, I was thinking of the French girl, that's all.'

'You want to come down to the school with me tomorrow? I can't stand those stuck-up posh kids.'

'I'm picking up her parents tomorrow morning.'

'Let's hope they'll hear how she died before you have to see them.'

'They won't. It's not something you can tell them by phone. Mitch told me that before. I have to inform them, whatever the latest news.'

'Well rather you than me, girlfriend.'

Nina shrugged. She had to leave this minute.

The traffic was bad and she knew her mother would keep her talking, while the kids would be over-excited. They were always worn out after a day with their grandparents. In the past she'd been rather critical of Hazel leaving Liam with his grandmother so much of the time, but now she understood that for a single mum that would be out of necessity not choice.

As she'd anticipated, the boys were running noisily round the house much to their grandmother's irritation. With Rosie clinging to her, tired and emotional, Nina accepted a cup of tea.

'They've had their supper and I bathed the boys. They'll be ready for their beds when they get home.'

'I'll be ready for mine,' admitted Nina.

That was a mistake. Her mother began her usual tirade of how working for the police was not a fit place for a woman with children.

'I told your father, when you had Rosie, that you should give up work now you had a family. I said the same to Nigel and what happens? He goes off and leaves you to cope with it all.'

'He'll be back on Friday, Mum. And I can manage; it's just that it's a bit hectic at work.'

'What about the rest of the week?' her father asked. 'We can take Rosie to school.'

She squeezed his arm. 'Are you sure? What about the boys?'

'We can drop them off at nursery on the way back. It's no problem. Your mother enjoys the drive, don't you dear?'

The distance to her parents' in the morning was longer than taking the children to school and nursery herself but she accepted the offer gratefully. Repeating how much she appreciated their help, she piled her family into the car and left.

Nina was so busy getting the children to bed she hadn't noticed a text from Mills on her phone. Her friend was apologetic when she rang.

'Sorry it's so late, Nina.'

'Don't worry, I've only just got the kids settled.'

'It's about the DNA test on the bones. Donna told me they'd been reported but she wouldn't give me the results. She said I had to ask you.'

'That was very proper of her too. Well, nothing to say I'm afraid. No match. I got a missing person check on the area at that time but there was nothing, sorry.'

'Oh well, I suppose we'll never know who he was. I told Donna to send the bones back to you. What will happen to them?'

'We'll retain them for a while in case any further finds are reported at the site but I'll have to give permission for construction to proceed now.'

'Okay.'

'By the way, I spoke to Jo Rhodes and I've sent a message to the coroner. It's possible that the rue could have been a factor in Cecile Fleurot's death. He may wish to investigate further.'

'Hasn't she already been buried in France?'

'She has but if the coroner orders another PM she may have to be brought back.'

'Seriously?'

'Personally, I'm surprised there wasn't more interest in the fact she was pregnant, a young girl like her. In fact I wanted to ask you, is it possible to do a paternity test on the foetus?'

There was a long pause. 'I guess so. Why? Do you think it's important?'

'I don't know. I was just curious. By the way, Mills, Hazel is going to the school to get a written statement from the girls. I don't suppose you were going down there?'

'No, I've got a meeting at the lab. Why?'

'You know what Hazel can be like. I thought they might appreciate a friendly face that's all.'

Chapter 17

The Roberts family was already seated in reception when Nina arrived at the hotel. She was ten minutes late and apologised several times over. Madison's mother was smartly dressed, her hair immaculate and Nina noticed that her rose-coloured lipstick matched her nail varnish. She jumped up immediately and announced who they were, introducing the good-looking teenage boy with them as Austin, Madison's brother. Mr Roberts was chubby and had a friendly face. His hair was thinning and his jacket was crumpled. Austin stood up awkwardly in an ill-fitting suit and shook her hand.

Nina made her condolences as personal as possible, refraining from the usual clichés. Then she led them outside to her car hoping it didn't look too grubby. Her delay had been due to the time it had taken to remove the children's seats from the car and discard various items of rubbish that had accumulated on the floor.

Mr Roberts was in the front with her and immediately began commenting on the drizzling rain that had been falling all morning. However, conversation soon ran out and Nina was relieved that there were no serious hold-ups. She took them straight to Mitch's office, where he explained her duties as liaison officer to the family. They said very little except to confirm they understood what they were being told about the arrangements. Yes, their hotel was comfortable. Yes, they would be hiring a car. Yes, they would tell him if they needed anything. Mitch explained that a post mortem was taking place and Mrs Roberts, with great composure, asked when they might see their daughter. Austin's head drooped. Mitch added that there would be an inquest but he didn't know when that might take place. At present the investigation was at a very early stage and they were building up a picture of her movements in the days before – Mitch corrected himself – in the days when she was missing.

It was clear that Madison's parents knew nothing about their daughter's lifestyle while she was in England. They looked at Austin. Maybe their son could help them? He hadn't been able to tell them why she went missing. Mitch suggested that Nina take them to find a cup of coffee while he arranged for them to see their daughter's body.

He found them in the canteen and offered to drive them himself, allowing Austin, who did not want to go, to remain with Nina "for a chat".

She suggested they take a walk in the grounds. The rain had stopped and the sun was out. The air smelt fresh and earthy.

'You can take your jacket off if you're hot,' she said.

He looked relieved. He loosened his collar and rolled up his sleeves, slinging the jacket over his shoulder.

'That's better,' he said eventually.

'I understand you go to school over here?' Nina asked.

'Yeah but I'll be back in our home town from now on, Mom says.'

'That's understandable.'

'I guess.'

'It must be a terrible shock for all of you.'

He didn't answer but stopped and studied the ground. 'Do they know who… why…?'

Nina waited for him to finish but he set off again and she had to walk fast to keep up.

'We don't know why she was there, Austin. Just that she went out on Wednesday and didn't come back.'

'So when…?'

'The post mortem will tell us. We should get the results soon. Meanwhile, if there's anything that might help us? You probably knew her better than anyone.'

'You think? What do I know? I was back home. She should've been too.'

They sat on a low wall and Nina waited. She was wondering if he was older or younger than Madison.

'My sister was a party animal. She enjoyed life, you know? She was out there and sometimes she was way outta line.'

'Did you know any of her friends?'

'What, you mean at the school?'

'I meant outside, in the town. Where she went, what she did?'

'I tried not to know. Sometimes the older guys saw her in the pubs in Richmond. They got a kick out of telling me when she was drunk.'

'Did you ever talk to her about it?'

'No. She didn't listen to me.'

'She was older?'

'No, a year younger.'

'Did you know she took drugs?'

He turned to her. 'Only legal ones. No law against it.'

'Actually that's not true, Austin. We think she may have spent the time she was missing with a certain set of people in the town. If you know them I'd appreciate a list of names and addresses.'

'I told you. I didn't follow her around like some guardian. Perhaps you should ask Young, he spent more time with her than I did,' he mumbled looking down at the ground.

'Do you mean Jeremy Young, your drama teacher?'

'English teacher but he spent plenty of time over at High Fell with the girls doing drama rehearsals – at least that's what he said.'

'Was Madison in the play?' Nina asked.

'No but that didn't stop him seeing her.'

Mrs James sat between Mae and Fran across the table from the police sergeant called Fuller. She wasn't as friendly as the policeman they'd seen before. *My name is Detective Sergeant Fuller,* she'd said, *and I'll be taking your statements.* Mae had grinned but Fran was feeling nervous. She was scared about them hiding the fact that Madison was missing. A girl had told her they could be arrested for perverting the course of justice and she'd looked it up on the internet.

'So girls, I just want you to tell me what you told the other police officer, but this time I'll type it up and ask you to sign it for me.'

They both sat waiting. The woman looked up, impatiently.

'Let's start with your full names. You first.' She was pointing at Fran.

'Frances Jemima Elizabeth Steel.'

Mae giggled.

'I'll talk to Frances first then.' The sergeant looked at Mae. 'Can you wait outside?' She watched her leave the room, shutting the door behind her.

Fran's voice was shaky when she began to answer the questions: *How did she know Madison? Were you good friends? Did you go out anywhere together? Who did Madison hang around with?*

The questioning began to focus on the nights when Madison went off and didn't return until morning. *Where did she go? Who was she with?*

'She went into town.'

'Richmond?'

'Yes.'

'Where exactly did she go?'

Fran looked at Mrs James who was staring straight ahead.

'The pub.'

'Which pub?'

'Any of them. I don't know exactly.'

'You didn't go with her?'

'No.'

'Can you think of anyone who might know who she met in Richmond?'

Fran and Mae had discussed the taxi driver who usually came to take Madison into town. There'd been the time when Madison had lost her bag and rang him: they'd heard her calling him a pervert.

'She knew the taxi driver; he might know who she went to see.'

More questions about Madison's friends but there was nothing she could add and there was no way she was going to mention the rumours about Mr Young.

Then she was asked about Madison's last day at the school. Fran tried to remember what Madison had told her about going to see Diane Young and how she'd said she was going on holiday.

'Did she say who she was going on holiday with?'

'No, it was a secret.'

'Did she have a boyfriend?'

'I don't know. She didn't tell me anything. We'd just become room-mates.'

Finally, it was over and she was dismissed.

'Ask the other girl to come in now, will you?'

Outside, Mae rushed down the corridor. 'What did she ask? Did you tell her about Jeremy Young?'

Before Fran could answer, the door opened again and Mrs James summoned Mae to come inside.

Fran waited until she heard the door open and saw Mae emerge. They went into the garden together and exchanged accounts of their interviews.

'I told her about the taxi driver,' Mae announced.

'So did I.'

'Did you say anything about Mr Young?'

'Only that she was going to visit Mrs Young.'

'So did I. The other thing was only a rumour and I don't want to get him into trouble.'

Hazel went straight back to Newby Wiske to finish typing up the statements. It had been a frustrating morning and she was ready to tell Nina what she thought of teenage girls. But the office was empty. Presumably her colleague was still on liaison officer duties. She sat and stared at the various notes that had been left on her desk. Madison Roberts' computer had been accessed, could she review? The post mortem results had come in, take a look. Samples had gone for forensics, check when they'll be back.

'It wouldn't harm to say please, Mitch,' she muttered as she accessed the files containing the girl's email messages. She was still working through them when Nina arrived two hours later.

'I'd forgotten how mentally exhausting it is, looking after the relatives of a victim,' Nina said, slumping down at her desk.

'What are they like?'

'A nice American family, grieving. Mrs Roberts was pretty devastated after she'd been to see her daughter.'

'What are they doing now?'

'They're being driven back to their hotel. They'd had enough. Mitch is going to see them again tomorrow.'

'I've been going through the girl's emails.'

'Anything?'

'Nothing much to help us with *our* investigation, it would be more helpful if we could find Madison's phone, but there is communication with the French girl that died.'

'Cecile Fleurot?'

'Yes, she seemed to be in a bit of a pickle.'

'What d'you mean?'

'Look for yourself.' She turned the monitor round so Nina could see the messages, a stream of one-liners back and forth between the two girls.

As Nina absorbed the nature of their conversation, she realised that it could help explain Cecile's pregnancy. She asked Hazel if she could give her a print-out and half an hour later she handed her three pages.

Nina read them several times over, with a lump in her throat. Cecile was begging her friend for help: her period was late and she was scared. Madison said she should've been more careful.

Cecile: Careful? I should have been careful not to go out with you to your disgusting taxi driver and his friends again. You knew what they were up to with those drugs.

Madison: It's not my fault. Herbie only deals in legal highs and you didn't have to take them.

Cecile: You left me in that horrible place with those men. I didn't know what to do. I didn't know what was happening.

Madison: What happened?

Cecile: I think I'm pregnant.

Madison: That's your fault not mine.

Cecile: He raped me and you did nothing. You must help me.

Madison: It's your own fault but I can get Mae's help.

Cecile: Don't tell anyone.

Madison: Don't worry.

Nina turned to Hazel. 'This proves that Madison gave Cecile the rue to terminate her pregnancy.'

Hazel looked up. 'But not that she took it, of course.'

'No but it links the two girls.'

'But not necessarily their deaths.'

'I know.'

'So why didn't you get this from the French girl's phone?'

'Because up to now her death was an accident. At least I can tell the coroner we have proof that she took the rue and ask him for another PM.'

'It's a big deal.'

'Tell me about it. Her family will be devastated and she'll have to be exhumed for examination by a French pathologist.'

Nina went to tell Mitch what she'd discovered but he was on the phone. She knocked and waited outside. When he'd finished his call he came to the door and suggested they went out for some air.

'The sun comes right in and my room is unbearably hot this time of year,' he complained.

Nina showed him the messages between Cecile and Madison.

'And who is Mae?'

'She concocted the tincture that Cecile took to stop the pregnancy. We didn't know this at the time of the inquest; this is new information.'

'You should contact the coroner.'

'I already have.'

He gave her one of his looks.

'Just to let him know of the possibility. Now I can confirm it,' she added.

'It could mean another PM.'

'I know.'

'We'd better be sure of our facts. Get a statement from this Mae. Is she still at the school?'

'Yes. I'll go over right away.'

'Hold on. We need more information about these friends of Madison Roberts: the taxi driver and this Herbie character. It sounds as though they may be important in our investigation of *her* death too.'

'So you think they are connected?'

'Open minds, Nina, open minds. By the way, we've been appointed a researcher on the case. I think you know her?'

'Not Ruby?'

'Yes. She'll be with us later today. Ask her to get hold of the French girl's phone.'

When Mills contacted Fran to suggest they meet later in the week, the girl mentioned she was being interviewed by the police again the following day.

Mills immediately rang Nina on the pretext of asking if the coroner had responded to her.

'I'm waiting to hear from him.'

'But the rue *was* significant.'

'Yes, it could be. We now have evidence that she probably was offered the tincture by someone. I can't say more than that.'

Mills wanted to ask more questions but she recognised Nina's tone. It meant she didn't want to discuss it further.

'Is that why you want to speak to Fran again? She told me she was being interviewed tomorrow,' Mills added quickly.

'You don't miss much, do you?' Nina laughed. 'Actually I'm going over to see Fran and her friend Mae to find out about some dodgy-sounding acquaintances that Cecile and Madison shared.'

'I might see you there then. What time are you going?'

'Eleven.'

'Then I will.' Mills hoped it sounded like a coincidence.

They arranged to meet up afterwards for lunch.

Alex looked up when she put the phone down. 'I thought you said you were at the lab tomorrow?'

'I was but something's come up.'

'At the school?'

'Yes. I'm going to meet Nina there.'

She didn't mention that she wanted to talk to Nina about his plan to leave her to work in London.

'So did you let them know that you're taking it?' she asked.

They'd agreed that he would accept the job offer that day.

'Yes. They said they were pleased.'

'So when do you start?'

'Soon I expect. They'll send me an offer by email this week. At least I don't have to hand in my notice to anyone.'

'No.'

'It'll take a while to find somewhere to live,' Mills pointed out.

'That's easy. I've got a mate that has a flat in Streatham. There are three of them and one is moving out at the end of the month so I can move in there. Meanwhile he says I can sleep on his sofa.'

'You do know where Streatham is, Alex? It's south of the river, for a start.'

'He says it's easy to get into the middle of London.'

'Right.' Already plans were being altered to suit him. 'So where would I stay if I come down? On the floor?'

'No, you would have the sofa obviously.'

He was laughing at her but she wasn't in the mood for jokes.

'Well it sounds as if you will have to come up here at weekends to begin with at least.'

'Yes, of course I will,' he promised, picking up his iPad. 'I'll look up the train times.'

Chapter 18

Mae and Fran had decided to tell the police officer everything they knew about Madison's lifestyle this time. Fran insisted they leave nothing out, not even their suspicions about Mr Young.

'And you must say how she stole the rue out of your cupboard and then admitted it afterwards.'

Fran was still troubled by the fact that they hadn't ever reported Madison missing when she'd stayed out at night. Mrs James had banned them both from going out at all unless accompanied by an adult and their parents were coming to fetch them the following week. It wasn't entirely clear whether they would be returning. Certainly Mae's parents said they were considering sending her to an international boarding school in Beijing.

Their headmistress summoned them to her office to meet Sergeant Featherstone, who turned out to be the complete opposite of the other woman officer. She was pleasant, taking pains to put them at their ease; soft spoken and sympathetic. When they discussed her later they agreed she was probably born in this country but with parents from India and Mae declared she would grow her hair so it looked like hers.

Unlike Sergeant Fuller, this one said to call her Nina and didn't try to confuse them with jargon. She didn't mention the fact they'd not reported Madison missing but wanted to know about their friends and hers and whether they mixed socially. Fran admitted she once went into town with Madison.

'And where did you go?'

'Just into town.' Mrs James leaned forward. Fran blushed. 'We visited some pubs.'

'Did you see any of Madison's friends there?' the police officer asked.

'Yes,' said Fran. 'She knew lots of boys. They drank a lot and I didn't like it. I didn't go again.'

'So did Cecile go into town with her?' Nina asked.

'Yes,' Mae and Fran answered together.

'She came with me that time,' added Fran. 'I told her not to go again but she liked Madison's attention. She went several times before she stopped.'

'Why do you think that was?'

'Because Madison was mad, that's why.' Mae was animated. 'She drank too much and it was obvious she took different substances…'

'Substances?'

'I don't know what but she used to boast about getting stoned.' Mae stared defiantly at the Head, who looked shocked at her outburst. 'Everyone knew.'

'Do you know where she got these substances?'

Fran and Mae looked at each other. They'd already spoken together about the taxi driver and wanted to tell her about him. They took turns to explain how he always picked her up and brought her back until the argument over her bag. They described what they'd overheard and how Madison had threatened to report him to the police, saying she had witnesses that he tried to abduct her.

The sergeant was making notes. 'Do you know how to contact him?'

'It's the number for the taxi firm the school recommends. He often appears when we ring.' Mae was looking at Mrs James.

'I can give you the name of the firm and its number,' she said, going to her desk.

'Is there anything else you think might be relevant?' asked Nina.

Mae spoke up. 'I want to tell you about the medicine that Madison stole from me.'

Nina nodded.

'Well, I made it as an insect repellent, a strong concentration. It was never made to be used in a neat form.'

'This is the rue?' asked Nina.

'Yes. Well she – Madison – stole it from the cupboard next to my bed. She admitted it later. She said she'd given it to Cecile for her period pains but I thought she'd taken it herself because we thought…' she looked at her friend.

'We thought Madison might be pregnant but it was Cecile all along!' Fran couldn't stop the tears.

There was a pause in the proceedings while Fran was provided with tissues and the Head handed Nina a note of the taxi firm's name and contact details.

'Can I ask why you assumed Madison was pregnant?' Nina asked at last.

Mae straightened in her seat. 'She didn't exactly admit it but we're pretty sure she was having an affair with someone and we think that it was...' she hesitated.

'It was Mr Young.' Fran could feel her face burning as the Head stared at her in horror.

'That's absurd!' Mrs James was standing.

Fran burst into tears again and Mae shouted something about her never listening to anything they said. Nina suggested they had a break and they left the room, rushing to the toilets together. Now they were in real trouble.

*

Nina related some of the events of the morning over a sandwich lunch in Richmond. Mills had arrived at the school in time to see the girls rushing down the corridor. Assuming the interview was over, she knocked on the headmistress's office door and found Nina comforting a distraught Mrs James. Deciding to call it a day, Nina had suggested they leave and find somewhere to eat. Much to Mills' frustration, Nina was being very discreet about what had occurred.

'All I can say is the girls made an accusation that caused the poor woman to become hysterical. I can see how Hazel found it difficult to cope with them all.'

'Did you say the girls' deaths might be connected?' Mills asked.

'I did not.' Nina smiled. 'But yes, I wanted to see if they had any mutual friends outside the school.'

'You mean in the town?'

'Maybe.'

'And had they? You said "dodgy-sounding" on the phone.'

'Did I?'

'I might be able to help you there. I did see a young man in a hoodie passing her a small packet on the school premises when I was there once.'

'Really? Would you recognise him again?'

'Sorry, I didn't see his face.'

Nina sighed. 'Never mind, I have another lead I can work on.'

Nina asked her about work and when Mills told her the bones were on their way back from the lab, she confirmed they would be archived in the absence of any DNA match.

'They've stopped work on the building site for the time being,' said Nina. 'We're doing a quick forensic search around the area where you were working, just in case we find anything.'

'I just wish I'd removed the bracelet before it was taken.'

'Good point. I'll ask uniform to question the workmen; someone may have some intelligence. In fact it's something our researcher could get her teeth into, although she's been assigned to Madison's case really.'

They chatted until Mills managed to work the conversation round to Alex's job offer and poured out her reservations.

'It sounds like a really good opportunity,' Nina said.

'Good for him, I agree,' Mills said.

'It's always a difficult one but if your relationship is strong, it will survive.'

'That's what worries me.'

'Oh, that reminds me: it seems that Cecile Fleurot's body will be exhumed to look for toxins. The coroner is putting the wheels in motion now. In fact Dr Moreau told me to let you know.'

'Why me?'

'I'm really not sure except that you were involved before. They will do the post mortem in France and send the details over to the UK, with an expert to explain the findings to the coroner.' Nina smiled mischievously. 'And she said you know the person: a certain Phil Freedman?'

'He's coming here?'

'Of course!' Nina grinned. 'I thought it would be best and she agreed.'

Mills was speechless that her friend had deliberately influenced events in such a way.

'And, naturally, you'll want to meet him,' Nina continued. 'To discuss the outcome.'

Mills shook her head slowly in disbelief.

'Changing the subject,' Nina began. 'You were right about the DNA test on a foetus: I've requested one as part of the new PM on Cecile.'

'Have you any idea who the father might be?'

'No, although a name came up today that was interesting.'

'And?'

Her friend looked at her watch. 'I'd better go. I need to make enquiries at some of the pubs here.'

'And I'd better get off to the lab.'

'If you are seeing Fran in the week, let me know if she says anything to you about Madison Roberts or Cecile Fleurot and particularly about a teacher called Mr Young.'

'Good luck with the pub crawl then,' Mills called as she left.

'Hello stranger!' Ruby called from her seat at the spare desk when Nina returned to the office.

Her hair was a different shade of blonde but otherwise she was the familiar streak of bright colours. Today she was in a flowery sleeveless dress with large plastic beads round her long neck.

'So how are you?' Nina asked, going over to give her a hug.

'Fine. I've got some good intel for you.' She thrust a sheet of paper at her. 'The calls list for the girl's phone.'

Nina looked at the numbers. 'Have you identified them?'

'Not yet. I'm working through them now.'

Nina busied herself writing up the morning's interviews until Hazel appeared.

'How did it go, Nina?' she asked.

Nina gave her a quick report of her meeting with the schoolgirls.

'Not much more than I got out of them, then.'

'Except,' Nina said, 'we have intel on two men: the taxi driver and a teacher. I've got details of the taxi firm. I was going to see them this afternoon but it took longer to go round the pubs than I thought.'

Hazel guffawed. 'Sounds like an excuse if I didn't know you better.'

'Actually I could do with your help. There was one, called "The Fleece", where they identified Madison. In fact she was quite a nuisance, that's why they knew her. She used to hang out with a young man called Herbie. There's a group of lads who can be a handful on occasions.'

'Sounds promising.'

'They are there most evenings. I don't suppose you fancy coming along with me?'

'Yes but not tonight though.'

'Got a date?'

'I wish! No, Liam's in the school play this week and he needs a lift back from the dress rehearsal. What about tomorrow? You can do the taxi firm this evening.'

'I do have a home to go to!'

The researcher interrupted them. 'I've got the taxi number on the list. I could call them. And I can probably locate the drivers from the times when she called the company.'

'Welcome back Ruby,' replied Hazel. 'We have so missed you!'

The office went quiet as all three of them worked at their computers. Nina could hear Ruby giving the taxi firm the dates and times of Madison's calls to them, asking them to get back to her with a list of drivers. She was sceptical of the researcher's success.

A little later Ruby came to Nina's desk.

'I've listed the contacts against the calls,' she said. 'There aren't many apart from the taxi company. Mainly her family, school friends and retail outlets.'

Nina looked down the names. Ruby was right.

'What are these?' she asked, pointing at "PAYG" against a few items.

'Sorry – pay as you go. Not traceable.'

Nina's finger reached the bottom of the list; the last call she made – a text message. A familiar name.

'That's Jeremy Young. He's a teacher at a school in Richmond,' Ruby said.

'Yes, I know. His name came up this morning in connection with Madison. Hazel, we need to speak to him. But Ruby, can we get the details of that last text?'

'It will take some time.'

'All the more reason to get it moving,' called Hazel, as she answered her phone.

Still treating Ruby in the same assertive way, Nina noted. She could hear her friend chatting to the pathologist about Madison's post-mortem and waited for her to finish the conversion.

'Are the results through?'

'Sending them this afternoon.' She looked at her note-pad. 'High levels of alcohol in her body so unlikely she could have staggered far. Cannabis also present and evidence of recent sexual activity.'

'Time and cause of death?'

'Time: Friday night or early Saturday morning. Cause: Repeated trauma to the head, unlikely to be inflicted accidentally.'

Nina eventually broke the silence. 'So she had to be driven there. Mitch says there are no useful tyre tracks but whoever took her there had use of a vehicle.'

'The taxi driver?' asked Ruby.

'Or the boyfriend called Herbie,' said Hazel.

'If she'd had sex, is it possible to test for DNA, I wonder?' asked Nina.

'You could ask your forensic friend,' said Ruby.

'Yes I could,' said Nina and immediately sent Mills a question about a DNA test on semen.

The reply came back almost immediately. *I have no idea but I know a girl who does.*

The phone rang a few minutes later.

'Nina! Donna says it would be viable for up to five days.'

'Good, that's ok then. Can she do it?'

'Of course.'

'Then I'll arrange it as soon as the boss gives the authorisation.'

Nina went straight to see Mitch to update him with progress and to ask for further forensic work. He'd already heard about the PM results.

'If we can identify who she was seeing, at least we'll know who to focus on. Someone must know where she was from Wednesday to Saturday.'

'I've asked Ruby to get the details of her last text; it was sent on the Friday night.'

'Good.'

She returned to her desk. Nothing left to do on the Madison case that day, except to arrange a visit to the family. It was important to keep in touch and she'd remembered that Madison's brother had mentioned the drama teacher. At the time it hadn't seemed important but the name kept cropping up and she needed to talk to Austin again. She left a message on Mr Roberts' phone asking for a meeting.

At last she had a moment to open the email from the uniformed officer who'd been talking to the builders. His report was very brief: just one person had anything to say and was reluctant at first. Apparently one of the men working on the site, an old man doing menial tasks, had acted suspiciously. He'd been poking around the excavation area when Mills wasn't there. The report named the informant but not the old man. Nina emailed a "thank you", saying she would follow it up.

Hi Mills. I'm going to the building site to talk to someone who may have been tampering with your burial site. If you want to come along, give me a ring at home later. We may have found the man who took the bracelet! She clicked "send".

Mills received Nina's message as she finished a call with Fran, arranging to meet her the following morning. The girl's archaeology project had lost momentum and Mills wanted to get her back on track, somehow. It wasn't clear how she would do this in view of the fact that the excavation was of a recent body. However, Fran had unearthed a lot of information about the use of the site prior to the new build and it might be helpful to the police investigation. She would call Nina to ask if Fran could accompany them to the site since her background research could be useful.

Mills had been surprised when Nina agreed to Fran joining them at Gilling West. But it seemed she had an ulterior motive: she wished to speak to Fran without her headmistress present.

'Just a few minutes without the poor girl being pressurised will be plenty,' she'd said.

There was a light drizzle and Nina was sheltering in the foreman's hut when they arrived.

'They're fetching him now,' she said.

'I've left Fran in the car,' said Mills.

'Yes. I think that's best. We can chat afterwards.'

A white-haired man in a muddy yellow jacket appeared in the doorway.

'Mr Thomas Weston?'

'Ay.'

He came into the hut and they shuffled along to make room.

Nina introduced herself and began to explain who Mills was.

'I seen 'er,' he said.

Standing in an awkward line, Nina began to speak about the excavation and how they had reason to think he had been interfering with it. 'So we wanted to have a chat about it.'

At first he denied it, insisting he was never anywhere near the skeleton. When Nina said he'd been seen, he changed tack and admitted he'd taken an interest.

'So why were you curious about the skeleton?' Nina asked.

He feigned interest in the archaeology but soon became flustered.

'You knew the place when it was a remand home?' Mills tried.

He looked round at her sharply. 'Who told you that?'

'I just…' Mills began.

'Mr Weston? Thomas?' Nina asked gently.

'Tom, they call me.'

'Well, Tom. It would be very, very helpful to us if you know something about the skeleton this lady was working on. To be honest we can't identify the poor man and any help you can give…'

He stuck his hands in his jacket pocket and bowed his head, as if deep in thought.

'I'll tell you. Yes, I'll tell you. That wasn't a poor man, it were a poor boy. A young lad left to rot like a rat.'

Chapter 19

'Sorry to keep you waiting, Mills,' Nina said, climbing into the back of the car.

'Was it him that took the bracelet?'

Tom had asked to speak to Nina alone. Mills had been waiting in the car with Fran for half an hour while she finished interviewing the old man.

'Yes, it was. I've arranged for him to be brought to Newby Wiske tomorrow so I can record the information.'

Mills knew better than to probe further in front of her tutee.

'And now I've got a rather more important investigation to address concerning your friend Madison,' she said, turning to Fran.

The girl moved round in her seat to face Nina.

'I want to get a better picture of her and her friends. I know she liked to go out and sometimes she stayed out all night. Do you know where she was on those occasions?'

'No. She drank a lot and... Well I assumed she just crashed out on someone's floor.'

'Was there anything else in addition to alcohol?'

'Mae said Herbie is a druggie but Madison swore he only gave her legal highs.'

'They're still very dangerous,' Nina said. 'And no longer legal.'

'I know. I don't think she cared.'

'And is there anyone else she was involved with?'

She didn't answer.

'At the school the other day, you mentioned someone – a teacher,' continued Nina. 'A Mr Young?'

'Yes.' Her answer was barely audible.

Mills watched the girl's face. She was biting her lower lip.

Nina was talking gently to her. 'I know you are a sensible girl and you wouldn't say something like that out of mischief. Understandably Mrs James was upset but I'd like to know why you think he was involved with her.'

'Mae told me she saw them arguing… and then Madison was talking about going away with a man. We thought it could be Mr Young.'

'Would you say Mae was reliable, she wouldn't have made that up to get Madison into trouble?'

'Oh no, I believe everything she says. You can ask her yourself.'

'Thank you Fran, I probably will.'

Mills waited until Nina had gone before asking the girl if she was ok. She nodded. They walked across to the excavation site to take a few last photographs for Fran's report. There was police tape across the area and nothing left to see but a piece of disturbed ground.

'Shall we to go back to school?' Mills asked as they returned to the car. 'We'll go through what you've found out about the history of this site. And you can make me a cup of coffee.'

'Do you understand why I've brought you back here for interview?' Nina asked the old man.

Tom Weston nodded and she asked him to speak up for the tape. He seemed more nervous than he had been the day before. His bony hands were shaking slightly.

'Yes.'

'I'd like you to repeat what you told me about the boy you call Ginger, whose body was found at the site of the old remand home.'

He coughed nervously. 'He was a little scrap of a lad. We called him Ginger on account of his hair. He was pale except for his hair. That was red, a fiery red. His face would go red too because of his stutter. He must've been the smallest lad there but not the youngest.' There was a faint smile on his lips as he remembered the boy.

'You said he was bullied.'

His expression changed to one of anger. 'We all were but he got it worse than all of us. If there was trouble he would be punished with the rest, though he kept himself to himself.'

'So was he a friend of yours?'

He seemed to consider the question. 'No.' He put his head on one side. 'But I left him alone, so I suppose he thought of me as one.'

'How do you know the skeleton uncovered at the site belonged to him, Tom?'

'I didn't at first, although I guessed it might have come from the old days.'

'Why was that?'

'Because it was a cruel time. People got beaten up.'

'Who beat them up?'

'The lads got into fights. The officers punished them. It was a hard place.'

'When were you there, Tom?'

'May sixty-one to November sixty-three. And I remember every day of it.'

'So Ginger was there all that time too?'

'No. He arrived after me. It was probably in the summer; he had freckles. He went freckled in the sun, see.'

'And how long did he stay?'

'Not long. He got sickly in the winter and went very thin. He was always shivering. I thought it was the cold but he seemed withdrawn like.'

'He left before you?'

'Yes. It was still cold but it was cold all the time in the winter. He left sudden like while it was still wintry outside.'

'Do you know where he went?'

'No. That's the point. I thought he went too sudden. One day he was there and the next – gone.'

'Didn't you think that was odd?'

'Yes but you didn't ask questions or you got a clip round the ear, or worse. Some of them officers were right cruel so you kept your head down.'

Nina changed her position and left a pause before continuing.

'So, when you saw the skeleton, what did you think?'

'They said it was some ancient burial so I went over. When I saw something glinting there I took a closer look. It seemed to me it could be an ID tag of some sort. They were popular in those days. Some boys even swapped them. Suddenly it all came flooding back. Of course I knew what the site had been but I'd blotted it out.'

He put a hand over his face and lowered his head.

'Would you like a break, Tom?'

He looked up defiantly. 'No, I want to do this.'

'Go on, then.'

'I admit I scraped round it and took it.'

'You mean the bracelet?'

'Yes. It belonged to him, I'm sure. It didn't say Ginger, but I knew the surname. It said "Gregory Lee" but he was Ginger Lee to us boys.'

'Do you still have it?'

He looked embarrassed. 'Yes. I was going to report it.'

'Were you?'

A tear ran down one side of his face. 'He was so little and he couldn't hurt a fly but they made his life a misery.'

'What d'you think happened to him, Tom?'

He was sobbing gently. 'I don't know. But whoever hurt him deserves to be punished, that's the truth.'

'Why do you think someone hurt him?'

'Because that's what they did and he was a thin, sickly boy, wasn't he?'

'Was there anyone in particular who might have hurt him?'

He appeared to consider the question as he rubbed his eyes. 'There was one officer, a short Scotsman. He enjoyed bullying the younger ones, more his size I suppose. He was vicious. They sacked him in the end and we were glad to see the back of him.'

'Do you know when he left?'

'It was before I got out,' he said, 'because we had a party to celebrate.'

'Do you remember whether Ginger was at the party?'

He shook his head.

'And can you remember the name of the officer who was sacked?'

He shook his head again. 'I've been trying but it's gone. I wouldn't have remembered Ginger if I hadn't seen his name on that identity bracelet.'

They left him in the interview room with a cup of tea while they reviewed the situation.

Mitch agreed that it would do no good to bring charges; he was a good witness and had been a great help to the case. Nina sent him home with an officer to pick up the ID bracelet and returned to her desk to ring Mills.

'Was he any help, Nina?' Mills asked.

'Yes, we've got a name: Gregory Lee, Ginger to his mates. It was on his bracelet, apparently.'

'So the old man had it!'

'He knew the lad.'

'Does he know what happened to him?'

'I'm getting Ruby to find out about the inmates and officers at the time.'

'I see. Fran might be able to help you; she's been studying the history of the site.'

'If there's anything you think might be useful.'

'Will do. Are you off to collect the children now?'

Nina laughed. 'No. I'm going to Richmond with Hazel. We're meeting at a pub in the town at seven o'clock.'

'Sounds like fun.'

'Fun? We need to talk to the young lads who Madison associated with.'

'You mean the one who supplied her drugs? The one I saw at the school?'

'Possibly. By the way, Cecile Fleurot will be exhumed tomorrow and the PM results will be available early next week; in case you wanted to know.'

'Thanks, Fiona has been asking.'

'I thought you might be interested too. It means your friend Phil Freedman will be coming over quite soon.'

"The Fleece" was empty when Nina peered in so she waited outside, hoping her colleague would be along soon. She sheltered in the doorway away from the cold breeze, watching for Hazel's car as she called her mother on her mobile.

'Sorry I'm late!' Hazel announced her arrival.

'No problem, I was just checking on the kids.'

She followed Hazel in and stood aside while she talked to the girl behind the bar.

'They aren't in yet,' Hazel reported. 'Have you eaten?'

'I had a sandwich on the way.'

'I had a snack before I came out too but I'm starving.'

She grabbed two menus and passed one to Nina.

'I'm having scampi and chips. What d'you want? My treat.'

Nina protested but Hazel insisted so she accepted a bowl of chips.

'How did Liam's dress rehearsal go?' Nina asked while they waited for their meals.

Hazel shrugged. 'Fine, I think. You know teenage boys, everything on a "need to know" basis.'

'What's the play?'

'Some Shakespeare thing. It's his birthday this year apparently.'

'Anniversary of his death, actually,' Nina corrected her.

'Whatever. Liam is a Roman soldier.'

'Julius Caesar?'

'No, just one of the troops.'

'I meant is the play "Julius Caesar" or maybe "Anthony & Cleopatra"? It could be "Coriolanus" if there are Roman soldiers.'

'I'd assumed it was Julius Caesar. I didn't know there were others.'

'Well there are but it probably is. Are you going to see him?'

'Of course, although it's not my thing.'

The food arrived and Hazel fetched two orange juices.

'I'd kill for a large glass of red,' she muttered.

They turned to look at the door as two men came in and went to the bar.

'Too old,' Nina said.

A few more men drifted in over the next hour. They all seemed to know each other to nod at and pass the time of day. The girl came to take their plates.

'No sign,' she said. 'They're usually here by now.'

'Just let us know when they arrive,' said Hazel.

It was just before eight when two scruffy young men tumbled through the door, laughing and pushing each other. Both wore grey hoodies, denim jeans and trainers, their heads shaved to a shadow. They would have looked almost identical except one was a good eight inches taller than the other. They argued at the bar about whose round it was then stood silently watching the drinks being poured into pint glasses. The smaller lad carefully counted out his money and put it on the counter, ready to exchange for the two pints of lager. Sipping from their full glasses, they headed for the pool table and began an apparently established routine, tossing a coin then beginning the game.

Hazel nodded at Nina to follow as she made her way over. She stood beside the table, watching. Nina hung back. The lads stopped chatting and the short one looked sideways at Hazel as he aimed at the ball with his cue and missed.

'Did you want something, missus?' said the tall lad.

'Just watching. It's not a crime.'

Nina hated it when Hazel played these games. Her colleague liked to wind people up, especially if she thought they were up to no good. She believed it rattled them into tripping up. It certainly worked this time. After a few hopeless attempts, the two players put down their cues, glared at her and uttered a few expletives. At that point she produced her ID.

'Come and join us, boys. We just want a chat.'

Their demeanours changed. Suddenly the two bolshie teenagers were walking nervously over to their table and the four of them sat observing each other. Nina took a note of their names: Herbie was the tall lad, his friend was called Robbie. They both lived with their parents on Gallowgate.

'We're police officers investigating the death of Madison Roberts,' Hazel began.

Robbie looked puzzled, the other muttered *Mads* under his breath.

'Yes, she was found dead – but perhaps you heard?'

They both shook their heads.

'But you knew her?' Nina asked.

Robbie nodded hesitantly. Herbie stared at the table.

Hazel straightened up. 'She was found on Sunday but she was missing from Wednesday. Perhaps you know where she was?'

No answer.

'We understand she used to come in here?' Nina said.

'Yes.' It was Robbie. 'She was a laugh.'

'So was she here last week?'

Nina spotted Herbie kicking his friend's leg under the table. He shook his head. 'I don't remember.'

'We're trying to build up a picture of what she was like,' began Nina. 'She's been described as a party animal. Did she drink when she was here?'

'I can't say,' Robbie replied, looking away.

'Why not?' Hazel asked sharply.

No answer.

She repeated the question.

'I don't want to get anyone into trouble.'

'Underage drinking is the least of our problems at present, young man. If Madison was drinking, what else was she using?'

Herbie leaned forward. 'We don't have to talk to you. So shut up, Robbie!'

Hazel raised her voice so everyone could hear. 'This is a murder investigation and you do have to talk to us. If you were with Madison during the time she was missing, you need to tell us or I will have you dragged in for a formal interview. Do you want to add anything now?'

Robbie looked at Herbie but neither spoke.

'Come on, Nina,' she called before walking over to the bar. 'How much do I owe you?' she asked the barmaid.

Nina waited by the door while Hazel settled up. A middle-aged man came over and asked if he could have a word. She followed him out into the street.

'Were you asking about the American lass found in Scorton?'

'Yes.'

'I've seen her in here before. I'm sure it was Friday night, possibly the night before.'

She made a note of his name.

'Can I ask whether she was with those boys we were talking to?'

'Oh yes. She hung about with that tall lad. If he weren't in, she'd go off again.'

Nina thanked him for his help and took his phone number. 'Just in case we want to speak to you again.'

Hazel appeared and the man hovered as if undecided whether to go back inside. As they returned to their cars, Nina saw him walking off in the other direction. She told Hazel what he'd said.

'Give me their addresses and get back to your family,' said Hazel. 'I'll get the local officers to bring them in nice and early for interview tomorrow morning.'

Hazel watched Nina's car drive off before making the call to bring the boys in. Her day was now officially over. It was only just after eight-thirty, she could be home in time to watch a bit of telly with a glass of wine before Liam returned from performing in the school play.

She was about to put the key in the ignition when she noticed two figures in hoodies crossing the square: it was Herbie and Robbie. She automatically sank down in her seat and observed them. She guessed they were only Liam's age, certainly not much older. Who knew what they were involved in; at least underage drinking and drugs but possibly murder? She knew Liam drank with his mates at house parties but she thought he was sensible about it. She'd drilled into him not to try drugs and he knew about the dangers, they'd even had a talk at school, but that didn't mean there weren't temptations and opportunities – plenty of occasions as she was out much of the time. She pulled her mobile from her pocket and sent him a text. *I'll pick you up at school after the play has finished.*

The boys had disappeared from view but as she turned the car down the hill, she saw them standing beside a taxi parked on the side of the road. They didn't notice her slowing down to read the registration number as she passed by; they were too busy chatting to the driver. She parked further down the road and walked back up. Herbie saw her and pulled Robbie away, running up the hill and out of sight.

'Good evening!' Hazel addressed the driver seated in the taxi.

'Where to, love?' he asked, throwing something out of the window.

She stamped on the glowing cigarette end.

'I'm not going anywhere,' she replied, showing him the ID card. 'You know those lads?'

'Yes. I see them about.'

'Did you know Madison Roberts?'

'Who's she?'

'The schoolgirl who was found dead at Scorton on Sunday.'

'I don't think so.'

'No? What's your full name?'

'Why are you asking me these questions?'

'Just trying to find who saw her last. Do you pick fares up from the posh girls' school called High Fell?'

'Sometimes.'

'An American girl?'

'They have all sorts there: Chinese, French...'

'This girl was an American called Madison Roberts.'

'I don't know, honestly.'

'I can check with your firm. Presumably they log the calls?'

'Yes.'

'Good. So I need your name and address – just for the record.'

He drove off as soon as Hazel was walking back to her car. She would ask Ruby to check with the taxi company to see whether he'd picked up Madison in the past week. At last there were connections; finally the investigation was going somewhere.

Chapter 20

The final report of Madison's PM was on Nina's desk when she arrived for work. She already knew most of what was in it but she was looking for the additional DNA results that might tell them who she'd had sex with before she died. The results were apparently not particularly good. Certainly there was no match on the database. She immediately rang Yardley Laboratories.

'Mills? I'm looking at the DNA results for Madison Roberts. The report says it's inconclusive.'

'Yes, Donna explained to me that even with a potential match it's impossible to produce a clear identification. Madison's DNA is mixed up in it.'

'Does that mean if we find a suspect it might not be possible to match it?'

'It's possible.'

'You don't sound sure.'

'I'm not. Not one hundred percent.'

Hazel had arrived and was waving at Nina to finish the call.

'We're going to Richmond now!' her friend called. They've got Herbie, Robbie, and maybe even a taxi driver, ready for interview. I'll explain on the way.'

Nina waited until Hazel was driving them towards Richmond before asking about the taxi driver. Her friend explained how she'd met him the night before in Richmond.

'And guess what? I go in this morning and Ruby is waiting to pounce like a little cat. She tells me she's computed all the calls Madison made to the taxi firm against the times of call outs and discovered that more often than not it's the same driver. The poor girl is about to give me the name of the driver when I go *Stop, let me guess – Jim Scallion*. She was actually speechless. One more victory for practical policing.'

'Did she have the same name?'

'Of course.'

'So we're speaking to him this morning?'

'If they found him at the address he gave me. They had a problem locating young Herbie. Apparently he doesn't stay at his parents often and they eventually hauled him out of a grotty flat belonging to a known user.'

They reached the police station at nine-thirty.

'We'll take Robbie first,' said Hazel. 'He might even answer our questions honestly. He's with one of his parents.'

Robbie had been accompanied to the police station by his mother, who was anxious to know what trouble he was in. Nina reassured her that if he answered their questions truthfully there was nothing for her to worry about. She hoped she was right. The lad looked as though he'd not slept. Hazel led the questioning after assuring him that he was only there to help them with their enquiries. He looked at his mother nervously.

'I have three simple questions,' Hazel began. 'If you can answer me clearly and honestly, then you will be out of here in ten minutes.'

His mother looked relieved.

'The first question is whether you knew Madison Roberts. She was an American girl studying at High Fell School.'

'She called herself Mads.'

'So you did know her?'

'Yes.'

'Ok. Secondly, did you see her between Wednesday the twenty-ninth of June and Saturday the second of July?'

'No.'

'Are you sure?' asked Hazel.

His mother leaned forward. 'He wasn't well last week. I wouldn't let him go out.'

'Thirdly, have you ever given her drugs or seen anyone else give her drugs?'

He was shaking his head vigorously. His mother looked alarmed.

'I haven't done anything illegal,' he said. 'And I never gave her anything.'

'What about sex?' Nina asked, looking directly at him.

His mother gave a quiet involuntary squeal. The boy reddened.

'No way!'

'Then tell me about Herbie,' she asked.

Robbie's mother leaned forward. 'I'll tell you about that Herbie,' she said suddenly. 'He's a good-for-nothing with no parental control. I've told Robert not to go about with him and from now on he won't be going anywhere near him or his father won't be responsible for his actions.' She sniffed loudly.

Nina looked at Robbie's downturned face. 'Is it possible that Herbie and Madison were having sex?'

He shrugged.

'Is that a yes?'

'I don't know, honestly.'

'And was he supplying her with drugs?'

'Legal, yes – probably.'

Nina warned him that "legal highs" were no longer legal before letting him go and as she led them out, Robbie's mother thanked her profusely, promising to ground him for the next six months. Nina wished her luck with that, knowing very well from Hazel's experiences how difficult it was to keep a teenage boy at home in the evenings and weekends.

Nina re-joined her friend, who was busy interrogating Herbie in her inimitable style.

'… so you are saying that Madison joined your house parties of her own free will, that she was drinking heavily and taking these so-called legal highs like they were going out of fashion?'

'Too right, she was.' The young man seemed to be enjoying himself. 'She was a fun-loving girl.'

'And when these parties went on all night, did she sleep anywhere?'

'She'd just crash where she was – at the flat usually.'

'Were you two in a relationship? Would you say that you were her boyfriend?'

He laughed. He had a nasty cruel laugh. 'No way!'

'You didn't fancy her?'

'No.'

'Did she have a boyfriend?'

'Don't know. She didn't mention anyone, except…'

'Yes?'

'She sometimes went on about someone when she was really pissed. Sounded like he might've been a married man, you know.'

'So, you didn't ever have sex with her?'

'No.'

'We'll know if you're lying.'

'How?'

'Science, Herbie, science.'

'What *were* you talking about, Hazel?' Nina asked when the interview was over. 'Science? What was that about?'

'Sorry, I got a bit carried away. But did you see his face? That's why I asked for a sample of his DNA. Interesting that he refused at first.'

'Will you get a sample from the taxi driver too?'

'Probably. Let's see what he's got to say.'

They returned to the tiny interview room where a middle-aged man was now waiting. His jacket was crumpled and his hair looked in need of a good wash. The room was beginning to smell of smoke. Hazel turned to Nina and explained, unnecessarily, that she'd met Mr Scallion at the taxi rank the evening before. Nina told him her name and explained that they wanted to ask him about Madison Roberts since he might have met her. He sat calmly with his arms folded, listening to her without responding, a hint of a smirk appearing as she spoke.

'Do you ever pick up girls from High Fell School in your taxi to take them into town?'

'Yes.' He nodded in an exaggerated way.

'Have you ever given an American girl called Madison Roberts a lift into town in your taxi?'

'I don't know all their names.'

'You would have to have a name when they gave you the address, surely?' Hazel asked.

'Not necessarily. They may just say pick up at the school.' He smiled at them.

Nina showed him the picture of Madison given to her by her mother. She was in skiing outfit, posing in front of a ski-lift.

'Do you recognise her?'

'Not sure. They all look alike to me.'

Hazel was getting ready to intervene. 'Changing the subject,' she began, 'how do you know Herbie Mason?'

'I don't.' His arms were resting on the table now, his shoulders were relaxed.

'But I saw you talking to him and his mate last night. They ran off when they saw me coming.'

'Them? I don't know them – well, I've seen them around.'

'What did they want?' she asked.

'Just a light, that's all. I told them to clear off. Druggies. You want to ask them about that young girl.' He pointed at the photograph.

'Have you seen them together?' Nina asked.

'Yes.' He was looking relaxed now. 'Now you come to mention it, I think they were quite close.'

He stood up and pushed his chair away. 'Can I go now, only I've got a job to do this morning at the airport? Can't let them down, can I?'

Nina looked at her colleague, who nodded. He was out as soon as she opened the door.

'No DNA sample then?' she asked.

Hazel sighed. 'I think he knew her but there's no grounds for taking a sample, sadly.'

She kicked the chair back into place and led the way out into the sunshine. They stood discussing the case in the car park. Hazel expressed the view that Herbie Mason was being implicated at every turn and she was going to speak to whoever had been behind the bar at "The Fleece" on Friday night.

'Are you coming with me? If we can prove he was there with Madison that night, he's the last one to see her alive and we're bringing him in.'

'Mitch wants me to update the parents, not that there's much to report. I have to get down there now. And there is one other lead we haven't really dealt with yet: the drama teacher, Jeremy Young. I spoke to Fran, one of the pupils from the school. She mentioned him again. There's nothing concrete but plenty of rumour about him having a relationship with Madison. I think we should follow it up.'

'Ok. I'll check him out when I've visited "The Fleece". You get off to your family liaison duties.'

Nina knew the reason her friend made disparaging remarks about her liaison role was because she had been unsuccessful at it herself. Somewhat lacking in emotional intelligence is how Nina would have put it. It was disappointing that she wouldn't meet this teacher but doubtless Hazel would establish if there was any truth in the rumours.

Nina parked on the cobbled street in front of the Georgian hotel where the Roberts were staying. Inside the smell of furniture polish combined with the scented roses on the hall table. She waited in the beautifully furnished lounge, expecting to see the whole family appear but it was just the middle-aged couple. Madison's father helped his wife onto the soft-cushioned sofa. She seemed frailer than before. The place was quiet, deserted except for a member of staff hovering by the door. Nina was offered coffee but declined, anxious to get to the point of her visit.

'Is your son joining us?' she asked.

'He went for a walk.' Mr Roberts looked out of the window. 'He's not back yet. We'll continue without him.'

'I thought it was best if we saw you alone.' Mrs Roberts' voice was thin, almost a whisper.

Nina was admiring the antique furniture. How she would love to stay here with Nige for just one night, although her husband would say it was too posh for him to enjoy. Mr Roberts joined his wife on the sofa. They sat stiffly, side by side and stared expectantly. Nina took the armchair by the large ornate fireplace.

'I'm afraid there's not a lot to tell you,' she began. 'We've been following a few leads and may have found the friends your daughter was meeting in town in the evenings.' She waited for a response but they remained quiet. 'My colleague is speaking to the barman now, to see if anyone saw Madison on Friday evening.'

'Who are these "friends" you speak of?' asked Mr Roberts, showing no emotion. 'Are they from her school – or Austin's?'

'No.' Nina took a deep breath. 'He…' She stopped and started again, forcing her voice down an octave. 'He's a local lad. I think they probably met in a pub he frequents.'

'Where is this pub?' he asked.

'In town, it could have been anywhere.' Nina quickly changed the subject. She didn't want Madison's father paying a visit. 'We are also talking to a taxi driver who she may have used.' She swallowed hard, wishing she'd accepted the coffee because it would have delayed saying the next bit for a few more minutes. At least Austin wasn't present. 'I have something rather delicate to say about your daughter and we thought you should know before it comes out in any court proceedings. Madison was not sexually assaulted before she died…'

'Yes, they told us,' said Mrs Roberts. 'It was a relief to hear that.'

'… but she had had sexual intercourse.'

'What do you mean?' the woman asked. 'How can that be if she hadn't been assaulted?'

'The pathologist believes it was consensual.' She took a deep breath. 'Did you know that your daughter was sexually active?'

'Of course she wasn't!' insisted her mother. 'She was only just sixteen, a schoolgirl for pity's sake.'

Her husband patted her shoulder. 'What my wife is trying to say is that we brought her up as a good Christian and in the way of the bible. We don't like to hear what you have to say.' He looked crushed.

'I'm very sorry to come with such information but it's important you are fully informed.' She smiled sympathetically, she hoped.

The smart American woman, who had appeared so composed when Nina first met her, seemed smaller as she shrank back on her seat, her face in a handkerchief. Her husband looked uncomfortable, unsure how to comfort her, embarrassed in the presence of a stranger.

Nina thought it best to leave them, ensuring they had her number in case they had any questions. It had been an awkward encounter and she was left feeling annoyed that she'd handled it so badly.

Outside she was greeted by a young man.

'Hi ma'am.'

She immediately recognised Madison's brother.

'Hello Austin. I'm sorry I missed you.'

'No, that's fine. Mom asked me to stay away and I wanted to speak with you on my own, if that's ok?'

'Of course. Do you want to go back inside?'

'No, it won't take long.'

Nina waited.

'I went back to school yesterday. I told my parents I wanted to see my friends. I did but I wanted to speak with them about my sister. See, there were boys who knew her. Well, they'd seen her outside. Just a few of them but I wanted to ask them whether it was true, what they'd said. I only found two guys but one told me that he'd seen her at parties using alcohol, cigarettes and tabs, you know?'

'Were you surprised?'

'Not really. She was getting out of control when we came over to England. That was three years ago. Pop's vice-president of a pharmaceutical company and we came over here for a year with him when he was working with the UK affiliate. At first we were based in London and went to a school in St John's Wood. It was fine at first but my sister was mugged walking home one day after school. It was dark and she was alone. The guy attacked her and she was lucky a jogger came along when he did.'

'Did they catch the man?' Nina asked.

'No. He ran off. She said she was glad because it meant she didn't have to face him again. I think it left a mental scar. She began to act a bit crazy after that. Pop was moved to the site up here and we were put into boarding schools because he didn't know where he'd be sent next.'

'Did your sister get any counselling?'

'No. I think her behaviour was caused by the attack. She never spoke about it to me or anyone else as far as I know. My mom didn't cope with it well.'

She waited. He stared at the ground. A car revved its engine.

'Well ma'am, I just wanted to tell you what I heard from the other boy at school because it's important. He said he'd seen her with our teacher, Jeremy Young.'

'Seen her?'

'Yep. She was with him, hanging onto him. They were kissing and such.'

'Really?'

'Sure. He was up on the moors near her school, doing nature study, bird-watching or something geeky. They were definitely together, didn't even see him. The guy went red when he was telling me what they were up to.'

'Do you think he's reliable?'

'Totally. He's a bit of a nerd. He didn't enjoy telling me. I had to kinda persuade him.'

'If what you say is true, I have to go and talk to Mr Young about this accusation. You do understand?'

'Look, my sister has been killed by someone. I'm not saying he has anything to do with it but if he knows something about what she was doing when she was missing, you gotta ask him.'

'Right. Thank you, Austin. I may need you to give me all this in writing.'

'You won't tell Mom, will you? She'll go crazy. She's already crazy with grief. You see, she blames herself for sending Mads away. And she's probably right.'

He walked slowly towards the hotel and then seemed to change his mind. Nina watched him amble back toward the town centre before calling her colleague.

'Hazel? I'll meet you at the school. I think Jeremy Young needs to give us some answers.'

'Is there somewhere we can have a quiet word?' Hazel asked.

The drama teacher looked ill at ease in the presence of his headmaster and Nina watched her colleague using the situation to make the poor man even more discomfited.

'It shouldn't take long but it does concern an important police matter.'

They followed Mr Young along the panelled corridor to a small room. The sign on the door indicated it was the Staff Library. He assured them they wouldn't be disturbed as they seated themselves formally at the highly polished table in the centre of the room. As usual Hazel took the lead while Nina made notes. She began by explaining that they were investigating the death of Madison Roberts.

'We understand you knew her.'

He looked blankly at them. 'Should I?'

'She was a pupil at High Fell School. You were producing their play?'

'Oh yes, of course. But I don't think she was in the cast.'

'How can you say, if you don't know her?'

He looked startled. 'Because I knew all the actors.'

'So are you saying you didn't know Madison?'

He seemed to be deciding how to respond.

'I have information that a witness saw you and Madison kissing. What do you say to that?'

He closed his eyes for a while. Eventually he opened them again and sighed. 'Yes, I got entangled with her. She threw herself on me and I was, well, flattered I suppose. At least that's what Diane thinks.'

'Diane?' asked Hazel.

'My wife. She found out and I stopped it. I told Madison it couldn't go on.'

'When was this?'

He thought about it. 'Last Wednesday. She came to the house. There was a scene. She left.'

'Was that the last time you saw her?'

'Yes.'

'You see, that might have been the last time anyone saw her. Do you know where she went?'

'I dropped her at the bus stop; she wanted to go into town.'

'One last question: where were you last Friday night?'

'At home, all evening. All night.'

'We'll want to have a word with your wife as well, Mr Young,' said Hazel.

Nina fetched her swab kit from the car and asked him to open his mouth. His forehead was glistening with sweat as she took a DNA sample from inside his cheek.

As he showed them out, he asked when they would be talking to Diane. Nina was deliberately vague. She didn't trust him and wanted to be sure to see Diane Young alone.

'Do you think she might have done something stupid – Madison, I mean. She was very upset when she left and I was worried she might… you know… harm herself.'

Hazel was unlocking her car. 'No, Mr Young, she didn't harm herself. Someone else harmed her.'

Chapter 21

DCI Mitch Turner wanted an update on the Madison Roberts case when Nina and Hazel were back in the office. They went over the interviews with Herbie Mason, Jim Scallion and Jeremy Young. Ruby was working on a timeline and wanted to know if they had any more intelligence on where Madison had been between Wednesday afternoon and Saturday morning. Hazel told them what she'd discovered at "The Fleece". It seemed that after Jeremy Young left her at the bus stop on Wednesday, she ended up in the pub for the evening, getting drunk with Herbie and his friends. The barman threw them out at ten, threatening to call the police.

'If only he had,' said Nina.

'We can track where they went on CCTV,' said Hazel.

Ruby snorted. 'You'll be lucky, they turned off the town cameras two years ago through lack of funds.'

'Listen,' Hazel continued. 'They were back in on Friday night, the same crowd. This time they'd obviously been drinking when they arrived. They were loud and abusive and were ejected immediately by the landlord and barred from the pub altogether.'

'He remembered Madison?' asked Mitch.

'Oh yes, she was worse for wear. They were almost carrying her.'

'Then someone will have seen her in town. We should do a reconstruction,' suggested Nina.

The subsequent silence was broken by Mitch. 'This Herbie character was the last person to be seen with her alive. We'll bring him in now as a suspect.

Meanwhile we need to know where he went with her after that.'

'I can go back to the list of taxi bookings to check if she used a cab that night,' Ruby suggested.

Mitch was surprised that the company would know such details but she explained they had to keep records of every booking for six months, including where the journey started, the destination, the name of the person hiring the vehicle and the time the vehicle was allocated to the booking.

Hazel suggested to Mitch that they take DNA from Jim Scallion, to clear him from their list of suspects.

'You don't need to,' said Ruby. 'He was arrested for affray in 2010, so he'll be on the database already.'

Nina reported on their talk with the drama teacher but Mitch simply told her to speak to his wife to confirm his story. No-one else shared her view that he was also a plausible suspect. She went back to her desk, where a pile of paperwork was waiting, including full details of the French post-mortem on Cecile Fleurot. The pathologist had translated the French before sending it on but the original text was included and Nina noted that the French common word for the herb rue was "rue de grace". It struck her as both beautiful and chilling. Wasn't there a song that went: ...*and darling there you go, slipping away into a state of grace*?

She shook herself and began to read the report, slowly and carefully. There was a lot of scientific experimentation included, apparently to test what residues they might be looking for. It wasn't one hundred percent definite but they did find some matching toxins in her body. The conclusion of Dr Moreau was that there was no liver damage, that could be expected, but, importantly, rue can cause seizures and that might have been a possible cause for her drowning. However, there was no physical evidence to confirm that proposition. The conclusion remained "accidental death".

Nina read on, expecting to see the results of the DNA test on the foetus but there was only brief mention of it. It appeared there was nothing to report yet. The final section told her that the French pathologist would be sending an English colleague over if it required giving evidence at a second inquest. Nina was fairly sure that wouldn't be necessary if the verdict remained the same: an accident.

When she explained the outcome to Hazel, her colleague had questions about the implications of Cecile consuming a dangerous amount of rue extract. Did the dead girl know what she was doing? Did Madison know the consequences of giving her the rue? Was it possible that the American girl knew how it would affect her? Nina agreed they might never be able to answer that but it could be relevant to Madison's own death. Was someone taking revenge?

'In my opinion, the person responsible for Cecile's death is the father of her unborn baby,' announced Hazel. 'If she hadn't been pregnant, she wouldn't have taken the rue.'

'That's why we must find out who it is. When the DNA comes through we'll have the answer. Herbie Mason will be on the database tomorrow.'

Ruby had waited until there was a pause in the discussion. 'I've been through the taxi bookings,' she said. 'There's nothing on Wednesday evening or after that.'

'Not even on Friday night?' Nina decided to try her suggestion out on Hazel. 'We could go down tonight and see if anyone remembers her.'

'We could ask Mitch to get uniform onto it,' her friend replied. 'And *he* can organise an appeal on TV. If we're working through the weekend, we need some time off.' She didn't mention her ticket for Liam's school play as she went to find her boss.

'Oh well, I'm off to see Diane Young,' said Nina to Ruby, gathering her things, including Cecile Fleurot's pathology report. 'Tell Hazel I'll see her tomorrow.'

As she drove to Scorton, Nina rang Mills to find out where she was working. She left a message on her mobile. *I have the results of the French PM. If you're at the university, drop in on your way home and I can talk you through it.*

In half an hour she was parking outside the neat cottage, hoping that Mr Young didn't get home early on a Friday. She was relieved when a young, heavily pregnant woman opened the door and waved her into a small sitting room.

'I'm sorry, Jeremy isn't here yet.'

She waited for Nina to sit before lowering herself down onto the arm of the sofa.

'That's fine; I just wanted a quick chat with you to check on some timings. You understand we are investigating the death…'

'Yes, I know. That poor girl. I felt physically sick when I heard about it and realised it was her. Such a young, lively kid. And I'd only seen her a few days before she was found. How horrible.'

'This is rather delicate but your husband said…'

'That they'd been in a relationship?' She straightened up. 'I knew all about it.'

'I understand he finished with her last Wednesday?'

'Yes. She came to the house and we discussed it. We… he decided it was the right thing to do. Is he in trouble because of her age?'

'I can't comment on that at present. Can you tell me what time she left on Wednesday?'

She considered for a moment. 'I suppose it was around five.'

'Did she leave alone?'

'No. I told my husband to take her back to the school.'

'And did he?' Nina asked.

'Yes.'

Clearly he hadn't told her that he'd left her at the bus stop.

'How long did it take to drive to the school?'

She was standing now. 'I don't know. Not long. He was back quite soon.'

Nina was finding the next question difficult to express. 'We are trying to establish whether Madison might have seen your husband in the period between Wednesday afternoon and Saturday morning.'

'No.'

'So it wouldn't have been possible for her to have had a relationship with your husband after last Wednesday?'

'No!'

She was standing with her hands folded across her bump. It occurred to Nina that she had a lot to lose if her husband had continued to see the teenager. He had also jeopardised his career. It still could cost him his job.

'When she left here…' Diane's voice was shaky. 'When Jeremy took her away from here, that was that. He came back, he said he was sorry and that was the end of it.'

Nina could tell the poor woman was close to tears and decided to ask one last question and leave it there.

'Can you tell me where you and your husband were last Friday night?'

'Here. We were here all evening.'

'And overnight?'

'Of course.'

She thanked her, gave her a card with her number on, and saw herself out, relieved that a difficult interview was at an end. She sat in the car for a few minutes before calling Ruby with the important details of her conversation with Diane Young. If Madison had gone back to school, no-one there had seen her again on Wednesday. There were witnesses who'd seen her in the pub that evening and again on the Friday night before her body was discovered. Nina wanted to know where Madison had been but it wasn't as important as knowing who she was with after she was ejected from the pub on Friday night with Herbie. The lad would be in custody ready for interview the following morning but for now it was time to collect the kids and get home ready for Nige's arrival from the airport.

It took Hazel much longer than anticipated to liaise with uniform over the hunt for witnesses in Richmond town centre that evening. By the time Mitch had persuaded the duty inspector to round up sufficient officers for the job and to arrest Herbie Mason; she was already late for Liam's performance. Friday traffic was worse than usual and she was twenty minutes late when she tiptoed into the hall and felt her way to an empty seat in the back row.

She couldn't see what was happening on the stage unless she leaned to one side and even then she couldn't hear what they were saying. Not that it would make much sense to her anyway. She could see a row of soldiers shuffling on but from that distance it was impossible to tell which one was her Liam. She wished now she'd volunteered to take witness statements back in Richmond. Instead she passed the time until the interval by going over the facts of the case in her head without interruption.

In the interval parents were greeting one another like long lost friends. The noise level rose as conversations became more animated. Hazel bought herself a glass of wine and stood against the wall, surveying the mass of thirty- and forty-something men and women. She knew no-one. She'd met some of Liam's friends but she'd never been introduced to their parents. Being a single mother and a police officer was a life of juggling which, fortunately, Liam was perfectly accustomed to. Tempted to rush home but obediently returning to her seat when the bell rang, Hazel closed her eyes. She concentrated on the case, only to be woken by loud applause. The play was over and the soldiers were taking their bow. Hazel clapped as Liam traipsed off the stage after his peers.

Herbie Mason was accompanied by a duty solicitor who had clearly advised him against saying too much. Nina and Hazel had agreed they would focus on the Friday night, since it was the key to Madison's final hours. Hazel took delight in explaining to Herbie that they knew he was with her in "The

Fleece" on Friday and that they were thrown out at around nine o'clock. He sat placidly picking his fingers.

'So can you tell us where you went then?'

No reply.

'Do you know where Madison went?'

'No.'

At last, a response.

'When did you last see her?'

'When we left the pub. I wanted another drink but she said she was getting a taxi. She just went.'

'You let her go in that state?'

He shrugged.

'And you didn't see her after that?'

'No.'

Hazel looked at Nina, who asked, 'Herbie, did you have sex with her that evening or in the days before that?'

'No.' He was barely audible.

'Can you repeat your answer, please?'

He looked up and yelled, 'I told you before... No!'

'I should warn you that we have your DNA and will be able to confirm whether what you are saying is true.'

After that he refused to answer their questions.

They left him with his solicitor and made their way back to Newby Wiske together, where Mitch was waiting for them with news from the police activity in Richmond on the previous evening.

'Something positive from the taxi rank,' he said. 'A driver had Madison in a very drunk or drugged state, trying to get into his taxi. He refused to take her and she staggered down the line. He wasn't sure whether she got someone to take her but he gave a list of the cabs on the rank and Jim Scallion was there that night.'

'Yes!' shouted Hazel. 'I knew it. And if he picked her up it wouldn't necessarily appear as a booking if he didn't tell his boss.'

'True. Ruby, we need to do a trace on his phone to find out exactly where he went on Friday night. And you two get him in for formal interview. His name is cropping up too frequently for it to be a coincidence.'

Hazel organised for Scallion to be picked up while Nina sent a text to find out if Mason's DNA had been registered on the national database. Mills rang back immediately.

'Are you working today, Nina?'

'Yes. It's a murder enquiry.'

'Still no news?'

'Not really. We've arrested a couple of men but to be honest we've not got much to go on. We really need a DNA match.'

'Well, Donna has finished the sample and entered it on the national database, so if you haven't heard anything…'

'There was no match this morning. By the way, I've got the report from France and they've made some progress on the DNA from Cecile's baby. How do we test that against the database?'

'That's easy. We can get it through the Interpol Gateway. Just tell them to submit it and we'll be able to access it.'

'We need it as soon as possible.'

'Ok, send me their contact details and I'll arrange it.'

Five minutes later, Mills was emailing the French pathologist, requesting the information. She was surprised to receive a reply so quickly, particularly from a name she recognised: Phil Freedman. He was looking after the case while Dr Moreau was away on holiday. The message was rather formal but she understood that it would be in the official records so she replied in the same vein, asking him to transfer the DNA profile of the unborn child through Interpol. She then rang Nina back to let her know the information was on its way and told her she would drive to the lab so she could carry out the check as soon as the results came in.

Ruby quickly confirmed that Scallion's phone had been triangulated to an area around Scorton on Friday evening from nine-twenty-three to nine-thirty-nine.

'At last we're getting somewhere,' Nina said when she was updating Mitch with their progress. 'Scallion is in custody and there's just one more thing I need to check before I go over to interview him.'

Mitch agreed, it sounded as though they had solved the case. She went back to her desk to have one more look at her inbox, just in case the DNA database had magically matched Scallion as Madison's attacker. She left a message for Mills to check if he was a match for the sample taken from the dead girl and to call her the moment she had any information. Grabbing her bag, she rushed off to interview the taxi driver.

Scallion had spoken to a solicitor and refused to answer any of her questions. She put it to him that he had been in the Scorton area where Madison was found dead. She had witnesses that placed the girl in the middle of Richmond, in a drunken state, looking for a taxi on the Friday night. She asked him if he gave her a lift. 'No comment.' Did he have an alibi for Friday night? 'No comment.' She listed her questions about his movements and received no reply to any of them. Eventually she left him to remain in custody, hoping she would have sufficient information by the morning to charge him with the murder of Madison Roberts.

Returning to Newby Wiske, she brought Mitch and the others up to date then made a call.

'Please say you've got something for me, Mills.'

'Actually I've got two,' her friend replied. 'The DNA you sent from Mr Jeremy Young is a reasonable match to that from Madison Roberts. Donna says it will never be perfect because of the presence of Madison's DNA but it is quite good.'

Nina made a quick note before asking for the second piece of news.

'It's about the sample from Cecile's foetus. There is a match to James Scallion.'

'Really?'

'Does that make sense?'

'No… Well yes, I think it might. Thanks Mills, that's really interesting.'

'I'll send the reports over when I get the signatures for you.'

Nina called Nige and told him not to expect her home just yet. Hazel was due in soon and now they had a link between Scallion and the rape of the French schoolgirl, it seemed the taxi driver was not as innocent as he wished to appear. She hoped Hazel could help her persuade him to answer their questions now.

Chapter 22

The clock was ticking, literally, as they sat opposite Jim Scallion in the stuffy interview room. Hazel was looking uncomfortably hot in her ribbed sweater, Nina noted. The taxi driver's face was shiny with sweat and the solicitor had loosened the neck of his shirt in an attempt to keep cool. Nina felt relaxed and calm, pleased they had something to rattle Scallion with.

'… so we're waiting for an answer, Jim,' Hazel was saying. 'Can you tell us how you knew Cecile Fleurot?'

She was pushing a photograph of the girl in front of him but he seemed unwilling to look at it.

'I am showing you a picture of Cecile. You recognise her?'

He shook his head.

'You don't think so? She was a pupil at High Fell School, like Madison Roberts. And she's dead, sadly. Are you sure you never met her?'

No answer.

'She was pregnant when she died. She'd been raped. Did you know that paternity cases can be determined even from an unborn child?'

He was wiping sweat from his forehead with the palm of his hand.

'Would it surprise you if I told you that the unborn child carries your DNA?'

The solicitor looked at Scallion, his face expressing shock.

His client shook his head and rested his arms on the table. 'No comment.'

Hazel then arrested him for the rape of Cecile Fleurot and he was returned to custody.

'We'll get him for the rape charge *and* the murder of Madison Roberts,' said Hazel as they returned to Newby Wiske.

'You think?' asked Nina. 'We've got no proof yet.'

'He was in the area; he lied about knowing her and he is clearly a man who preys on teenage girls.'

'I suppose so but we need to talk to Jeremy Young,' replied Nina. 'He said he'd finished with Madison but we've got evidence they'd been together soon before she died. I'd like to know where he was on Friday night.'

'You go home and get some sleep, we'll sort the drama teacher out in the morning.'

'What about you?'

'I had a kip this afternoon while Liam was doing the matinee performance of his play.'

'Is there one tonight?'

'Oh yes, and the end of show party. I suspect he won't be back tonight.'

'Don't you worry about him being out late?'

'Of course I do but I trust him. I have to, don't I? I can't leave him with the babysitter now he's grown up!'

Nina left Hazel and went home to catch some sleep. The children were waiting up for her and she helped Nige get them into bed before collapsing on the sofa.

'Hard day?' Nige asked.

And before she could answer, he described the hectic time he'd had with the boys and Rosie. She agreed it was no fun at the supermarket when Tomos and Owen were overtired and irritable. Rosie had tried to be helpful but even placid Nige had been exasperated by the experience. He'd taken them to the park in the afternoon but the boys were bickering on the way home. Only ice-cream had restored calm and they had all fallen asleep in front of a video, including Nige.

Nina woke to hear the landline phone ringing. Looking up she could see her husband had his "irritable" face on.

'That was Hazel,' he said when he'd thrown the handset down on the sofa. 'She wants you to go in tomorrow morning.'

'That's ok,' said Nina, sitting up.

'I thought we were going to have a day out somewhere. I haven't seen you for a week.'

'Do you know why she wanted me there?' said Nina, ignoring the jibe.

'It's something about interviewing someone again.'

Nina picked up the phone. By the time she'd finished speaking to Hazel, Nige had taken himself off to bed and appeared to be asleep.

'It's important, Nige. He's asked for his solicitor and he says he's going to talk to us.'

Mills had spent the rest of the afternoon at the lab sorting out paperwork. It was a perfect opportunity to get up to date while no-one else was around to disturb her. Alex was at a stag do and she wasn't picking him up from Northallerton station until later. She was going through her emails when she spotted the message from Phil. It was a shock yet again to see his name after such a long period. Once, she had been certain he was "the one" but time was a great healer and she was sure they would be good friends. He had probably changed a lot since she'd last seen him. Working on mass graves in Colombia was a grim job, although clearly he was now in Paris helping the French pathologist. And he was coming over to see her about Cecile's inquest.

She spent a long time compiling her reply to Phil. There were several false starts and it took a while to get just the right tone of friendliness without familiarity. She said she was looking forward to seeing him and asked when he would be arriving. She carried on with her work but found it difficult to concentrate, telling herself he wouldn't reply immediately. In fact it was only half an hour before she was alerted to his message.

Hi Mills, great to hear from you and can't wait to be back in the Dales. My flight is booked for Tuesday. I'm flying into Manchester & staying in Harrogate.

Mills wondered whether he'd be in a hotel, or maybe he had a friend in town – a woman, perhaps. But encouraged by the tone of his email, she replied, asking where he was staying and how long he'd be around. The answer came back immediately: he was booked into the "Cairn Hotel" until the following Monday. He was happy to come to the lab whenever it was convenient for her. She replied that she was free any time on Wednesday morning and would expect him.

As she drove to the station, she found herself thinking about what to wear to the lab on Wednesday. Would she look overdressed in her new top? Should she look more "business-like"? He never dressed smartly. He'd had to borrow a suit when he was best man at his friend's wedding... was it really five years ago? And spending time in Colombia excavating graves of victims of the paramilitaries would hardly have refined his dress sense. She was still thinking about him when Alex appeared by the car.

'Had a good time?' Mills asked, not really wanting to know what he'd been doing.

He spent the entire journey relaying juvenile antics he and his friends had been up to over the weekend. Mills wasn't listening until he began to tell her about this amazing flat his friend lives in.

'It's in Streatham, nearly in the middle of London.'

Mills didn't argue, even though his geography of London was so disastrous.

'It's got three bedrooms and I can move in at the end of the month. London is so amazing.'

'I know – I used to live in Purley,' Mills said. 'About seven miles away.'

'So you know what a buzz the place has. You'll love it.'

It appeared the flat was shared by Alex's best mate, Bill, and two other university friends: Roisin and Dot. Roisin was moving out to get married and so it would be her room he would be taking over.

'Are Bill and Dot an item?' she asked.

'No, just mates.'

So Alex was leaving her to live in London with a girl called Dot.

'You'll get on well with her,' Alex added. 'You'll like her.'

'Will I?' Mills asked.

Nina left before the rest of the family were properly awake. Closing the front door gently behind her and pulling the car door as quietly as possible, she felt a guilty sense of relief as she set off through the empty streets to Richmond.

Hazel was waiting for her with a paper cup of coffee. 'It should still be hot. I've only just drunk mine.'

They went into the police station together, where Scallion's solicitor was waiting. He looked tired and greeted them with a limp wave.

'Let's get it over with, shall we?' said Hazel briskly. 'Then we can all get back to bed.'

He smiled wanly, followed them to the interview room and waited for his client to appear.

If they'd had little sleep, Scallion appeared to have had less. There were bags under his eyes and his unshaven face was drawn and anxious.

'My client would like to make a statement,' the solicitor began.

'Fine,' said Hazel. 'Let's get on with it then.'

She switched on the tape and sat upright looking expectantly at Scallion. Nina was poised with her note-pad. There was a pause while the solicitor whispered something to him. Then Scallion took a deep breath.

'I want to make a statement,' he said. 'I want to make it clear that I may have had sexual relations with the French girl but it was consensual.'

Hazel looked at Nina with raised eyebrows. She said nothing.

The taxi driver continued. 'I also want to say that I might have driven the American girl on Friday night but I left her alive and well in Scorton.'

Silence. That was the end of his "statement".

Nina looked at Hazel, who nodded.

'Mr Scallion,' Nina began. 'We have evidence, from Cecile herself, that she was raped. You have admitted that you had sex with her and, whatever you say, she was underage and therefore you will be charged with rape. Do you understand?'

He sank back in the chair, his head dropped onto his chest. His solicitor indicated that his client understood.

Now it was Hazel's turn. He had admitted that he drove Madison as far as Scorton. What time was that?

'I dropped her off about half nine.'

'Was she with anyone?'

'No.'

'What did you do then?'

'Drove back to Richmond.'

'Straight away?'

'Yes.'

'What state was Madison in when you left her?'

'Her usual state – half cut.'

'And where did you leave her?'

'In the middle of Scorton. She said she wanted Scorton. She didn't give me an address.'

'And you just left her there, on her own?'

'Yes.'

They probed and pressed him but that was his story and he was sticking to it. They had proof he'd been in Scorton at that time for fifteen minutes, long enough to drag Madison to the quarry and kill her. After calls back and forth, Mitch informed them he was to be charged with the rape of Cecile Fleurot and the murder of Madison Roberts.

They grabbed a late breakfast in a small café on the edge of town. Hazel was jubilant about the success of their investigation but Nina pointed out they had no forensic evidence to prove that Scallion had harmed Madison and wondered if the CPS would accept the charge.

'What about DNA? We can look for a match, now we know who we're looking for.'

'We already have one, Hazel,' Nina explained. 'Mills rang yesterday. The DNA belongs to Jeremy Young.'

Hazel shrugged. 'Well, we know he was having it off with her.'

'Yes, and he was at home all evening with his wife so Madison didn't go to Scorton to see him. But I'm still puzzled since he swore he had stopped seeing her.'

'So Scallion didn't rape Madison but he still murdered her. Perhaps she put up a fight.'

'There would've been forensic evidence in that case, Hazel. You know: under her nails... bruises on her wrists... There wasn't anything like that.'

'What are you suggesting?'

'Let's assume Scallion is telling the truth and Madison went to Scorton, hoping to see Jeremy Young but his wife is at home. She goes up the lane to the quarry – perhaps they used to meet there. It would still be light. Loads of people go there dog walking, bird-watching, jogging. Anyone could have taken her by surprise and attacked her.'

'That's right, Nina, blow the case wide open again when we have a perfectly good suspect in custody already.'

'I just think we should talk to Young again, to establish when he did last see Madison, in view of the DNA results.'

Hazel suggested seeing Jeremy Young immediately as it was on the way back to Newby Wiske. Nina wanted to ring him first but her colleague relished the prospect of surprising the poor man in his own home.

'His wife will be upset if we just descend on them out of the blue,' protested Nina.

'Good,' Hazel responded.

Nina saw a curtain move as they parked outside the house and the door was opened almost as soon as she pressed the bell. Jeremy Young was dressed in shorts and polo shirt.

'I was just on my way out,' he said, opening the door wider to let them in, while looking up and down the street.

'We won't keep you long,' promised Hazel.

They were ushered into the tiny sitting room and joined by Diane. Nina introduced her colleague and explained they wanted to tie up a few loose ends. She asked if Jeremy would prefer to have the conversation in private but he shook his head and everyone took a seat.

Nina began, nervously. 'We have received forensic evidence taken from Madison Roberts that suggests you had intercourse with her within a few days of her death.'

She let the sentence hang there, waiting for a response. When there was none she felt compelled to continue.

'You told me that she came here on the Wednesday before she was murdered but you finished with her and took her back to school. Is that correct?'

'Yes.' His response was barely audible.

'Did you have sex with her on that occasion?'

He looked at Diane and then at Nina. Taking hold of his wife's hand he sighed and cleared his throat.

'We're waiting Mr Young.' Hazel was pushing, as usual.

'Look, this is awkward. She was upset and I tried to comfort her.' Diane pulled her hand away. 'It was a rash moment.' He turned to his wife. 'I'm so sorry.'

But she didn't seem crushed. She wasn't crying. She didn't even look upset. She looked angry.

'The forensic evidence suggests you did more than comfort her, Mr Young.' Nina had hoped she wouldn't have to go into details. 'The sample was of an intimate nature.'

He bowed his head. 'I know. It was unforgiveable.'

Hazel looked triumphant. 'It could also result in a prosecution if we find you have abused your position of trust to engage in sexual activity, Mr Young. It will be the end of your teaching career, that's for sure.'

Nina, who was keen to finish the interview as soon as she could, asked them to confirm that they hadn't seen Madison again after Young had taken her back on Wednesday. She checked again that neither of them had gone out on Friday night and signalled to Hazel that they should leave.

Diane followed them to the front door. 'Will he really be in trouble? It was obvious she was leading him on.'

'I'm sure he'll hear if we intend to prosecute,' Hazel replied as they left.

But when she was in the car, she added, 'Too right he'll be prosecuted. Did you hear her blaming the teenager? She was barely sixteen! What is the woman thinking?'

'If the poor girl hadn't come to Scorton to try and see Jeremy Young, she wouldn't have been in Scallion's taxi and wandering around the nature reserve alone on Friday evening. He's partly responsible for her death. I hope he does get punished, although I do feel sorry for the wife.'

'Well, there's nothing more we can do today,' said Hazel. 'I'm off home for a nice hot bath and a kip.'

'And I'll get back to make a start on that pile of ironing, I suppose,' said Nina.

It was Fran's last meeting with Mills before she was going home for the rest of the summer. Most of the girls had left and there seemed to be a melancholy air in the old school as Mills walked down the corridor to meet her pupil in the music room.

'Is there any news about Madison?'

It was the first thing Fran asked each time they spoke.

'I haven't heard anything.' Mills lied, knowing full well they'd arrested the taxi driver.

It would be all over the news later today, as Nina had warned her last night. Her friend had sounded uncertain about whether the charge would stick but the fact he was the father of Cecile's baby was surely an indication of his involvement in what appeared to be a case of grooming.

'What about the skeleton?' Fran asked. 'Have they found out what happened to him?'

Mills explained that the police had been too busy to spend time on such an old case but they would be looking into it. All they knew was that his name was Gregory Lee, Ginger to his friends.

Fran opened a large file and flicked through its contents. There were photocopies of documents and newspaper articles.

'Did you show them this article in the newspaper?' she asked, pointing to the report of the prison officer being sacked for excessive punishment at the borstal.

Mills had given it to Nina but it had not been acted on, she was sure.

Fran was not to be deterred. 'I did a bit of research on the man in the newspaper article. He must be really old. I checked the address but he doesn't live there anymore.'

'You went to his house?'

The girl laughed. 'No, I looked it up. I've been doing my family tree so I know how it works. I checked the address but the house was sold six years ago. He was there before that though. He lived with his wife in Aldbrough St John for a long time before he moved. She died ten years ago.'

'So is he still alive?' Mills was taking notice now.

'I couldn't trace a death certificate, so I guess so, but I don't know where he went when he left Aldbrough St John.'

Mills considered for a moment. Fran was clearly motivated by the investigation, exactly as she would have been at her age and was now, if she admitted it. Nina and Hazel wouldn't be looking into the death immediately and so they had the opportunity to do a little digging first. She knew Nina wouldn't approve but...

'So do you have his Aldbrough St John address?' she asked Fran.

'I do.'

'Good. Let's go and see if someone knows where he's gone.'

Fran looked incredulous. 'Really? Can we do that?'

'I don't see why not.' After all, they'd be helping Nina wind up an unsolved crime if they got to the bottom of it.

The light drizzle had stopped and the sun was quickly drying the damp roads. Aldbrough St John was just a few miles from Gilling West, across the A66. It was formed of a mixture of small pebble-dashed terraces, stone cottages and larger houses.

Fran directed Mills across the other side of the green where she parked in front of a semi-detached cottage.

'It doesn't look as though anyone is in,' Fran said.

Mills thought she sounded hesitant. 'Let's see, shall we?'

She walked confidently up the short path and knocked loudly. Her companion hung back at the gate. There was no answer.

Fran sounded relieved. 'Never mind, we tried.'

But Mills wasn't going to be deterred and walked along to the cottage next door. She didn't need to knock, she'd hardly gone through the gate when the front door opened and a woman appeared in a floral apron.

'They're not in,' she said cheerfully, wiping her hands on a teacloth. 'Are you from the council?'

'No, we're… we're trying to trace the gentleman who lived here six years ago.'

Her demeanour changed. 'Are you now? Why would that be then?'

'My grandfather knew him,' she said, glancing at Fran who was out on the pavement. She hoped the girl couldn't hear.

'Did he now? Well good luck to him. He was a cantankerous old man. We never got on and we were neighbours for fifteen years. Glad to see the back of him to tell the truth.'

'Do you know where he went?'

She appeared surprised that Mills didn't know. 'He's gone to "The Gardens Care Home" and good riddance.'

Chapter 23

Fran had wanted to visit the old man immediately but Mills thought it wise to contact the care home first and offered to take her the following day, if the staff agreed. As it turned out, there was no problem and, before she'd really thought it through, Mills and Fran were being led along the corridor to Mr Webster's room.

'He doesn't like to leave his room,' the care worker explained, knocking gently on the half-open door.

The television was on but Mr Webster was lying fully-dressed on his bed with his eyes closed.

The care assistant called him softly, repeating his name with increasing volume until he opened his eyes. Still he remained horizontal.

'You've got visitors, Mr Webster,' she called. Turning to Mills, she explained, 'He's a bit hard of hearing and he doesn't always want to communicate, poor love. Call me if you need me.'

And they were alone with the old man.

'Hello Mr Webster.' Mills stood beside the bed and raised her voice.

His watery eyes opened again and he looked across at her.

'Who are you?' His voice was strong but rasping.

'I'm Dr Sanderson,' Mills replied, conscious that he might accept her presence more readily if she used her title.

'What d'you want?' he asked, looking at them warily.

'We'd like to ask about your life,' said Fran, moving towards the bed, looking at Mills for reassurance before continuing.

He pushed himself up a little and wriggled up the bed until he was sitting propped up with pillows.

'What's your name?' he asked, peering at her.

'Fran; it's short for Frances.' She smiled at him.

'What d'you want to know?' His tone was friendlier.

'About your work as a prison officer.'

He showed no surprise that she knew about the nature of his job. He wheezed as he talked and sometimes stopped to catch his breath but he gave them a complete resume of his working life, starting at the age of eighteen. They listened politely until he reached the point where he started work in a borstal, as he called it.

'Was that at Gilling West?' Fran asked.

'It was, my girl. Fifty-five that would have been,' he confirmed. 'That was my last job. I retired in sixty-four.'

He went quiet for a minute, apparently catching his breath. Mills hoped that Fran would wait for she felt sure he would continue. But he didn't.

Eventually Fran asked, 'What was the borstal like?'

'Young tearaways,' he said, resting back on his pillows. 'Nothing but trouble the lot of them.'

'There was a boy there,' Fran began. Mills tried to catch her eye to warn her to stop but she continued. 'He was called Gregory Lee. We thought you might have met him.'

The man's eyes were closed, his breathing was audible. They waited and Mills wondered if he'd fallen asleep. Despite Fran repeating her question several times, there was no response and while they waited for him to stir, the care worker returned.

'He gets tired easily,' she explained. 'He probably needs a nap.'

Mills, disappointed, took the hint and reluctantly left his room with Fran. Walking back to the car, Mills expected Fran to express her frustration but she was surprisingly buoyant.

'Never mind,' the girl said. 'I've found out where Ginger Lee's mother lives and it's only a few miles away in Piercebridge.'

'And what exactly do you propose to do with that information?' Mills asked.

'I thought we could let her know that her son has been found.'

Mills sighed. 'I think we should leave that to the police,' she said. 'But if you give me the address, I'll pass it on to them.'

Now Fran did look disappointed.

'You need to concentrate on getting your report written up,' said Mills. 'We'll grab some lunch then go back to school to finish discussing what you still need to do before you go back to your family.'

'But you will tell the police about Mr Webster, won't you? I'm sure he knew Ginger and if we could just…'

'I'll tell them everything. As soon as we get to school I'll ring Sergeant Featherstone and tell her where to find Mr Webster and Ginger Lee's mother. The police can do the rest.'

Nina had been busy writing reports all morning, tying up loose ends on the Madison Roberts case. Jim Scallion was still denying raping Cecile Fleurot or murdering Madison, despite admitting he'd driven her to Scorton the night she died. However, they had been able to go ahead and charge him on both counts and it was just a matter of completing the paperwork. When Mills had rung about the skeleton at the building site, she'd been mildly irritated by the distraction but jotted down the names and addresses before pushing the note to one side. Looking at the time, she stretched, picked up her lunch box and made for the door. She had half an hour before she needed to go and meet Madison's family for an update.

It was warm outside and the brightness almost blinded her at first. She didn't recognise the figure walking towards her until she spoke.

'Sergeant Featherstone, you gave me your card. Diane Young. Perhaps you remember?'

She seemed very composed compared to their previous meeting.

'Of course.' Nina put her lunch box under her arm and extended a hand.

'I don't mean to interrupt your lunch.'

Nina shook her head. 'I was going to sit over there,' she said.

She led the way to a seat in the shade, placing the box to the end of the bench. Diane Young sat down beside her.

'Did you want to ask me something?' Nina assumed the woman wanted to find out if she'd reported her husband's misdemeanour.

'Yes and no. I wanted to tell you something,' she replied.

Nina waited.

'But I wanted to know something first.'

Again Nina waited.

'Is it true that someone has been arrested for Madison's murder?'

'Why do you ask?'

Diane shook her head.

'What did you want to tell me?'

'I need to know if someone's been arrested.'

'Yes, they have. Why?'

Nina heard Diane take a deep breath before she spoke. 'That night, the night Madison died, I said we were at home all evening.' She took another breath. 'We had a row and I went out and drove around for a couple of hours. I left about eight and didn't get back until later… when the BBC news was on.'

'So why did you say you were at home?'

'Jeremy asked me to. He said it was important we should say we were home together because if there was the slightest suspicion he was still involved with the poor girl, he'd lose his job.'

Nina reassured the woman that her visit would be treated as discreetly as possible and asked her not to mention her concerns to her husband.

'By the way, Diane, where is your husband today?' She would have to follow up Young's lack of an alibi even though they had their suspect in custody.

'He's at work. At the school.'

As soon as the woman had left, she bolted her lunch and set off for Richmond. If she mentioned her meeting with Diane Young to Hazel, her colleague would either dismiss it as unimportant or be off after Jeremy like a terrier after a rabbit. She felt some sympathy for the wife and would prefer to handle it a little more sensitively.

As it turned out, her meeting with the Roberts family was quite brief. She explained that the man who had driven their daughter to Scorton was in custody. He'd also been charged with the rape of another girl at the school. They appeared content that someone had been arrested for the crime and asked when they might have their daughter's body. She promised to put the appropriate arrangements in motion.

Driving back to Newby Wiske, she rang Hazel to tell her about Diane's visit and suggested they both went to question Young again as soon as possible. Her friend was waiting for her in the car park.

'We'll take your car,' she said, climbing into the passenger seat.

'Ok.'

Nina turned the car round and set off for the boys' school.

'So what's this all about?' Hazel asked.

Nina described her conversation with Diane Young.

'...so he doesn't have an alibi for Friday night,' explained Nina.

'And nor does his wife. Do you think she's trying to have revenge by getting him into trouble?'

'She seemed genuine.'

The school grounds were deserted and the corridors echoed as they made their way to the Head's office. The administrator said he was away but she would fetch Mr Young from the tennis courts. He arrived breathless a few minutes later, in a pair of creased shorts and a T-shirt.

'You wanted to see me?' he asked, wiping his red shiny face with his towelling wrist band.

'Just a few things we wanted to clear up,' began Nina.

'We understand that your wife was out of the house for a couple of hours on Friday evening, Mr Young. You told us you were both at home that night.'

He looked puzzled. 'Did she tell you that?' he asked.

Before Hazel could reply, Nina asked again. 'Is that correct, Mr Young?'

He smiled. 'I see. Well, yes, she did pop out for a while. Not long.'

'How long exactly?'

He shrugged. 'Maybe an hour.' He was watching her response.

'Could it have been two hours between eight and ten?'

'If she says so.'

'So we'd like to ask you again. Did you meet Madison Roberts that night?' Nina kept the questioning light.

'No.'

'And did you go out while your wife was absent?' asked Hazel.

'No.'

To Nina's surprise, Hazel finished their questioning at that point and they left the building.

'What's the matter, Nina?' she asked, as soon as they were outside.

'Shouldn't we do a search of his car?'

'We know Madison has been in his car and we have someone in custody for the murder. If you ask me, his wife has more motive than he does.'

'Surely you don't think…'

'No, I don't. I'm just saying he's a sad man caught up in a scandal that he's trying to hide from his employer. Jim Scallion, on the other hand, is a much sadder paedophile who will be proved to be the killer when it reaches court.'

'Does that mean Young won't be prosecuted for inappropriate relations?' asked Nina.

'Oh no, he'll get done for that and quite rightly too.'

*

Mills spent far too long deciding what to wear and arrived at the lab late. She noticed that Brenda had finally bought herself a dress that fitted her new reduced frame. Mills had forgotten that Phil Freedman had been a colleague of Brenda's at the Forensic Archaeology Unit years ago and when she was informed of his visit, she insisted on being there to meet him.

It seemed that neither of them could settle down to work that morning and Mills found herself reminiscing with Brenda about that terrible woman, Claudia, who had owned the lab before Brenda took it over.

'That was five years ago,' said Brenda. 'She could be out on licence in a few years, despite murdering Phil's university friend.'

'You won't mention it when he's here, will you?' Mills begged Brenda. Sometimes her boss could be rather blunt.

'Don't be daft, pet.'

They were drinking coffee in Brenda's office when there was a gentle tap on the door.

'I'm a bit early.'

Mills recognised the voice immediately and jumped up, nearly knocking over her mug. He hadn't changed at all and she said so, without thinking.

'Hello Phil,' said Brenda, rushing round to give him a hug. 'Still messing about with dead bodies?'

He grinned. 'Are you still fiddling with rags?'

'I still dabble in textiles, yes,' she replied.

Mills let them talk before suggesting they grab something to eat. Brenda excused herself, saying she would catch them later and waved them out, offering suggestions of where they could get a good pub lunch. An awkward moment followed when neither of them wanted to choose, until Mills suggested they wander into town and she could point out one or two places. To be honest she wasn't hungry but she knew Phil could eat at any time of the day or night and would want at least a substantial sandwich.

She took him to a little Italian café where she knew they would have the choice of bruschetta and panini with a selection of Italian hams and cheeses that were always fresh and tasty. Also they served alcohol and she definitely needed a glass of something to get through the meal. Her choice of venue was a success and a glass of wine helped relax her a little. Phil asked what she was doing now and she prattled on about the new university post and her work with Brenda. She told him how ill her boss had been with cancer and how she was recovering slowly.

'I thought she looked very slim,' he said. 'I hardly recognised her. I suppose the scarf hiding her hair should have given me a clue.'

She asked what he was doing in France. Had he finished working in Colombia?

'My final job started in July last year. After that I was beginning to grow tired of disinterring bodies or parts of bodies from mass graves year after year. I wasn't well and they advised me to have a break. I was offered a temporary post in Paris and jumped at the opportunity to do less gruesome work.'

'And then you get involved in the exhumation of Cecile Fleurot!'

'That wasn't a problem. The toxicologist needed someone to take samples and I was happy to do it. And the DNA… some people don't like handling, you know…'

'Well the DNA results were brilliant. We were able to identify the father and he's been arrested for that and another even more serious crime.'

She was explaining why the toxicologist had been asked to look for plant toxins when their food arrived and the topic was parked while they ate.

'I expect the food is great in Paris,' Mills suggested.

Phil shook his head, his mouth was full and it was a while before he answered. 'I miss it here,' he said. 'I miss the food and the countryside. That's why I thought I'd spend a few days up here before I go back.'

So he was going to be around for a short while. She could hardly invite him to stay but there was no reason why they couldn't meet up for a drink or a meal, Mills thought.

'And then you'll carry on working in France?'

He shrugged. 'Maybe. It's only a temporary arrangement. My contract in Colombia was for five years so I don't have any commitments.'

No commitments? Did that mean he wasn't with anyone? She could hardly ask him that.

'So there's nothing to keep you there?'

'No.' He drained his beer glass. 'So are you still in the same place?'

'Yes, still in Laurel Cottage. Are you thinking of visiting Arkengarthdale while you're here?'

'I thought I might look up my old neighbours.'

'You must let me know when you're coming and we could meet or something.'

'Yes, that would be good.'

When lunch was over they walked back in the sunshine. Brenda was anxious to show Phil round the laboratories and whisked him off. They were gone for over an hour and when they returned Brenda insisted on making tea. Finally Mills was able to sit down with Phil to discuss the report on Cecile Fleurot.

'Dr Moreau was anxious to have a representative to explain the findings to the coroner. I've got an appointment with him tomorrow but I wanted to go through it with you first. I think Dr Moreau felt I would cope with the language better than she could.'

He pulled a large file out of his bag and opened it at the first page. Mills saw it was in French.

'Don't worry,' said Phil. 'There's a translation here.' He turned over a few pages, removed a thin document and handed it to her. 'The rest of this is just the appendices with all the technical details.' He indicated the remaining pages in the file.

Mills read through the paperwork quickly. It gave the procedures the French laboratory had used to try to identify the toxins in Cecile's body. It wasn't conclusive.

'How sure are they that the rue affected Cecile?'

'If you look here…' He turned a few pages and pointed to the figures. 'The levels of toxins are high. It is not conclusive that they come from the rue but it is certainly from a plant source. At those levels it is perfectly possible that she was unwell or had a seizure, causing her to drown in the pool.'

'Wouldn't there have been evidence of the seizure?'

'Apparently a seizure can't necessarily be detected in a post-mortem.'

'Really?'

'I'm only repeating what I've been told.'

'So the conclusion is that she had dangerous levels of an unidentified plant toxin in her body that might have affected her so badly in the pool that she drowned? I suppose that will still be recorded as accidental death?'

'Dr Moreau didn't know. That's why I have to speak to the coroner. Do you want to come?'

Mills hesitated. She wanted to but knew it would be inappropriate for her to attend a meeting with the coroner without good reason.

'Yes, I think that would be a good idea.'

As he was leaving, Phil asked whether she would like to join him for dinner. Mills mumbled an apology but said that she could be free the following day, thinking she could concoct something to tell Alex about where she'd be. It wasn't that she wanted to hide her friendship with Phil, of course not, but she wanted to avoid the inevitable questioning that would result.

Chapter 24

'There's been a development.' Hazel looked unusually cheerful.

'What's that?' Nina asked, putting her bag down at the side of her desk and removing her jacket.

'You'd better ask Ruby'.

The girl was looking across at her with a broad smile. 'A call came in to 101 last night from a Mr and Mrs Booth,' she said. 'They passed it on. A sighting of Madison Roberts on the Friday night in Scorton.'

'We know she was there, Scallion admits that.' Nina was disappointed.

'They recognised her,' Ruby went on. 'They'd seen her before, in the same taxi.'

'Well that's something.'

'We're going down to see them now,' announced Hazel. 'A definite sighting of her with the taxi driver will seal his fate, that's for sure.'

'We?' asked Nina.

'Yes, girl. You and me.'

Hazel offered to drive, so Nina gave directions once they were in the village. She located the neat terraced house just down from the green and the door was opened as soon as they stepped out of the car. They were welcomed in and offered tea before they could say a word and Nina could see that Hazel was becoming irritated by the fuss the old couple were making.

'You see, we'd seen her about a week before when she was having an argument with the taxi driver outside our house,' Mr Booth began. 'It was quite a commotion for so late at night.'

'I was all for calling the police then,' his wife added.

He looked across at her, waiting to continue his story.

'Anyway. We saw the sign up at the quarry, asking for information about the girl who'd been killed on Friday the first of July. Now, we'd been away since then. We went on holiday on the second and we had to make an early start…'

'We were flying from Manchester at nine,' Mrs Booth interrupted.

'…so we were in bed but I heard a taxi pull up just down the road and the same girl got out, just like before, only this time she got out quietly and the taxi went off again.'

'When he told me, I got up to look,' said Mrs Booth. 'The reason being that the last time she went off to visit a house down the way and I wondered if she was going there again.'

'Did she?' asked Hazel.

'Yes, just like before. She went off in the direction of Diane Young's house. Very unsteady she was.'

'And what time was this?' Hazel asked.

Mrs Booth looked at her husband. 'Around nine-thirty d'you reckon?'

He nodded.

'Did you see her go in?' asked Nina.

'Oh no, you can't quite see the house from here.'

Her husband leaned forward. 'We weren't sure whether to report it. We weren't sure it was her. The photo in the paper wasn't a good likeness.'

'It's a school photo,' said his wife. 'She looked very different all dolled up.'

Hazel looked at Nina and nodded. 'Thank you very much. You were right to contact us. We'll be back to take a statement but for now we must get going.'

Mrs Booth looked disappointed as she showed them to the door. 'Diane's house is across the road on the other side a bit further down. It's got a green door.'

They thanked her and leaving the car where it was parked, they walked the short distance to the house and knocked. Jeremy Young appeared looking tired and dishevelled as if he'd only just got up. He invited them into the sitting room, quickly pulling bedding from the sofa and dumping it in the hall.

Hazel took the lead, once they were seated. 'Some new intelligence has emerged and we need to ask you some more questions.'

'Fine.'

'We have witnesses who saw Madison get out of a taxi at nine-thirty on Friday the first of July and make her way to your house. What do you say to that?'

They waited while he considered his response. He was looking at his hands, clasped in his lap until he suddenly seemed to make up his mind.

'Yes she did come to the house that evening but I told her to clear off. She's ruined my life with her stupidity and I wasn't going to let her in.'

'So what *did* you do?'

He considered for a moment.

'I told her to go home and leave me alone.'

'And did she?' asked Hazel.

'Yes. She must have got lost and wandered into the quarry.'

'Is that what you really think?' said Hazel. 'That she wandered in her drunken stupor along the lane and up to the quarry on her own, without help? It seems unlikely, doesn't it Mr Young? I think you told your wife to cover for you by saying she was with you on Friday night because you did see Madison and you took her to the quarry where you had sex then bludgeoned her to death.'

'No!' He was holding his head with his hands and shaking it from side to side.

'Why else would you ask your wife to lie?'

No answer.

'We can do a thorough search of your car for forensic evidence,' Nina said. 'That will tell us if Madison was in it that night.'

He laughed. 'She's been in it many times, that doesn't prove anything.'

'It will prove something if we find any fibres from the clothing she was wearing that night. Apparently her outfit was brand new when she went missing.'

After a long pause, he said he needed to talk to a solicitor. Hazel fetched the car and they took him with them. Nina noticed that Mrs Booth was watching them from her window as they drove back out of Scorton.

'I don't know about you, but I'll be glad to be finishing at a reasonable time today,' Nina said to no-one in particular.

She spoke too soon. Ruby immediately gave her an urgent message from a care home she'd never heard of. An old gentleman called Mr Webster in their care was very ill and wanted to speak to a police officer urgently about a serious crime he had been involved with. Curious, she set off, hoping it wasn't a wild-goose chase resulting from the ramblings of someone with dementia.

The care home owner was anxious to let her know that the old man had little time left. He'd had another heart attack and was confined to his bed. Another one was likely to kill him and he knew it. That was why he wanted to speak to the police. She led Nina down a long corridor to his room, where the old man lay in bed. His thin white hair framed a drawn grey face. The woman explained he was very weak, as she moved his pillows to raise his head a little before leaving her alone with him. He had a tube fixed to his nose, providing oxygen from a cylinder behind his bed.

Nina tried to attract his attention. 'Mr Webster?'

His head turned slowly and she was looking into his pale blue watery eyes.

'Mr Webster, I'm Nina. I'm a detective sergeant in the police force.'

She waited. He tried to sit up but flopped back on the pillows.

'Police?' His voice was just a whisper.

'Yes. You wanted to tell us something.'

'That woman, she asked about the young lad at the prison.'

'Prison?'

He nodded. 'Prison. Borstal. They were asking about the young lad called Ginger.'

'D'you mean at the borstal at Gilling West?'

'Yes. I want to tell them what happened.'

Nina sat down on the edge of his bed. 'You can tell me. I can pass the information on.' She had no idea who he was referring to.

'I'm an old man. I'm not religious...' He coughed weakly and Nina waited until he'd recovered his breath. 'But I need to make my peace before...' His voice, almost a whisper, trailed off but Nina knew what he meant.

'So what about Ginger? Do you know what happened to him?'

He looked at her sideways, studying her face. 'Do you?'

Nina shook her head. He waved in the direction of the bedside table where a glass stood. She offered it to him but he didn't take it, just moved his head forward and sipped at the water. When he'd had sufficient he lay back and licked his cracked lips.

'It was an accident.' His voice was stronger now. 'He was on the allotment, trenching.'

'Trenching?'

'Digging a trench for composting. He was a lazy type. I told him to get on but he refused, he said he couldn't breathe. I kept him working for about an hour but then he lay down and pretended he couldn't get up.'

The old man indicated he wanted more water and Nina responded.

'So what did you do?' Nina asked when he'd finished.

'I told him I'd fetch the governor unless he finished the trench down to three feet. I left him to it but when I came back after an hour or so, he'd collapsed. He wasn't breathing.'

'Did you fetch the governor?'

He shook his head. 'Too late. He'd gone.'

'Gone?'

'Lying in the trench.' He had another coughing fit. 'He wasn't breathing.'

'He was dead?'

He didn't answer.

'Mr Webster, did you leave the boy in the trench?'

He lay back on his pillows with his eyes closed and nodded.

There were details she needed to know. 'Did you tell anyone?'

His head was moving slowly from side to side on the pillows.

'Did you fill the trench in?'

He nodded.

'So you didn't report it?'

'Now. I'm reporting it now, aren't I?'

She looked at the fragile figure lying in the bed. Mitch would tell her what would happen next. Mr Webster was obviously mentally fit to plead but his physical health was another matter.

His left cheek relaxed against the pillow and the sound of regular breathing indicated he'd fallen asleep. There was no point trying to question him further. She picked up her bag and tiptoed out of his room, pulling the door gently behind her. The owner must have been waiting close by because she appeared immediately to show Nina out.

'He's asleep,' Nina reported.

'Poor man. The doctor says he's on borrowed time and he obviously wanted to get something off his chest. He'll be happier now.'

Nina didn't answer. He won't be happy if he's arrested for manslaughter, she thought.

'Can I ask you about his visitors?' she inquired.

'Oh, you mean the young woman who came yesterday?'

'Possibly.'

'The only visitors he's had and *she* came twice.'

'Really? Did she have red hair by any chance?'

'Yes, that's right. Do you know her?'

Nina sighed. Mills had been there before her. As soon as she reached her car she rang her for an explanation.

'It was Fran,' explained Mills. 'She found out where he used to live and the neighbour gave me the care home address. I popped in to see him.'

'Why?'

'Just to ask if he knew Ginger.'

'Did he tell you anything?'

'No, he refused to talk to me. I may have mentioned I was going to talk to someone about it.'

'Well, he spoke to me, if you want to know. And you can tell Fran that she was right.'

'While you're on the phone, is there anything I should know about Cecile Fleurot? I'm seeing the coroner tomorrow.'

'Are you? Does that mean Phil is over here?'

'Yes. Is there anything?'

'As it happens, there is. The taxi driver has finally admitted rape. The evidence against him in Cecile's emails is pretty damning, even though it doesn't mention him by name.'

'I think the coroner made the pragmatic decision,' said Phil, topping up their glasses. 'Even if there was any malicious intent in the American girl giving Cecile the tincture of rue, she's no longer around to prosecute. Cecile's family will be able to bury her finally this time.'

'I don't think Madison meant any harm,' said Mills. 'It was just an unfortunate accident.'

The waiter came outside to take their order but they hadn't even looked at the menu. Mills felt surprisingly relaxed as they sat silently choosing what to eat. When at last they'd ordered their food, Mills asked Phil what he planned to do in future.

'You know, I realised when I saw Brenda again, how much I've missed working with forensic scientists in a range of disciplines. She could be a pain at times but her interest in textiles was so different to working with bones. What about you?'

'Me? I'll just carry on with my teaching and part-time work at the lab.'

'So do you do much research?'

'Not really. There never seems to be time.'

'You shouldn't give up. I'd like to get my work published as a monograph.'

'You mean a text book?'

'Yes, something on the examination of mass graves.'

'You've certainly had enough experience.'

'Too much, I sometimes think.'

They chatted easily, watching people passing in the street and enjoying the last of the sunshine. Their meals arrived and Mills realised how much she was enjoying Phil's company.

'I assume that you're not driving back tonight?' Phil said as he drained the bottle into her glass.

'Donna said I could stay with her, so I could have a glass of this delicious wine!'

The morning had been rather tense with Alex enquiring why she was wearing a posh frock to work. She'd explained that she was seeing the coroner in Harrogate and that she was dining with the French pathologist. It was rather naughty of her to let him assume it was Dr Moreau. She'd told him she would stay with Donna to avoid driving home afterwards.

Perhaps it was the wine or because she was reminded of the conversation, Mills found herself speaking to Phil about Alex and his decision to move to London; how he was going to share a flat in Streatham and expected her to be travelling down to see him every other weekend. He sympathised, asked her how she felt about it and she told him she was going to finish with him as soon as he went down South. In fact, she might even do it before he moved so he took all his stuff with him.

Despite her protestations, Phil insisted on ordering another bottle. She'd noticed that he'd been drinking quite fast and wondered if the distressing work he'd been doing had led him to develop a dependency on alcohol. The time flew by as they ate ice creams and drank coffee and finally, at past ten o'clock they left the restaurant to wander through Harrogate. Soon they were outside his hotel and that was when he suggested she came in for a nightcap.

Nina was late but Hazel had waited for her to arrive before starting the interview. Jeremy Young was accompanied by his solicitor, a woman who she recognised as a smart cookie. Hazel anticipated having a hard time and told Nina so. They went in together and initiated the recording equipment before introducing everyone on the tape. Hazel kicked off by explaining why Young was there and reiterating the charge of murder. She and Nina had prepared well and worked out exactly how they would share the questioning. So Nina began gently on his relationship with Madison.

'She loved you and she thought you loved her, isn't that so?' she said when he denied any bond between them.

'She was a hysterical teenager,' he said. 'She was infatuated and I told her to grow up.'

Nina explored the extent of their relationship and he eventually agreed that their liaison had lasted several months and on a number of occasions they had engaged in sexual activity. She explored how guilty he felt at their affair and how it impinged on his marriage, including his wife's pregnancy. He agreed it was not his finest hour.

'More than that, were you not concerned about the impact it would have on your job if the truth came out?'

'Of course.'

'Did Madison ever threaten to tell the school about your affair?'

He refused to answer so she moved on to the Wednesday before Madison was killed, when she came to the house and confronted his wife.

'I told her it was over and that was that.'

'You told us you didn't see her again but on Friday night she came back to Scorton and she came to your house, didn't she?'

He didn't reply.

Hazel took over. 'We have witnesses who saw her. We'll bang on every door in Scorton if we have to. You made your wife give you an alibi. Why would you do that if it wasn't because Madison came to see you at home?'

He wouldn't answer. He seemed to have diminished in stature. Nina suggested a break and they left him with the smart solicitor. Hazel was unhappy, certain that the woman would persuade him to make no further comment. Their evidence was weak and the CPS wouldn't be happy.

Nina was more optimistic. 'The thought of Diane sitting at home about to produce their baby while police swarm all over the village asking the neighbours about his movements seemed to affect him. We may be lucky.'

'Lucky? Listen to yourself! When will forensics finish with his car?'

'It will be a day or two before we get the results, even if they find anything.'

They drank coffee and waited until half an hour was up then went back to the interview room. Young's eyes were red; the solicitor looked nervous.

On went the tape again.

'So, Jeremy,' Hazel began, 'do we get the boys in blue over to Scorton?'

Nina cringed inwardly but it had an effect.

'My client has prepared a statement,' the solicitor said, producing a sheet of paper which she handed to Young.

On the evening of Friday 1st July 2016, Madison Roberts came to visit me at my house in Scorton. She was very drunk. I wanted to take her home by car but she felt sick so I drove to the quarry for her to get some fresh air. There she seduced me into having sex with her before telling me she was going to report me to my employer. I lost my temper and struck her.

'That is all my client wishes to say.'

Nina was stunned. 'Was she unconscious? Was she dead? Why did you leave her there?'

Hazel was grinning.

'That is all he wishes to say at this time,' said the solicitor, packing up her papers.

'I didn't mean to kill her,' he wailed.

Out in the corridor Hazel gave a whoop. 'That's enough for me and Mitch and the CPS.'

Nina sighed. 'I'll go to tell Mr and Mrs Roberts. They can begin their arrangements to take Madison home.'

Mills had driven over to High Fell School to see Fran for the last time. The grounds felt empty and it hardly seemed possible that just two weeks previously they were full of actors and their parents gathering for the production of Hamlet. The events that had begun that night had unravelled into a nightmare, particularly for Fran, which was why Mills felt it was important to explain to her what the outcomes were.

Obviously it was a shock to hear that Mr Young had been charged with Madison's murder but Fran was comforted to know that Cecile had not been deliberately poisoned by the American girl. Mills had been unsure whether to mention Cecile's pregnancy but when Fran asked directly, she told her that the taxi driver had admitted rape.

It was a relief to turn to the more mundane matter of the archaeology report but there remained the question of poor Ginger's demise.

'I went to the care home again but Mr Webster wouldn't talk to me. However, he confessed to the police before he died.'

'He died?'

'Yes, he had a heart attack following Sergeant Featherstone's visit but he told her what happened all those years ago. We know Ginger was asthmatic. Apparently Webster made him dig a trench until the boy collapsed and at that point left him alone. When he returned much later, the boy was dead.'

'So he buried him there?'

'He was making a composting trench so it must have been several feet deep. I suppose he just filled it in. It was amazing they didn't find him until the site was excavated.'

'Well at least we can tell his family what happened to him.'

'Fran…'

'I've got his mother's address so we could …'

'I've given it to the police, Fran. I've been in sufficient trouble with Nina already.'

Driving back to Mossy Bank, Mills wasn't looking forward to breaking the news to Alex. She would explain that it would be better for both of them to have a clean break and that he should take all his belongings with him to Streatham. And she would like them to be gone by the time she returned from her trip to Paris.